Redferne Lane

Redferne Lane

Sarah Scholefield

This first edition published in 2017 by:

Thistle Publishing
36 Great Smith Street
London
SW1P 3BU

www.thistlepublishing.co.uk

For Dyl

September 2014

Flicking through the pages of an old sketch book it was strange to find drawings of my husband. The contours of Ezra's face had once been so familiar. But as I ran my fingertips over the sketched pencil lines I could barely remember drawing these pictures of him. His features were foreign; he was a stranger. Yet the house we had shared was still my home and his things were all around me. But our house was no longer filled with love and care, and Ezra would have chided me for the dust and mess I had let accumulate.

I'd spent the last few years drawing nothing real only doodling patterns as though I could order my life with the geometric shapes I laid on the paper. On finding a blank page in the sketch book an unusual urge to draw a living thing took me. Before I could question it I went outside to pick one of the flowers that had survived in my neglected front garden.

With the solid stem of a lilac-blue daisy in my hand I was about to return inside when a sigh of wind caught my cheek. I turned my face into the breeze as though there was something of interest in the air. The flower fell from my fingers as I saw a figure walking down Redferne Lane. It was not Noah or Josie coming from Redferne House, but still a familiar form I recognised straight away.

Torin, Ezra's brother.

He raised his hand in greeting but he did not speak until he was at my gate.

'Alright Gracie?' he said, rolling the 'R' in my name with his Scottish burr. He looked me up and down slowly before speaking again. 'Are you going to invite me in?'

Ezra and Torin had looked similar; the same reddish tint to their brown hair, the same dark, near black eyes, a well-moulded torso, and they each had an energy they brought to a room that lit it up with intrigue. But where Torin had a beard and moustache that seemed to pull his mouth down into a serious line, Ezra had been clean shaven and it had lent a lightness to his demeanour.

'What are you doing here?' I asked.

'I've come to see you Gracie.' He spoke as though it was obvious, and I suppose it was. I just didn't know why he'd come now. I hadn't seen him since the funeral. Josie and Noah had mentioned he was coming to stay at Redferne House, but they hadn't said when. And I hadn't really believed he would actually ever come.

Torin pushed open my small blue gate, like he was a giant come to steal all I had. He let it bang closed.

I thought about staying in the doorway of my cottage for a moment, not letting Torin in, but it wasn't really an option so I turned and walked inside allowing him to follow.

Torin shut the front door with another bang.

He stood in the doorway of my sitting room and surveyed it, rubbing his bearded chin with thick knuckled fingers.

'Ach Gracie, you live like a pig,' he told me with a small chuckle.

'And?' I said, affronted.

'And you should clear up.' His Scottish lilt lessened as he said more.

'I wasn't expecting anyone,' I mumbled. I felt jittery.

'Obviously.'

There were piles of books and magazines, dirty plates and mugs, cushions slumped on the sofa and a dusty film covered the surfaces. Sketch pads full of my doodles lay wherever I'd left them. Pens and pencils littered the table, the window sill, the floor; dirty smudges on the door frames and the arms of the sofa. Ezra had been the tidy one.

'So how are you?' Torin said, pushing the sleeves of his checked shirt higher up his arms, revealing the swirls and patterns of his tattoos.

'Fine,' I said, as I sank down on my shabby sofa. I wore one of Ezra's T-shirts over my jeans; it was big and had holes in places and I imagined it still smelt of him. It had when I'd started to wear it. I hugged myself, gathering in the soft fabric.

Torin finally came into the room. He made it feel crowded. He moved a sketch book off the armchair, glanced at it for a moment before placing it on top of the debris on the low table and sat down.

'Is that work?' he asked, nodding toward the sketch book.

'No.' I couldn't earn a living with patterns I drew, their purpose was purely to occupy my hands and mind in the solitary hours; I did not draw people any more.

'Are you working?'

'Yes.' I frowned and leaned over to close the sketch book.

'What you doing?'

'Admin.'

'Where you doing that?'

I shrugged. 'In an office.'

'Wow, well it's great of you to tell me all about it Gracie,' he said, raising his reddish eyebrows.

I regarded him on the edge of the chair, elbows on knees clad in black denim. His gingery brown hair had begun to recede into a widow's peak, but a wave of a few inches disguised it well enough. I was sure there must be some grey hairs too, but I couldn't see them. Torin looked around the room, his eyes flitting from the Indian wall hanging to the gilt-framed mirror, to the dusty and broken paper lampshade.

'I'd love one,' Torin said, looking back at me.

'What?'

'A coffee. Black with a wee bit of sugar,' he said with a smile, crow's feet gathering at his eyes.

He never used to take sugar. I sat for moment contemplating whether I could just tell him to leave. But there was a part of me that didn't want him to go. I got to my feet and padded to the kitchen.

I tipped two scoops into the coffee machine then stopped. I so rarely made coffee for anyone but myself any more.

'You'll wash a mug for me Gracie,' Torin said.

'You can wash one yourself.' I turned to him. He leant against the doorframe with his arms crossed, smirking at me.

I felt heat in my cheeks. I was being rude. I should apologise. But I was angry. He looked so smug, and he'd just turned up; I'd not seen him in nearly two years. He was acting as though that was fine. It was not fine with me.

'I'll wash one for you too,' he said, coming into the kitchen and opening cupboards. 'Got any biscuits?' he paused. 'Where's your food?'

'In the fridge.'

He opened the fridge, then looked at me, 'No wonder you look like shite. You must just live off white wine and fancy yogurt.'

I pushed the door of the fridge from Torin's hand and closed it. 'The mugs are over there.' I pointed to the sink.

The coffee machine bubbled and hissed behind me as I watched Torin.

He put a squirt of washing-up liquid into a dusky pink earthenware mug that Ezra and I had bought when we'd gone to Appledore for our honeymoon. Ezra had teased me for wanting to buy a pink one and a blue one. But I'd laughed and told Ezra the pink one was for him. I wanted to tell Torin to put the mug down. I wanted to tell him he shouldn't touch it. He had no right. But the words wouldn't come. Torin rinsed the mug and put it upside down on the draining board before picking up the blue Appledore mug.

I could hardly contain my anger. How dare he just turn up at me house?

'Coffee ready?' Torin asked. He turned and caught me watching him; my cheeks burned again.

I wished he'd just leave, but I poured the coffee anyway; Torin had the blue mug. Back in the living room, I curled myself onto the sofa, my feet tucked underneath me and held the pink mug with both hands. Torin perched back on the armchair, regarding me with a slight frown before he looked away.

He began a monologue about work, detailing the events his company had staged over the previous two years, as if this was excuse enough for his absence. He'd spent a lot of time in Canada and at home in Scotland. I said nothing. Could he not have even visited once in those two years? Or even a phone call? Yet I was not surprised; it was not the first time he'd disappeared without trace from my life.

'Noah and Josie send their regards,' Torin said.

I heard the accusation in his tone; I suppose he knew I'd not seen them for a few weeks. It riled me even more that Torin should accuse me. Why should I make the effort to see the family when he had not bothered himself? I'd never been close to Ezra's other brother Noah, nor his wife Josie. And although they lived only a few minutes' walk up Redferne Lane, weeks could go by without us meeting. They were kind to me, Josie had tried to welcome me into their lives but I didn't like to see their pitying eyes. Nor did I want to know that they hurt too. I didn't care if they missed Ezra. It didn't help me. Nothing did.

'They thought you might like to come for dinner tomorrow?' Torin said.

'I can't.'

'I told them you'd want to come,' Torin said, 'that you'd want to see us.'

I didn't want to go.

'Now don't look like that Gracie, you'll have a nice time.'

'I'm busy tomorrow.'

'Doing what?'

I couldn't think of an excuse off the top of my head.

'Then you can come.' He stated, his black eyes shone with amusement. 'You can have a few drinks, eat some good food. Christ, it's not you that's dead.'

I blinked, stung by his words.

'Besides, I'll be there. You'll want to see me of course.'

I did not respond but glared at him instead, incredulous.

He stared back. 'Why'd you cut off your pretty long hair?'

I floundered and put my hand to my head as though I'd only just realised my waist length hair was all gone. I would not tell Torin I'd hacked it all off four months ago. There was no way I'd tell him I'd stood at the kitchen sink and picked up a knife from the draining board. I held the blade against the white skin on the underside of my wrist. I thought to run the point of the knife along the blue vein. I don't know why I didn't. Instead I took hold of a clump of hair and sliced the knife through the strands, close to my scalp. I didn't stop until the sink was full of locks of my long brown hair. My head had felt light and cool.

Mum and Dad had come down from Surrey a few days later. They'd been worried about me. I hadn't answered my phone or e-mails for days. Dad wrote me a new prescription and Mum took me to a hairdresser in town. She asked the young woman if she could make me right. It was a lot to ask of the hairdresser, but she'd managed to make me look like more of a lesbian stereotype and less like an escaped convict. My hair had grown a little since then, lending something of the pixie to me. But I hated it. I missed my long hair.

'Well, you failed if you thought it would make you look ugly,' Torin said, without humour.

'Why are you here Torin?'

'I told you Gracie, I just came to see you.'

'But why now?'

'I have some work around here. I'll be staying with Noah and Josie for a time. Up at the house.' He paused. 'It'll be good to see you with the family tomorrow,' he said, and I noticed his Scottish accent had grown heavier again.

'They're not family,' I pointed out.

He rubbed his beard. 'Are they not? Do you not have Redferne as your name same as me? Am I not family?'

'Not anymore.'

'I see.'

'Do you?'

'Oh aye Gracie, I see.'

I licked my lips, turning away from him and swallowed. 'I have things to do.'

'Right, well I'll come and get you at seven then,' Torin said, making me look at him again. He placed the blue mug on the table and smiled.

'You don't need to come and get me.' I tried to tell him in my most assertive voice but I just sounded whiny and childish.

'You're going to come on your own?'

I shrugged, thinking I wasn't going to go at all.

'I'll come and get you when you don't turn up.'

'Fine.'

'Good,' he said, 'and wear something nice.'

'I'll wear what I want,' I snapped, unable to contain my frustration.

'You'll feel better if you wear something nice Gracie. I couldn't give a shit if you rock up in a bin bag, but I don't suppose you'll feel all that good about yourself.'

'I really do have things to do Torin.'

'Aye some cleaning I should think.' He chuckled.

'You should go.'

'Aye,' he said, 'I'm going. But I'll see you tomorrow.'

I didn't get up, only watched him walk out of the living room and waited for the bang of the front door. The bang of the gate.

I was glad that he was gone.

My next door neighbour, Sam stood outside her house, hands on hips, looking down Redferne Lane towards the railway bridge. Had I realised she was there I would have waited to return Ada's plates.

'Hello Sam,' I forced myself to say, and paused on the other side of her garden wall.

Turning she gave me a tight lipped smile.

Sam was only a year or so older than me. She must have had her teenage son Jerome when she was a teenager herself.

Sam wore tight jeans and a cerise halter neck that showcased her breasts. She was not a large woman, but she was blessed with more than a handful of soft tissue in front. Her blonde hair was twisted up into a do on top of her head and secured with a large blue tropical silk flower. Her face was perfectly made-up; she had something of a china doll about her.

Although we'd lived next door to each other for nearly two years we exchanged little more than vague pleasantries every once in a while, when required.

I readjusted the little stack of Ada's plates I held in my hands as Sam asked, 'Alright my love?' She and Jerome both spoke with the rounded brogue of the West Country; they were Somerset, born and bred.

I gave a stock reply not letting on that I'd been in bed most of the day with a terrible hangover that had forced me to call in sick at work. My response to Torin's sudden arrival the day before had been a long night alone with a vodka bottle. But now my hangover was subsiding and I felt the calming effects of one of my little white pills that Dad prescribed for me.

Jerome came under the bridge wearing the St Mary's school uniform and even through the tangle of dark hair that hung over his face I noted the roll of his eyes when he saw his mother. As soon as Sam noticed Jerome her attention was immediately snapped away from me to her son. I could almost see the waves of rage coming off Sam as Jerome approached.

'What've you done now?' she said.

'I haven't done anything,' Jerome replied.

'Then why's I got school phoning me to come in and see them again?'

'I dunno.' He pushed open the gate and stood before his mother so she had to look up at him.

'Why can't you behave yourself?'

'I didn't do nothing,' Jerome said, but without conviction.

'Don't you start with me,' Sam said.

Jerome muttered something I couldn't hear. Sam gave her son a stinging look and barred his way as he tried to enter the house.

I was not part of the conversation but neither did I feel as though I could just walk away, so I stood feeling awkward, watching Jerome being told off by Sam. I often heard her raised voice through the wall but rarely heard Jerome reply.

'That woman needs a bra,' Torin said, into my ear, startling me as I hadn't heard him approach. I dropped Ada's plates. The white porcelain hit the old tarmac with a high pitched crash, followed by a cascade of noisy tinkles as the fractured pieces of china bounced and fell again.

'What did you do that for?' I snapped at Torin.

'Sorry, didn't mean to make you jump.'

I bent down in the vain hope of salvaging something of the plates but they were beyond repair.

'Why are sneaking up on me?' I asked with a spiky voice, unable to contain my irritation.

Torin bent down next to me. 'I wasn't. I just came to see if you were ready to walk up to the house for dinner?'

'It's too early.'

'Aye, I know.' He paused. 'Actually, I wanted to clear the air. I'm sure it was a surprise to see me yesterday, I shouldn't have just turned up and barged in.'

'No, you shouldn't.'

'But you don't need to be so prickly.'

I shot him a look.

Jerome had disappeared inside their house but Sam lent over the wall and passed me a dustpan and brush. I thanked her but Torin took it from my hands and cleared up the mess. I felt another crest of rage as I watched Torin putting Ada's broken plates in the bin. He was only just back, and he was already making a mess of things.

Sam took back her dustpan and brush, gave Torin a disapproving look, then went back inside her house.

Torin followed me to Ada's door. He wanted to see her too.

'I haven't seen her for ages,' he reasoned.

'Since the funeral?' I threw at him.

Torin paused before answering but looked directly at me as he said, 'Aye, since the funeral.'

Ada opened her front door wearing an anxious frown, but once she saw me her face relaxed into a smile, her old loose skin gathered in powdery folds about her eyes.

'Hello Ada,' I said. My voice raised, and I enunciated carefully. 'How are you?'

She explained about a doctor's appointment she'd had that morning to check her blood pressure. Ada was deaf in one ear since she'd had mumps as a child. It affected her voice. Her words came out too loud as if she were speaking across a swimming pool.

'And you've brought your lovely young man to see me too.' She said looking at Torin.

'This is Torin, Ezra's brother?' I said, flushing at Ada's mistake.

She smiled as she made a noise of recognition and shook his hand. I wasn't sure who she thought Torin was, but she invited us in for coffee anyway.

The footprint of Ada's cottage was the same as mine. It's funny how two houses can be the same and yet so different. We both had an L-shaped hallway off the front door that contained the stairs, a door that led into the petite sitting room and another that led to the kitchen. At home, the space under the stairs was haunted by Ezra's mountain bike, untouched for nearly two years and all sorts of other stuff I didn't use. That same space in Ada's house was empty save for an ancient upright Hoover. Ada's own, much used, bicycle was kept outside in her front garden, under a worn piece of sky-blue tarpaulin. At 79 years old she still rode her bike into town every day.

As we followed Ada into her sitting room, I could smell a synthesised floral scent that cloyed at the back of my throat. Ada had a thick carpet over the flagstones, creamy with chains of large pink roses. It made her house feel warmer than mine. I slipped my boots off so I wouldn't mark the carpet.

Three china shire horses the size of rabbits, stood on the dark mantel piece. A small metal grate sat in a stone hearth, a neat scuttle of coal and a brass brush and pan hung on a stand, with tongs and a poker. The ashes from the wood burner in my house spilt onto the flagstones, so the room was dusty. If I'd run my finger along any surface in Ada's house, I wouldn't have found a speck.

'Sit down dears,' Ada said. 'I'll make coffee.'

'Can I help?' I asked, although I knew what the answer would be.

For around a year I'd been coming to her cottage for coffee every few days after work and she never let me help. I'd grown to like my visits to Ada. They had started out of guilt but once I'd worked out she was the closest thing I had to a friend, I held on to the comfort and security of my short visits. We didn't talk that much, we often just watched Eggheads or Countdown or other quiz shows together. Ada's general knowledge was vast, and she wasn't bad with pop culture either. My knowledge base seemed to be limited to art history but even that was pretty thin.

I watched Ada's slight frame walk across the room. Her ballet pink cardigan hung on her thin shoulders, her back a little stooped. The waist band of her woollen grey skirt was high and loose. There was so little of her, it was a wonder her skirt didn't descend to her nylon clad ankles. How she still rode her bike, I couldn't fathom. She didn't look too steady on her feet, let alone strong enough to power the pedals.

Torin and I sat on the beige settee and I tried to leave as much space between us as possible. But it was a small piece of furniture and there were only a few inches between us; I felt the heat coming from Torin.

'Are you going to just pretend I'm not here?' Torin said. As he spoke he shifted his weight on the settee. The movement forced me to turn toward him.

'Yes.'

'I don't remember you being so childish before.'

Ada came through with a tray, coffee in dainty white cups and saucers with a thin gilt band running around the lip. Matching side plates, jug and sugar bowl. I was glad they differed from the ones I'd dropped outside.

'That's a lovely tea set Ada,' Torin said.

'It's a coffee set dear,' Ada corrected.

'Of course,' Torin said.

I smiled to myself.

'Do you take cream?' Ada asked Torin, holding up the small jug.

'No thank you, I like it black.'

'Oh,' she said looking up, 'just like Grace?'

'Aye.'

Ada made a noise of approval in the back of her throat. With a slight tremor in her hand she lifted a saucer and offered the cup to Torin and then one to me.

'So how long have you two known each other?' Ada asked and gave me twinkling smile.

'Torin is a Redferne Ada. Ezra's brother. He's staying up at the house. With Noah,' I said, as Torin gave a small chuckle to himself as Ada's assumption.

The mention of Redferne was enough to set Ada off on one of her many Redferne related stories. She had been the house keeper at Redferne House since she was a young woman and her mother and grandmother before her. I'd heard the stories before. The first Redferne was meant to be a witch, but Ada said she was just a poor girl that married a rich man that had fallen in love. The portraits of Redferne's past all looked just like Noah's daughter, Eliza; pale skin, silvery blond hair and a beautiful way about them.

As Ada regaled us with tales of the Redfernes I could feel Torin looking at me and I wished he wouldn't. It made my heart beat in an irregular fashion. I still could not quite believe he was here.

'Ada,' Torin began, 'I had a wee accident with some of your plates.'

'Sorry dear?'

'Out on the lane, I dropped a couple of your plates that Grace was bringing to you.'

Ada looked confused. She smacked her lips together and placed her cup back on the saucer. She dabbed her powdery cheek with a hanky, where her eye was watering a little.

'I was bringing your plates back, but I broke them on the way, I'm sorry.' I said.

'I don't think I have any of your plates,' Ada said, as confusion wrinkled her brow.

'No, I had yours.'

Ada did not reply.

Unexpectedly, I felt my throat constrict. I'd noticed lately that Ada could get easily confused and sometimes forgetful. I didn't want to think she couldn't remember the lovely things she made me. Since Ezra and I had moved to Redferne Lane Ada had been giving me things; a slice of cake covered in a tea towel, sometimes a portion of some kind of pie, sometimes a few biscuits, or soup in an old ice cream tub. When Ezra died I didn't return any of the plates or containers or tea towels. But then she left a note with a slice of Bakewell tart, asking, in her shaky copperplate writing, if I could leave the plates on her wall so she might wash them up. Now when I came round for coffee she always sent me home with something and I tried to return her plates before she asked.

'I think it's time dear,' Ada said, picking up the remote control.

I smiled but I wasn't in the mood for TV quizzes today.

Ada reached beside her and opened a small drawer in the dark wooden occasional table. She drew out a pale blue cigarette packet and a box of Swann matches.

Ada pulled a cigarette half out of the packet and offered it toward me.

I shook my head. 'We should probably be going now.'

'Of course, I expect the two of you would like to be alone.' She grinned.

Torin chuckled again, and I frowned.

I told Ada I'd see her soon, and we left her watching TV and smoking her cigarette.

Torin and I walked in silence up Redferne Lane. Rich sun beams reached across the meadow on our right-hand side and made the old oak that stood in the middle a silhouette against a yellow candyfloss sky. The beech trees that lined the left side were illuminated by the golden light and seemed to hand out extra oxygen as we passed by, so my body felt a little more alive and my head a little clearer.

'Now you'll be good girl, won't you?' Torin said, as we reached the walled garden of Redferne House.

'What's that supposed to mean?'

'You'll be nice right?'

I ignored him and opened the wooden gate set into the old stone wall. It was like stepping into a children's book; the house and gardens had something magical and a sprinkling of whimsy about them. Redferne House was a red bricked Tudor building, a little squat and wonky, but elegant none the less. The large knot garden in front of the house lacked the well-kept precision of a National Trust property but was all charm and more endearing for the shabbiness. One could get lost in that garden, fall down a rabbit hole, or find a fairy. Perhaps all of those things and more.

I smelt the lavender and sage, thyme and marjoram, calendula and lemon balm that grew in abundance. The pea shingle covering the paths between each bed crunched under foot announcing our approach to the house.

The door opened before we reached it and we were greeted by Josie.

She wore a bright blue dress printed with large pink and orange flowers; it had a tight bodice and a full skirt. It left her solid arms exposed and showed her rounded shoulders red from the sun, the wide straps of the dress cut into her flesh, and her torso was dissected by the cut of the fabric and the pinch of her bra beneath. She had a scarf of flamingo pink holding back her blonde curls, tied at the nape of her neck, the ends trailing down her back. Her feet were sleeved in Birkenstocks of vivid green, her toenails painted electric blue.

I felt like a dull British winter's day in my grey top and black jeans, whereas Josie was a holiday in the Maldives.

'Where's that brother of mine?' Torin asked after greetings and hugs from Josie.

'Noah's out the back talking to Sam.'

'Sam?'

'The cleaner. She lives next to you, doesn't she Grace?'

Torin disappeared, seeking out Noah, leaving me with Josie and my young nephews, Barty and Godfrey. The following ten minutes were a dervish of the boys tearing around the kitchen while Josie was cooking, her face getting rosier by the second. I offered to help, but she refused, wafting me away with a tea towel and suggesting I could engage Godfrey and Barty if I wanted to be useful. I did not often play with the children; I barely saw them in all honesty. But both of the boys' faces lit up with excitement at having an aunt to play with. I smiled down at them and tried to understand the game they wanted me to play.

Noah came into the kitchen. He always walked leaning back slightly, led by his groin, his arms loose at his sides. Master of all.

He poured more than generous gin and tonics, patted Josie on the bottom and said to the room at large that we should come into the garden. I took the invitation and ushered Barty and Godfrey outside with me, their plump warm hands in mine.

Torin and Noah sat on the patio sipping their drinks and smoking cigars, ignoring the children and me. They were talking about Torin's work. He ran a stage building company that catered for all kind of events all over the world, providing anything and everything, from catwalks to business conferences to festivals. I understood it was quite successful.

My nephews as least seemed to relish my attention. I enjoyed an hour in the waning light playing with them on the luscious lawn at the back of the house. I was disappointed when Noah came to gather the boys and take them up to bed. I told myself that I should come and see the boys more often.

'Come and have a drink Gracie, you're flushed,' Torin said, from his seat on the patio. 'It suits you to have colour in your cheeks.'

I flushed further from his observation.

Torin stood up, picking up a glass and brought it to me.

I thanked him as I took it. The glass was cool in my hand and the ice tinkled. Torin watched me drink. He licked his lips as though he too was thirsty.

'So?' Torin began but Josie called from the house that dinner was ready.

I felt jumpy and went quickly inside, not waiting for Torin.

We sat down to dinner at the kitchen table; there was so much food I felt queasy at the sight of it; dishes of potatoes shiny with butter, a deep tart filled with plump tomatoes encased in baked egg, fancy breads, a platter of cheeses and meats, and bowls of salads all covered in oils.

I drank more than I ate and it helped the evening drift by with little input from me. I was probably being rude but all I could think was that Ezra was missing. He should have been there with his brothers; he'd have loved it. Instead I was there without him and I didn't know how to rise to the occasion. I couldn't think of anything to say.

Noah and Torin talked of the summer in their childhood Torin had spent at Redferne House. Torin had been ten when he'd stayed, Noah twelve and Ezra just a baby. Torin's father had been ill and Torin had been sent from his home in Scotland to stay the whole summer, much to the disgust of Noah and Ezra's father. Their father would have rather that Torin simply did not exist; he was solid evidence of his wife's year of adultery.

Their conversation drifted to another summer at Redferne house. It must have been after the car crash that killed their mother and Ezra and Noah's father, as the summer they talked of seemed to have been a period of drinking, smoking cannabis and parties when they invited local girls to the house. There was no mention of Ezra and I assumed he must have been in France with his grandmother. Ezra was almost a different generation to his brothers, ten years younger than Torin. Both Noah and Torin had been adults when their parents had died but Ezra had been only ten. He'd spent the rest of his childhood at boarding school, with a few summers in France before his grandmother had died too.

Throughout their reminiscing Josie smiled and nodded and laughed on cue. Occasionally she would catch my eye, expecting an indulgent smile in return to the one she gave. But my responses became less and less, my consumption of Chardonnay more and more.

'Had enough to eat?' Josie asked me. 'You've barely touched a thing all evening Grace.'

'I'm fine. Thanks.'

Josie shifted her chair closer to me and spoke in a conspiratorial whisper.

'There's nothing to you these days,' she said. 'You're wasting away. Is everything alright?'

'I really am fine,' I said and smiled.

She gave me a sympathetic look. We both knew I wasn't fine.

The kitchen door opened and Eliza slunk in, her face hidden by the sheet of her white blond hair.

'Darling, how kind of you to join us,' Noah called to his daughter.

Eliza was a Redferne in colouring, just like her father. Extremely fair haired and eyes the colour of bluebells on a shaded woodland floor. She was willowy limbed but petite in height, a wisp of ethereal teenage angst. She wore skinny black jeans, and a blood red top that skimmed the waistband of her jeans flashing glimpses of pale nubile skin when she moved. Eliza spoke to her father in looks alone, her pretty eyes outlined in heavy eyeliner and grey eye shadow. It was quite clear the contempt she held her father in.

'Come join us Eliza?' Torin said, 'There's plenty of dessert to spare.'

Eliza had at least the good grace to answer her uncle with words. 'I don't eat dessert.' Eliza said as though Torin had suggested she have some arsenic.

'Like your aunt then?' Torin suggested, gesturing toward me.

Eliza flicked a look my way before she went to fill a glass with water and slunk back out of the kitchen.

'Dear me, what am I to do Torin?' Noah said, indicating his departing daughter. 'She doesn't listen to a word we say!'

'How old is she now?' Torin asked.

'Fifteen,' Noah said, with defeat.

'Well, what do you expect?' Torin laughed.

'I suppose.'

'And she's a fine-looking girl too. I bet the boys are knocking down your door?'

'Thankfully not,' Josie said. 'She is the foulest creature to live with but the one good thing we can say is that she is totally not interested in boys.'

'Not yet,' Torin muttered.

They continued to talk about Eliza for a time, and then about Noah and Josie's boys, Godfrey and Bartholomew. They both had angelic fair hair and blue eyes like their half-sister but where her skin was as pale as summer bleached grass the boys had the warm golden skin of their mother. Then the talk fell into a conversation I didn't quite understand to begin with. Not until Josie spelt it out for me.

'Haven't I told you Grace?' She said and didn't wait for an answer before she continued. 'We're expecting number three.' She patted her stomach. 'He's due at Christmas.'

'Congratulations,' I said.

I should have known Josie was pregnant, it just highlighted how long it had been since I'd seen her or Noah.

'So when are you going settle down and give my children some cousins?' Noah asked Torin.

'When the sun starts going around the earth.'

'Then a woman? A wife? Another Mrs Redferne?' Noah continued like a plough through a field of wild flowers.

'I don't think so,' Torin said.

'No one you've fallen in love with?' Noah was teasing and Torin didn't look impressed.

'Once upon a time a beautiful witch stole my heart and now she won't give it back,' Torin said. 'They'll be no more falling in love.'

Noah laughed loudly, 'Christ man, have you turned into a poet?'

I didn't want to hear about Torin's love life and turned away. I saw Josie rub her abdomen. Now I looked properly, it was unmistakably laden with more than a few extra meals. I wondered how that weight must feel inside her. I wondered if I would ever know how that felt. But of course I wouldn't. Not now. Not without Ezra.

'I need a cigarette.' I stood up so fast I knocked my chair to the floor.

Unexpected tears suddenly stung my eyes as I fled outside. I pinched my arm with my nails so I wouldn't cry. I didn't even know what I was crying about. I took a deep breath. And another.

I sat on a bench next to the lavender hedge that ran along one of the old stone walls. Running a palm over the bushes, I inhaled and took the scent into me. The stars had just begun to come out and the sky itself still held a remnant of the day's light, not yet dark navy but inky blue.

I heard Torin before he reached me. The night was so still and the air so tranquil, I would have heard an ant approach. I knew it was him without looking.

'You alright?' He said.

'Fine. I just wanted to smoke.'

I pulled the tobacco pouch out from the pocket of my hoody and made a show of making a roll-up. My hands were shaking and my throat hurt from unshed tears.

'So?'

'Don't start Torin,' I snapped.

'Gracie, don't be like this.' He used a soft and gentle tone.

'What would you like me to be like?' I found myself using the tone back at him, taking the venom out of my words.

'A little less hostile would be a start.'

'It's my default these days.' I smoked my roll-up and looked up at the stars.

'Aye, so I'm gathering.' He reached over and plucked my tobacco from my pocket.

'You could just ask.'

'Aye, I could.' He said, putting tobacco into a paper. 'Thing I'm wondering Gracie, is why you're so angry with me?'

I was momentarily thrown by his question. No one was direct with me anymore as though they didn't want to upset me with honesty. No one in the past two years had even mentioned my foul behaviour or my anger.

I was about to tell Torin that I was not angry with him specifically, but I realised that wasn't true. I was angry with him. I was really pissed off about a lot of things, and Torin was definitely one of those things. And as he'd decided to turn up in my life unannounced again, I felt I owed him some of my wrath.

'Do you really have no idea?' I asked.

'I have some. But I want you to tell me.'

'Well I'm not going to.' After I'd spoken I realised I sounded like a child and Torin was grinning.

'Did you miss me Gracie?' he teased.

I gave him a playful hit on the arm and smiled, 'Not as much as you've missed me.'

He gave a small laugh.

Silence relaxed around us, only the soft far-off sounds of a Friday night in town mingled with the odd hoot of an owl and the scurry of an unknown mammal in the bushes at the edge of the garden. I could smell the dry earth mixed with sweet floral scents of lavender and stocks. Torin lit his cigarette and blew smoke rings into the still air as though he was Gandalf.

He pointed out a couple of constellations and told me the story of how Orion came to be in the sky. He told me of the night sky in Australia where he'd just returned from. It was nice listening to him talk.

I had missed him.

December 2013

The flagstones were cold and unforgiving against my cheek. I blinked to see a pair of sensible black court shoes in front of my face.

'Up you get dear,' Ada said. Her voice was unique with its squeaky nasal tones. I felt her grasping at my arm. But she was too weak to help me up off the floor. 'I was just coming to give you a nice chicken pie, and I found your front door wide open. I called, but you didn't answer.'

Shame washed through me as I pulled myself to sit up and my foot knocked the empty vodka bottle from the night before across the kitchen. I had no recollection of why my front door had been open but it was likely related to the empty pill packet next to Ada's left shoe. As I brushed my hair back from my face I found a cigarette end tangled in it. That Ada should find me in such a state on my kitchen floor was humiliating.

'There's a good girl,' Ada said, and pulled a chair from the kitchen table out so I could sit down.

Sitting with my head in my hands, partly because my head was throbbing from my excesses but mostly because I couldn't look at Ada; I was so embarrassed and ashamed.

I heard her running the taps, filling the kettle and opening cupboards before she presented me with a mug of tea and sat on the other chair. I wished she'd leave.

We sat in silence for what felt like an age. The train rattled over the bridge at the end of the lane.

I really wished Ada would leave.

'My Patrick was knocked down by a car,' Ada said. 'He died on the pavement by the market cross surrounded by strangers. I buried him at the same church where we'd been married seven weeks before.'

Now I looked at her.

'He was a good man, my Patrick. He didn't deserve to go when he did. I didn't deserve to be left behind. But we don't have a choice about these things. Not that I could see that at the time. Mother scolded me for not being to get up in the mornings, for not being able to do the things I had to do. But she didn't understand.'

I knew Ada's husband was no longer alive, but I'd assumed they'd had a long life together, that he'd died relatively recently, not over fifty years ago.

'I'm sorry,' I said.

'You don't need to be sorry dear,' she said. Her pale blue eyes were full of empathy.

I felt tears roll down my cheeks. She squeezed my hand with her gnarled fingers that still carried her wedding band and offered me a smile.

'It does get better dear.'

'When?'

She shook her head. 'When you're ready.'

September 2014

Godfrey strained against the straps of the pushchair before the gateway to the park had even come into view. Barty's hand had grown sweaty in mine and as he pulled forward in his eagerness to reach the park he nearly slipped from my grasp. I hastened my step to keep up with the small child and listened to his babbling excitement as he told me all the things he was going to do in the park. Godfrey's frustration at still being restrained peaked into a toddler roar and Torin stopped pushing the pushchair and looked at me.

'Shall I let him out?' he asked.

'I think so?' I replied with a shrug.

'Mummy doesn't let Godfrey get out until we're in the park,' Barty told us with an admonishing tone, already pulling my hand toward the gates once more.

Torin picked up the pace to a near run, stopped just inside the gateway and released Godfrey. As soon as the straps were off the crying and shouting ceased and Godfrey started a determined waddle toward a rainbow coloured climbing frame. Barty joined his brother and scaled the red and blue rope ladder.

Torin and I stood side by side, our arms almost touching, as we hovered behind the children, our hands raised, ready to catch one should they fall.

'Christ, I'm knackered,' Torin said.

'This was your idea,' I pointed out, 'playing at doting auntie and uncle.'

He'd turned up at my house with Godfrey in the pushchair and Barty by his side. As though rehearsed, in unison the three of them had asked me to come to the park. It was a lovely sunny day, perhaps the last before autumn. I could hardly refuse.

'If you'd seen the state of Josie this morning you'd have offered to take the boys off her hands. She's exhausted,' Torin said.

'Why?'

'These two,' Torin said, indicating our nephews that were still climbing. 'Plus being pregnant, having a useless husband and a foul tempered teenager skulking around the place can't be easy. She runs that house single-handed.'

'Oh,' I said, frowning. 'But doesn't Noah help?'

'Noah's about as helpful as kick in the head when it comes to domestication.'

'What about Eliza?'

'From what I can make out, she hates the boys. And she doesn't seem too fond of Josie either.'

'Poor Josie,' I said. I had no idea she might be struggling; I'd always thought she had everything she could ever want. She always seemed so happy and bubbly.

Torin reached up and held Godfrey steady as he performed a tricky manoeuvre over the top of climbing frame. I watched Torin smile and talk with his youngest nephew. Something about the way Torin moved, of how he played with Godfrey reminded me of Ezra. Ezra had only met Godfrey a handful of times when he was but a babe in arms, he'd never seen him walk or talk. I'd never taken a child to the park with Ezra.

'Keep your eye on the ball Gracie, you've lost your charge,' Torin said with a grin and pointed across the play area to where Barty was now climbing the steps to the top of the slide.

I gave myself a mental slap to the cheek; this was not the time to dwell. Instead I went to Barty and smiled as he said, 'Watch Auntie Grace, watch me go down the slide.'

He launched himself down the yellow plastic and flew down at such a speed he continued off the end and landed with a bump on the rubbery flooring. I ran around expecting tears but Barty was laughing with his head thrown back.

'Again!' He roared and jumped to his feet.

The exercise was repeated time and time again until Barty requested my participation increase from observer. I climbed up then descended the slide. Unlike Barty, I found the bump from slide to floor jarred and hurt, and I wasn't inclined to repeat the experience, especially when I realised Torin has witnessed the event. He stood, pushing Godfrey in the swing, grinning, as I sat slightly stunned on the floor at the bottom of the slide. Barty too seemed to find it hilarious.

An hour or more slipped by as the four of us played together, in a whirl of primary colours and childish laughter. I'd forgotten how easily Torin and I always clicked with one another even if we'd not see each other for months. From the moment I'd met Torin I'd felt relaxed with him, as though I could really be myself.

Torin and I took the boys from the playground into the other side of the park that was set out formally with a lake and a bandstand and manicured lawns. We kicked a Thomas the Tank Engine football between the four of us; an exercise than consisted almost entirely of Torin and I retrieving the ball from various hedges. Then Godfrey fell over on the tarmac path and after a second of agonizing silence wailed his pain for the whole world to hear.

I scooped him up and felt his little arms go around my neck. I stood and cradled his body against mine. He was solid and heavier than I'd thought he'd be. I could feel the precious life in him; his breath against my neck, the heat of his body, the sound of his crying. He was fragile and yet bursting with life. He lifted his head and his sobbing subsided enough for him to say, 'Have ice cream Gracie?'

Torin was the only one who called me that. I glanced at Torin, already knowing he was watching me; one hand on the pushchair handle and the other clutching Barty's hand.

'Yes, we can have ice cream,' I said, and shifted Godfrey onto my hip.

We sat at a wobbly metal table outside the café, overlooking the lake. The boys were silent as they concentrated on the bowls of ice cream before them.

'What beautiful little boys you have,' a lady of middling years next to us said, leaning over from her table. 'And so well behaved.'

'They're not ours,' I said.

'Our nephews,' Torin added.

'Practising until you have your own?' she said.

Both Torin and I both began to explain that we were not together but stopped and smiled, catching each other's eye.

'It all comes quite naturally when they're yours,' the lady said.

'Right,' I replied, not wishing to prolong the conversation.

'You'll make lovely parents,' she continued at the same moment Godfrey got down from his chair and started toward the lake.

I stood up fast and followed, halting his progress before he could launch himself into the algae green waters of the lake. I held his sticky hand, and we skirted the lake toward a gathering of mallards.

'We'll catch you up,' Torin called.

By the looks of it the lady was still talking to him and I was glad to leave her and her misguided comments behind. But I couldn't help but ponder the notion of Torin and me as a couple, with a child. Smiling to myself, I dismissed it with a shake of my head.

Not far from the ducks were a group of teenage boys. A couple of them were mucking about, play fighting, while their friends looked on, smoking conspicuously. Despite the warmth of the day they all wore hoodies, with the hoods up. I recognised one of them as my neighbour Jerome. He took a hard drag on his cigarette, making his cheeks hollow and exhaled through his nose before dropping the butt to the floor. He spoke to one of his friends and smiled at the response, before he looked up and caught my eye, lifted a finger in greeting and nodded at me. Jerome watched Godfrey and me for a moment as we walked around the edge of the lake then turned back to talk to his friend.

By the time Torin and Barty had caught up with us Jerome and his mates had gone, sauntering off across the grass. But Jerome had turned and given me another one finger wave before his departure.

After a small diversion to play on the empty bandstand the four of us made our way back to Redferne House. Godfrey was now content to sit in the pushchair and sprawled like a man after a long evening in the pub, his foot dangling off the footrest so I was wary of catching it against an obstacle. I didn't feel qualified to be in charge of the pushchair but Barty had persuaded Torin to carry him on his shoulders. He kept putting his hands over Torin's eyes as he held on.

Back at Redferne House the two tired boys were allowed to flop in front of a Thomas the Tank Engine DVD. As Josie settled on the sofa between them, an arm around each boy, she thanked Torin and me. I was delighted to witness her genuine gratitude as she told us she'd done nothing more than sit and read while we'd been out.

As the theme tune began Torin and I pulled the door to the living room closed and escaped to the kitchen.

'Gin and tonic?' Torin asked.

I'd been thinking I would go home but the sound of a cold drink was inviting.

Torin made up a large jug with slices of lemon. The ice tinkled against the glass as he carried it out to the front garden. The sun had warmed the stone bench and bathed both Torin and I in golden light as we sat down in the last of the day's rays.

'Alright?' Torin asked.

'Yes,' I said, with a true smile. 'I am.'

'Good,' he replied, with a faint frown of puzzlement on his brow.

'Thank you for today,' I said, by way of explanation. 'It's been a long time since I did something nice like that.'

My words made Torin look sad, and I wished I could take them back. I rolled my eyes and turned away from him.

'What?' He asked.

'You.'

'What did I do?'

'You gave me the look of pity.'

'What you said was sad.'

'I don't need your pity Torin.'

'I don't pity you. I was just sad that you haven't done anything nice for ages. That's shite.'

I rolled my eyes again and turned my face to the sun.

I jumped to my feet, gasping as I felt something wet and cold slipping down my back. Shaking my top, I reached around to extract what was left of an ice cube.

Torin was chuckling. 'I really don't pity you Gracie.'

I cuffed his arm with the back of my hand and sat back beside him. 'That was uncalled for,' I said, but I was smiling again.

'But it stopped you from sulking.'

'I wasn't sulking.'

'Uh, huh.'

I gave him shove. He shoved me back. I elbowed him. He elbowed back. I pushed him. He pushed me so hard I fell off the bench onto the pea shingle.

'Ow,' I muttered.

'Any damage?' he asked, coming over.

I looked at my palm and found a small cut.

'Nothing much,' I said.

'You always hurt yourself,' Torin scolded and chuckled as he offered me a hand. I put my hand in his and let him pull me to my feet.

'You remember that Star Wars party we went to?' Torin asked, as we sat down again.

'Of course I do. You went as Han Solo. I went as Leia and Ezra was Luke Skywalker.'

'Aye,' Torin said. 'But do you remember falling off the bench?'

'I remember you pushed me off the bench.'

'I did not.'

'Yes you did. And I got glass in my arm.' I said, and eased up my sleeve, 'Here's the scar.'

Torin looked at my arm, then traced the two-inch scar with his fingertip. 'Did I really push you off the bench?

'You know you did.'

One of Ezra's colleagues had hosted the Star Wars Party at their large Victorian house and Torin and I hadn't known anyone. We'd ended up in the garden with a bottle of tequila, while the rest of the party carried on inside. We'd been playing with light sabres and somehow that had ended with Torin pushing me off the end of the picnic bench. I'd smashed my tequila glass on the paving slabs and ended up with a good portion of it in my arm. Torin and I had spent the rest of the night at A & E.

'Well, I'm sure there was a good reason,' Torin said. 'But you always were good at hurting yourself quite spectacularly.'

As we reminisced about my many and various accidents we worked our way through the jug of gin and tonic. Torin told me a little of the work that had brought him to Redferne House for a few months. It was a couple of separate but interlinked jobs, one of which was very local, the others in Devon and Cornwall. He was going to Cornwall in the morning, to get one of the jobs under way, he would be there all week. He asked me if I'd like to go for a drink when he got back. I just smiled. Being with Torin today was like old times as though we'd somehow managed to sweep all the unsightly feelings under a large rug. But sooner or later my clumsiness would mean I'd trip over the rug revealing all sorts of messy emotions.

December 2012

'Hey Grace,' Ezra called, after the front door of the cottage banged shut.

'Hey,' I called back, putting another neat circle of pastry into a hollow in the baking tray. I heard him taking off his trainers and coat, the jangle of keys, the slump of his bag. 'Good day at the office dear?' I joked.

Coming to the doorway of the kitchen, he laughed. 'Yeah, it was good. And how was your day?'

'Fine.'

'You're *baking*? What a novelty.' He grinned, his dark eyes wide in mock surprise.

He loosened his tie, slipped it over his head, and hung it on the back of the chair.

'Ada gave me some jam. She made it herself. So I thought I should put it to use.'

'Wow, we have jam tarts for dinner then?'

'Maybe,' I admitted. Ezra knew there was no chance I'd have embarked on baking jam tarts as well as making dinner.

He came up behind me, and laid his hand on my abdomen, 'I'm sure I'll manage, besides I have other things on my mind.' He nuzzled his face into the crook of my neck; his cheek was cold from the cycle home. He placed warm kisses on my skin, the stubble on his chin prickling against me.

'Do you now?' I asked, my floury hands pausing on the pastry, turning my cheek to lean against his shoulder.

'Uh huh.'

'You smell of winter,' I said and inhaled the crisp chill embedded in his grey fleece top.

'It's cold out there.' He pressed my body back against him, 'but you must be toasty with all these layers on?' He slipped his other hand under my tops and jumper.

'Cold.' I gasped, as his chilled fingers connected with the warm skin of my stomach.

'Sorry.' He chuckled and removed his hand and kissed my neck again. Another kiss and he held my hips in his hands, 'Grace?'

'Yes Ezra?' I said, mimicking his tone.

'You know what we talked about? That once we'd moved to Redferne Lane…?' He spoke in almost a whisper and finished his sentence with another kiss.

'Yes?' I answered, smiling.

'Well we've moved.'

'We have.'

'So?'

'So?' I felt my heart pick up pace.

'So,' the delight was evident in his voice. 'I think we should.'

He pressed his hips against me.

'Right now?' I asked, turning my head to look up at him.

'Uh huh.'

'But I have pastry hands.'

'Then let me wash them for you.'

With him still behind me, we walked to the sink. Ezra turned the tap on and let it run. Tiny droplets splashed up at me from the enamelled basin. He took the hard soap and lathered it between his hands, then began to rub his over mine. His slender fingers moved in between my own, sliding the flecks of pastry from my skin. He wound my wedding ring around dislodging hidden pieces. And pushed pale dough from the stone on my engagement ring with his thumb nail.

'Shouldn't you take these off when you bake?'

'I never take them off, you know that,' I said and leant my head back against him.

He made a sound of approval in his throat and placed a kiss on my neck. He moved our hands under the running water. It had warmed and fell over our skin as Ezra ran his hands over mine, washing the soap off.

He pressed his body against me. I felt the hard side of the sink against my stomach as he laid kisses down my neck. I turned and slid wet fingers into his hair as I reached up to kiss his lips.

His damp hand reached under my top and connected with the skin at my waist.

'Still cold,' I uttered, interrupting our kiss.

Ezra smiled and placed his other hand on my skin too before running both up to my shoulder blades. Then one slid down my back and around my waist, moving up, over ribs to my breast.

We kissed again, Ezra pressing me against the sink once more, his hands busy with lace and straps and hooks. The tap was still running behind me. He tasted sweet and slightly metallic, like water fresh from a spring.

'Too many clothes Grace,' he said and peeled off my jumper. He discarded it on the floor and pulled another top up over my head, leaving only my shirt.

I pulled the zip of his fleece down and Ezra hastily shrugged out of it. He reached a hand down my thigh and began pulling my skirt up. I felt the tickle of excitement. Then Ezra stopped.

'We can't conceive our first child against the kitchen sink.'

I laughed, 'I don't think it matters where we are.'

'It matters to me.' He took my hand.

'Wait, the tap.' I reached over and my hand twisted the cool metal, stopping the flow of water.

'Come on,' he said and lead me through to the living room, our fingers entwined.

He pushed me, as gently as he did everything, down onto the sofa and knelt between my legs. He lowered himself, bringing our lips close. I could feel his breath. He smiled before he began kissing me again. I felt the shape of his shoulders through his shirt, the weight of him on me as he lay between my legs. He unbuttoned my shirt and moved the fabric aside, hands on skin. Lips and tongues and kisses.

Fingers migrated. I undid his belt. He pushed up my skirt. He smelt of sweat and the dark winter's night outside, wild and untamed.

'Tights Grace?' he said, 'I hate tights.' He knelt up and pulled them, and my knickers off, flinging them across the room.

I popped the button on his trousers. Unzipped. Paused. Watched his lips part; breathing heavy. With a grin, he stood and let his trousers descend to the floor. I watched him slide black boxers down and with a flourish like a matador he threw them to join my tights.

'Socks,' I smiled, before he re-joined me on the sofa.

Without such elegance, he whipped them from his feet. Then stood proud before me.

He eased my knees apart and took his place between them. His hands journeyed from calf, up thigh and paused momentarily. I waited, my breath held.

His hands touched, moving, pressing, cool fingers on wet, hot flesh. A groan from me met by one from him.

He lay down on me once more, our hands caressing, bodies moving in rhythm.

He lifted himself up on one elbow and looked down at me, serious for a moment. 'No more condoms then?'

'No.'

'You're sure?'

I nodded, 'Are you?'

'Yes.'

He pushed inside me, slowly, like we had all the time in the world.

October 2014

'So Grace,' my boss, Simon said. He hitched his trousers a little before he perched on the edge of his desk. 'I thought it was time we had a little chat.'

'Right,' I sighed, wondering if I had any of my little white pills left in my bag. My palms were clammy and my heart was beating somewhat erratically.

'So, as I'm sure you're aware, you've been a touch late in once or twice this week…' he left his sentence hanging between us.

I'd been late every day this week. I hadn't made it in until midday on Monday. After I'd left Torin, after we'd taken the boys to the park, I'd felt good. We'd had a lovely time. I'd enjoyed playing with Godfrey and Barty and I'd so liked seeing Torin. Yet that pleasure had quickly disappeared. And I'd found myself sinking and felt the heavy blanket of despair laying over me. I'd sat up late into the night drinking, falling asleep on the sofa, then waking up long after the sun had risen, making me more than late for work. And the rest of the week I just hadn't been able to pull myself out of bed in time to catch the bus. That day with Torin and the boys in the park seemed like a distant memory.

'And, that's just this week…' Simon continued.

Simon was only a few years older than me but I always thought of him as significantly older. He liked to wear three-piece suits and sometimes a cravat or bow tie; the trousers were always tight fitting and the jackets tailored. And he had a silver pocket watch he carried in his waistcoat. Simon was tall and elegant and somehow didn't look as foolish as he might. His hair was a sandy colour, dead straight, cut to lay just on the tips of his ears and parted down the centre.

'I was wondering if everything was alright?' Simon asked, tentative and kind.

'Everything's fine.'

'I mean, if there was anything I should know?' He made a funny grimace. 'Anything you wanted to tell me, it would of course be in strict confidence.'

I looked down at my hands as they lay in my lap.

'I quite understand that I may not be the person you'd like to talk to so maybe I could set up an appointment for you with Tracey, from Human Resources?'

I glanced up at him.

He gave me an awkward smile.

'Uh, no, thank you,' I said, thinking that Tracey from Human Resources was the last person I would ever want to talk to. She was the scariest woman I had ever met, she reminded me of a hungry wolf; she had a piercing stare and a habit of licking her lips.

'Ah, right, well …' Simon sighed and shifted on the edge of the desk. I could hear how uncomfortable Simon was with this conversation and that only made me feel worse. 'The thing is, I know you haven't had the easiest of times since you've been with us and I feel terrible for even having to say anything but well, we need a little more commitment from you really.'

Tears pricked my eyes. I'd only been with the company for two weeks before Ezra died and ever since I was often late and took too many sick days. When I was in I couldn't concentrate and rarely completed anything. I made a lot of mistakes. My colleagues were still strangers to me; I didn't speak to anyone beyond formalities. I was quite possibly the worst employee they'd ever had.

A few tears escaped and I wiped my eyes with the back of my hand, sniffing.

'But obviously if you're not feeling up to it, I quite understand…' Simon said, as another tear rolled down my cheek. He was always so nice to me. Even when I was late he often made me coffee and brought it to my desk, quietly updating me on anything I might need to know.

'No, it's fine,' I said and raised my eyes to Simon's face. 'I'm sorry Simon, I'll try harder.'

He gave me the pity smile and thumped the air with his fist. 'That's my girl. Yes. Great.'

I nodded and forced a smile.

He sighed again. 'I'm so glad we've had this chat Grace.'

'Yes,' I mumbled, getting to my feet, knowing I was about thirty seconds away from a break down.

'We must do it again sometime.'

I nodded, uttered a goodbye, and all but ran to the door.

The wind stuck pins into my skin as I faced the open air outside the building. My face was wet with tears and my chest felt so tight I could hardly breathe. Rummaging in my bag I found a strip of pills and popped one, then another from the foil and dry swallowed them.

I walked, needing to be away from the office and found myself buying a bottle of vodka from the off licence next to the bus stop. I didn't even wait until I'd left the shop before I cracked the seal and took a swig, grimaced and threw back another. I swore at a man who witnessed my actions then left the shop, tucking the bottle into my coat pocket.

While I waited alone for the bus I smoked three cigarettes, popped another pill and swallowed more vodka. By the time the bus arrived I couldn't even remember what had been so upsetting about my conversation with Simon.

I woke up in my bed. I was naked but for my knickers and bra. They didn't match.

'Evening.'

Torin sat on my bedroom window sill.

'Why are you in my room?' I asked.

'So you didn't choke on your own vomit.'

'I've been sick?' I didn't feel like I had.

'No, but I wasn't sure what you'd been up to.'

'Nothing.' I said, but I felt like shite.

'Right.' Torin sighed and looked out of the window down onto Redferne Lane.

I tucked onto my side, my duvet made a lovely crinkly sound as I pulled it in close as if it would hug me, hold me and tell me everything was okay. It felt so nice to lose myself in the cotton folds of my warm bed.

'Don't go back to sleep,' Torin said, making me jump. I realised I'd been drifting off again, lost in soft thoughts of Ezra, cocooned in the safety of my bed, dreaming he was holding me. I felt a sudden hollow inside me as I remembered Ezra wasn't here. That my dream was just wishful thinking.

I opened my eyes and watched Torin get up from the window sill. He picked his way over the dirty clothes on my floor. A few boards creaked as he stood on them and a spring in my mattress twanged as he perched on the edge of my bed. The hole inside me seemed to get bigger and began to hurt. I remembered why I felt so awful.

'You should get up. Eat something,' Torin said.

'I'm not hungry.'

'Then get up at least.'

'What time is it?'

'Nearly midnight.'

I hesitated before I asked, 'What day is it?'

'Saturday.'

I held my arms around me as though I could squeeze the rising ache out of my chest, trying to fathom what had happened to the last twenty-four hours, since I'd left work.

'Did you take my clothes off?' I asked.

'Aye.'

I squeezed myself harder.

'No need to be coy, I've seen it all before Gracie.'

He looked at me, his black irises scolding me for something I had done wrong. But I wasn't sure what it was.

I ached. I felt uncomfortable and exposed. I wanted Torin to get off my bed. I wanted him to go. How was he even in my house in the first place?

'Have you got a key?'

'Aye.' He spoke as though it was obvious.

'How?'

'Ezra gave it to me. He said I was always welcome.' There was an accusation but also a question in his tone. Was he still welcome? I didn't know the answer.

'Can you pass me a top, please?' I asked.

He bent over and scooped up an item from the floor. It was one of Ezra's old T-shirts. I pulled it on but it had always been big and the neck was nearly as wide as my shoulders. It slipped off one shoulder and then the other when I tried to rebalance it. It was a bedroom T-shirt, not something to be worn in front of anyone else.

Just as I was about to ask Torin to leave, he said, 'So what's going on?'

'What do you mean?'

'Well I came round this afternoon so we could go for a drink, like we planned but obviously you had other ideas and I found you soaked to the skin, lying on the kitchen floor, off your head.'

He was angry with me.

Vague recollections of lying on the cold hard floor and of Torin's voice surfaced. My face tingly and my lips slightly numb. The pill packet on the kitchen floor beside me. The empty vodka bottle. Torin kneeling in front of me. The definition of his chest visible under the faded fabric of his T-shirt. Placing my palms and my cheek on his chest. The smell of tobacco and earth and just a little undercurrent of sweat. Torin's hands on my back, holding me against his chest.

He'd just held me.

It had felt so nice to be held.

I looked away from Torin embarrassed at throwing myself against his chest when I was shit-faced. 'I'd like to get dressed, could you leave?'

He didn't move.

I looked back at him. 'Please?'

'You've got two minutes.' Torin stood and walked around my bed and went out, leaving the door open.

It didn't take me two minutes to put on a pair of jeans and change my top to one that didn't descend down my arm. I had a sudden recollection of my little chat with Simon. I sat back down on my bed, overcome once more with the emotions that had sent me to the bottom of a vodka bottle.

A noise that resembled something of the tangled hollow inside me came out in a roar. I lay down on my bed and cried.

'Gracie?' Torin said, coming back into my room.

Torin climbed on my bed and lay down behind me. He put his arms around me and held me, stroked my hair and spoke soft words of comfort. And I cried soaking my pillow with my snot and salty tears.

When I had run out of tears Torin held me still. I could hear the wind rattling the window in the frame.

'Always better to have a good cry,' Torin said. As he spoke I felt his breath on the back of my neck.

'I don't want to cry.'

'I like to have a good cry sometimes.'

'You cry?' I asked and almost turned to look at him, so I might judge if he was telling the truth. Somehow I couldn't imagine Torin in tears.

'Aye sometimes.'

'When?'

'Usually when you girls break my heart.'

'Is your heart broken now?'

'Not as broken as yours.'

We lay awhile longer. I did not want to move. It felt so nice to be in someone's arms. Torin's arms. I was afraid that once out of his embrace I would crumble once more.

We did not move or speak. His body was firm and warm and alive pressed against mine. I relished the weight of his arm on my waist and the gentle rest of his fingertips on my arm.

Torin whispered, 'You should eat Gracie, let me get you something?'

I nodded and held myself as Torin slipped his arms from around me. Listening to him in my house, I remembered what it had been like to share my home with Ezra. I'd always know where he was even if he was silent as if I could just sense the heat of him coming from a particular room.

Mugs of coffee and a plate of toast were on a tray. Torin placed it on the edge of my bed and tugged the duvet underneath so it would sit flat.

'So?' Torin said. 'What's going on?'

I sighed. I'd been about to revert to my default response of *everything is fine*, but as I looked at Torin, the one person in the world that probably knew me better than I knew myself, I realised, that if nothing else it would be insulting to tell him I was fine when I so obviously was not.

After a deep breath I said, 'I think my boss wants me to leave my job.'

'Is that what this is all about?' He picked up a piece of toast and broke it in half with his fingers. Crumbs scattered on the plate underneath and a few escaped onto my pale blue bedspread.

'Not really,' I admitted.

'What is this all about then?'

I shrugged and shook my head, not because I didn't know the answer but because there was too much to put into words. Especially when my brain was befuddled and still under the influence.

'It's Ezra's birthday on Monday,' Torin said. His eyes were so dark I couldn't gauge any emotion from them.

I nodded. It was as much as I could say about Ezra then. I did not want to think about how he'd have turned thirty-two on Monday.

Torin held a piece of toast toward me.

I thanked him and took it. I'm sure it was good, but I felt so hollow I could hardly taste it and it cloyed in my mouth. But I forced it down and sipped coffee.

'Eat some more,' Torin said.

'I'd rather a cigarette,' I said.

'Eat that first,' he said and passed me another piece of toast.

While I chewed I watched Torin roll two cigarettes. I'd forgotten how nimble his thick fingers could be. He lit one of the roll-ups and passed it to me. I mumbled a thanks and inhaled gratefully. As the nicotine hit my bloodstream I felt muscles I didn't know were tensed, relax.

Torin watched me as he smoked his own cigarette. I became incredibly aware of his physical proximity. He leant against the board at the foot end of the bed and I sat, propped up on pillows, against the head board. Our feet met in the middle. Mine were bare and pale and striped with blue veins. His were covered in thick creamy woollen socks. I could almost feel the fibres from his socks against the sole of my foot.

'If things are doing your head in, you could tell me?' Torin said.

We looked at each other. Once upon a time, not so long ago, I had known every line and scar and blemish on his face, and every fleck in those ebony eyes of his. And yet now I wondered if I knew him at all. He was so familiar and yet everything was now so different.

'I wouldn't know where to start,' I admitted.

He nodded, as though he understood the mess inside my head.

'Maybe next time, instead of reaching for the bottle, you'll talk to me?'

I wanted to nod and say yes, of course Torin, next time I'll tell you everything. I wanted to say that actually, there won't be a next time. But it wasn't the first time I'd taken a cocktail of drugs and alcohol. It wasn't the first time I'd lost an entire day. It was just the first time that Torin had been around to witness my failings.

So I took a drag of my cigarette and then apologised. I wanted to reach out and touch Torin but I couldn't. Instead I apologised again; I was sorry that he'd found me in a heap on the kitchen floor. I'd rather he didn't know what a mess I was in.

He sighed and shook his head; his anger resurfacing.

We held each other's eyes once more. I willed him not to be angry with me any longer but I had no idea what he was thinking.

'I should go,' he said, looking away.

'Do you have to?'

'It's late and I'm tired Gracie.' He sounded exhausted, and I was sure it was more than just sleep deprivation. But I didn't want Torin to leave. I didn't want to be alone. And I realised I was going to start crying again. I sniffed and tried to swallow the tears away but they fell down my cheeks anyway. I wiped crossly with my sleeve and couldn't look at Torin.

The mattress creaked as Torin stood.

'Don't go.' The words were out of my mouth.

I heard him sigh and looked up.

'I could stay?' he uttered.

I nodded.

'I'll be downstairs,' Torin said.

'Stay here?' I asked it quietly so he could pretend to not hear if he wanted. Then I lay down in my bed, my cheek against my pillow and looked at the space where Ezra used to lie.

I felt Torin sit down behind me.

'I can't take his place,' he said, softly.

I moved over onto Ezra's side.

The pillow was cold.

Torin lay beside me, on top of the duvet. And he held me, his front to my back.

October 2012

'It's so nice of Noah and Josie to have us all at such short notice,' Ezra said, still trying to convince me that going to stay with his brothers for the weekend was just as good as going to Cornwall as we'd planned. 'Isn't it lucky we hadn't booked?'

If we had booked, we would still be going to Cornwall for a long weekend of beaches and a nice hotel. Just the two of us. But it was Ezra's birthday, and he'd wanted to be spontaneous. And that had brought us to Redferne Lane.

'Yes,' I mumbled as we got off the train.

The train hushed behind me and people bustled around. I looked up and saw Torin looking back at me. He was thinner and paler than since we'd seen him more than a year ago; dark circles under his eyes and his hair hung over his forehead in a tangled mess. He was back from Canada and was to stay at Redferne House for the weekend before he went home to Scotland. It was his fault we were not going to Cornwall. Ezra had wanted to see Torin. And I'll admit that I was pleased to see him too.

Torin smiled, but I noticed the dullness of his eyes. He inhaled one last drag of his cigarette before dropping it on the floor and took the few steps towards us.

'Gracie,' he said. He hesitated then kissed my cheek. 'You're looking well.'

I stepped back. 'So are you,' I lied.

'Big brother,' Ezra said, and gave Torin a long affectionate hug. 'It's so good to see you.' He clapped Torin on the shoulder. 'Man we've missed you.'

'Aye, and you little brother. And you.' Torin said. He glanced at me again, then looked back to Ezra. 'So I took Noah's car to come and get you, it's just over there. Let's get back to the house.'

We had lunch as soon as we arrived at Redferne House; seven of us seated around the handsome oak table in the kitchen. Noah sat at the head with Eliza on one side and Josie on the other, Barty in a highchair beside her. Ezra took the other end, with Torin and me on either side. It was near impossible for Torin and me to avoid catching each other's eye. I kept offering smiles to Torin and although he smiled back, those smiles did not reach his eyes. After lunch Josie and Noah suggested a walk down the lane. Torin rolled his eyes, and I was reluctant myself but we all left the house none the less.

The leaves of the beech trees that flanked Redferne Lane had turned a delightful orange, and some had fallen, covering the lane in a copper coloured carpet. We walked to the three cottages at the end of the lane. They had been built for the staff at Redferne House in the early 1800's. Two of them were still occupied by staff; Ada who'd been the housekeeper until a few years ago and Sam the current cleaner with her son Jerome. Ezra and I soon discovered that the motivation for the family walk down the lane was to show us the third cottage. Noah was thinking of selling it to fund building work at the house.

'Thought you might be interested?' Noah said. 'Thought it might be rather wonderful to keep it in the family too.'

Ezra looked as confused as I was; it made no sense for us to buy a house down in the depths of Somerset when we both worked in Bristol.

Noah was grinning like a boy with a bag of sweets. 'Before you say anything, there's something else I want to put your way.'

'What's going on?' Ezra asked, narrowing his eyes.

Josie looked at me, smiling and excited.

'I want you to come and work for me,' Noah said. 'With me.'

For a moment no one spoke. Ezra glanced at me as Noah talked about his offer and his plans for the expansion of his architecture firm. I smiled and shrugged at Ezra. I turned to look at Torin, wanting to know what he knew of this but he was already walking into the meadow, with Eliza and Barty.

'Shall I show you the cottage?' Josie asked, dangling an old fashioned iron key in front of me.

As we went inside Josie explained that the last occupant had been the gardener at the house but he'd died many years ago and the cottage had stood empty since. It was a sweet, petite and olde-worlde house, with a dinky fireplace and flagstone floors. The windows were small and had warped handmade glass. The ceilings were beamed and low, and despite the lack of furniture and the cool stale air, it felt like a home even though it had been empty for years.

'Of course, it'll need a full make-over, but structurally it's all sound,' Josie said, after we'd looked around downstairs.

I wondered if my mild alarm at the lack of utilities had shown in my face.

Josie was full with pregnancy, her stomach so big I couldn't quite fathom how she would last another month or more before she gave birth. She huffed and gave little groans as she moved up the stairs, telling me there were three more rooms.

We passed the doorway to a tiny box room that Josie said should most likely become the bathroom and went into a room at the back of the cottage that had a fantastic view of the meadow. I could see Torin smoking a cigarette by a large solitary oak tree in the middle of the meadow while Barty was bashing a stick against it and Eliza was skipping around it. For a moment I wished I was out there smoking beside Torin, talking about something irrelevant instead of looking at this cottage. It felt as though Ezra and I were being offered a place in the grown up's club while Torin still had to play amongst the children. I wasn't sure where I belonged.

Josie escorted me back onto the landing and showed me the hatch to the attic, informing me there was scope to make a third bedroom in the future, should we want to. Then she showed me the front bedroom.

It was a wonky room with not a right angle in sight. There was a small fireplace set into the wall and a deep window seat sat below the crooked window. The floorboards gave a welcoming creak as I walked around imaging our bed in the room.

'We thought maybe you'd be thinking about settling down?' Josie said, and I turned to look at her. She rubbed her stomach. 'Starting a family?'

'We haven't really talked about it,' I mumbled, although this wasn't true. Ezra had talked about it. He wanted to have children, but I was still hesitating, waiting for something, but I didn't quite know what.

'Well, maybe you will now?' She smiled. 'You couldn't find a better place to bring up children.'

I smiled back. Maybe it was time for me and Ezra to start a family.

I sat on the window seat and looked down into the lane. Ezra and Noah were talking and unexpectedly, I felt a fizz of excitement at the possibility of living somewhere like this.

A woman with bottle blonde hair and perky breasts came out of the cottage next door. She laughed with a flirtatious flick of her hair at something Noah said. She shook hands with Ezra. Then a lanky boy with dark hair snuck out of the door, threw a quick look at the adults talking and made off down the lane in the opposite direction, his hood up and his hands in his pockets.

Josie sat on the window seat beside me with a sigh, her hand bracing her lower back.

'So? What do you think Grace?' She asked.

'Well, obviously, it's a lovely cottage,' I said.

'Sorry, I don't mean to pressure you.' She reached over and squeezed my hand. 'It's just it would mean an awful lot to Noah if Ezra came to work for him. And we'd love to have you both closer. Us Redferne's seem so spread out these days.'

As evening drew in we sat in the living room back up at Redferne House with a stately fire crackling in the grate. We played card games with Eliza while Josie put Barty to bed. Then Noah announced it was bedtime for Eliza too. With a coy smile she asked Ezra to take her up and tuck her in. She was almost fourteen, although she looked and acted younger and I wondered if it would be the last time she'd want her uncle tucking her in. But for now she seemed content to still be a little girl and I could hear her and Ezra giggling all the way up the stairs. Noah stood up and excused himself, muttering something about going down the lane as he needed to speak to the cleaner.

Torin and I, suddenly alone, sat in silence.

'Are you going move here?' Torin asked, after a time.

'I don't know.'

'You should.'

'Why?'

'It's family right?'

'So why do you spend so much time away if family is so important?' I asked, my question more waspish than I'd intended.

He gave me a frown and pursed his lips.

'None of us have seen you since the wedding,' I said, with a gentler tone.

'I'm a fuck up and none of you can cope with me being around all the time. I'm best in small portions.' Torin gave a lazy smile.

I rolled my eyes. 'You're not a fuck up, you just like to think you are. It gives you an excuse to behave badly.'

'Is that so?'

'Yes. I mean look at you, you're a state. I bet you've been screwing your way around wherever you were, sticking coke up your nose every other night and drowning your liver in whiskey. You couldn't act like that if you saw your family all the time could you?'

'Insightful aren't we?' Torin ran a hand over his head, momentarily lifting his hair from his face.

I glanced at him. 'Right though?'

He sighed. 'Mostly.'

I waited to see if he wanted to tell me more. But he didn't.

'You look ill,' I told him.

'Thank you.'

'I'm only saying it because I care.'

He laughed. 'Right, of course you do.'

'Torin,' I said, a little hurt.

'Don't fret woman, I can look after myself.'

'Really? It doesn't look like it.' I stood up and made to leave the room. I was in no mood to play Torin's games.

'Wait Gracie,' Torin said, standing up too.

I turned to face him.

He looked at me with his sunken eyes and grey skinned face. Whatever he'd been up to it wasn't doing him any good.

'You are happy aren't you? You and Ezra?' he asked.

I nodded.

He closed his eyes then opened them again, trying to pull a smile to his face.

'What's the matter?' I asked. 'What's going on?'

He shook his head. 'I'm alright Gracie.'

'Really?'

'Aye,' he sighed. 'I've just been finding there's some shite missing in my life, you know? Since…' Torin stopped talking as Ezra came back into the room.

Ezra stopped and frowned as he saw Torin and me facing each other in the centre of the room. His face was full of questions.

'There you are,' Torin said, in a jovial tone he'd not used while he talked to me. 'I was just going to find your birthday present.'

Torin left the room and Ezra came to stand in front of me where Torin had been only a moment before.

'Everything alright?' Ezra asked.

I wasn't sure if he was referring to Torin or the offer Noah had made. 'Yes,' I answered but my voice betrayed my uncertainty.

He smiled and placed his hands on my hips. 'Are you freaking out Grace? I can't believe Noah has just thrown this at us without warning. We can say no, you know that, don't you?' He gave a slight pause but not long enough for me to reply. 'I mean I know it's a big deal and you'd have to find a new job and everything but it is a fabulous opportunity.' He paused again. 'But we can say no. If you were totally against the idea?'

I smiled. 'It's okay Ezra, I'm not totally against the idea. What are you thinking?'

He frowned. 'Am I crazy to even be considering it?'

'No, it is an amazing opportunity. And that cottage is lovely.'

'Are you into this idea Grace?' Ezra asked, his tone dripping with surprise.

'I don't know. I think I might be. A little bit.'

We lost the chance to talk any more as Josie and Torin came back into the room. Josie carried a chocolate cake with candles and a sugar craft bike in the middle. I think it was supposed to resemble the one I'd given Ezra earlier that morning before we came to Redferne Lane; a new road bike, faster and lighter for him to cycle to work on than his mountain bike. Ezra had been ridiculously pleased with it.

Torin held a magnum of Champagne in one hand and in the other, flutes upside down with their necks between his fingers.

'Where's Noah?' Josie asked.

'He said he was going down the lane to speak to the cleaner?' I said.

'Now?' She frowned.

I shrugged.

Josie sighed and rolled her eyes. 'Well we can't wait for him the wax is starting to drip all over the cake.'

We sang Happy Birthday to Ezra, and he blew out the candles.

'Have you made a wish?' Josie asked.

'I don't need to, I have everything I've ever wanted,' Ezra said and looked at me.

'Ah, how sweet,' Josie said, with a smiling sigh.

Torin popped the champagne and poured it into the pale pink flutes.

Noah burst into the room looking flushed.

'There you are,' Josie said, with a tone of annoyance.

'Right on cue,' Noah said to his wife and scooped up a flute. 'A toast to my baby brother. Happy thirtieth birthday, my dear boy.'

And we all raised our glasses.

October 2014

I sat on the window sill in my bedroom looking down upon Redferne Lane, dressed for work but needing a little longer to ready myself. I'd woken with the rising sun and a headache, exhausted from my excesses at the weekend. After two cups of coffee, some painkillers and I don't know how many cigarettes; I was beginning to feel a little more normal. Today I would not be late for work.

Eliza came down the lane in her St. Marys school uniform. She looked younger with her hair in a ponytail, wearing a blazer, tie and functional grey school skirt; a stark contrast to when I'd seen her before, with a tonne of eyeliner and her hair loose.

Jerome came out of his house next door, just after Eliza passed by.

Ada came from under the bridge on her bike. The sun appeared to dazzle her and she swerved heading straight for Eliza.

I could see what was about to happen but was powerless to prevent it.

Too late, Ada tried to swerve around Eliza, but caught her wheel on my niece's foot. Eliza screamed. Ada lost her balanced and crashed straight into Jerome. And both he and the old lady fell on to the hard tarmac.

With my breath caught in my throat, I ran downstairs and outside.

The shopping from Ada's basket had spilt across the path. A milk carton had split and a flow of white trickled out, forming a pool in a dip of the faded tarmac. Oranges had rolled in every direction.

Eliza was crying and gasping for breath, sat on the floor, holding her ankle.

Jerome sat up and leant against the wall, his legs out in front of him. His trousers, on his right leg, were ripped to the knee. His shin was an ugly mess. Grit from the path stuck to his broken flesh. Dark blood ran over his pale hairy skin and congealed on his black and white chequered sock.

'Are you okay?' I said, looking between both of the teenagers.

Eliza nodded but whimpered, 'It hurts.'

'You're going to be okay.'

Eliza nodded and her crying subsided a little.

'And you?' I asked Jerome. His tangled hair hung over his face.

He nodded. 'Is she?' Jerome said looking at Ada.

Ada wasn't moving. She lay on the path, her eyes closed like she'd decided to lie down for a little nap. She wasn't tangled up in her bike nor were any of her limbs lying at an odd angle. There was no blood. No wounds. But she looked dead. I didn't want to touch her.

Yet I knelt by Ada's side. Even before I put my hand to her neck I could see her chest softly rising and falling.

'Ada?' I said. 'Can you hear me?'

She didn't move. I tried again, still nothing.

I could see the fine dust of her face powder on her cheek. Her silvery curls still set in place around her head.

I pulled out my phone and dialled 999.

We sat on a row of orange plastic chairs with metal legs, a spare seat between us. There was no one else in the waiting area. I'd spent many hours in A & E waiting rooms throughout my life by this was the first time I was waiting for someone else.

'Does it hurt?' I said.

'Bit.' Jerome nodded, his voice was barely audible above the electronic hum of the strip lights above us. It was not a kind light, it did not flatter; the yellowy hue made his pale skin tone look odd, like he was unwell as well as injured. His wounded leg was stretched out in front of him. His trainers squeaked against the beige tiled floor every time he moved. The paramedics had covered his wound with gauze but trails of blood had escaped from underneath and dried on his skin. I hoped they'd call him in to check his leg soon.

Ada and Eliza were already being seen to. I had yet to hear the prognosis on Ada but Eliza had sprained her foot and was having it bandaged.

'Do you want a drink? I could get you a coffee or tea or something?' I said.

'You don't have to wait with me.'

'I don't mind.' Even though he was taller and broader than me, he had something of a child about him in that moment.

He brushed his hair from his eyes, holding it back from his face and looked up at me. He had the most fantastic blue eyes, not unlike Eliza's. Underneath his messy hair he was quite a handsome boy.

'Do you want a drink?' I repeated.

'Can I have a coke?'

I smiled, 'Sure, I'll go and get one.'

We sat for a while watching the hospital staff come in and out of the doors we weren't allowed behind.

'Have you called your mum?' I asked. I kept the plastic coffee cup near my face, even though I'd already finished it, so I could smell the remnants of my drink instead of the chlorinated air of the hospital.

'Nah, she'd freak right out, get well upset, think I was in trouble again.'

'You're not in trouble,' I said.

'Yeah, I know but she thinks everything's always my fault.'

'It was just an accident.'

He shrugged.

We sat with the sounds of the hospital; hushed voices and muted phone calls, the hum of the lights overhead. There were footsteps on the other side of the doors. It made me think someone was about to walk through any second but no one did, it only added to the odd tension of the place. You could feel the volume of souls nearby.

The last time I'd been to a hospital had been to see Ezra's body. He'd not looked as my husband should have, they could not hide the state he was in. I'd known the moment I saw his body lying on the hospital trolley that Ezra wasn't there anymore, despite him being right in front of me. All that was left was the broken shell of him, dressed in a pale green gown. I did not kiss him goodbye. The body before me was not the Ezra I loved. I'd wanted him to stay as my Ezra even though I knew he would never be mine again.

'Shall I call your mum?' I said.

'Don't.' Jerome looked at me, worry pinching his lips.

'But, I'm sure she'd want to know…'

'I'll tell her later. When she gets home from work.'

'Okay.'

'She's gonna go mental about these trousers, she only just got them.'

'I'm sure she'll understand.'

He scoffed. 'You reckon I could mend them?'

I looked at the flaps of fabric that hung either side of his shin. I didn't know much about sewing but it didn't look they could be salvaged. 'I doubt it.'

He sighed.

'But you could try?' I said.

'I ain't much good at sewing.'

'Neither am I.'

He looked at his hands. 'Can you phone my school? Tell them I'm not skiving?'

When Jerome was called in to see a doctor I phoned the school. I told them what had happened and that Eliza and Jerome wouldn't be at school that day. I'd phoned Noah as soon as we'd arrived at the hospital to tell him what had happened. He was in a meeting in London and was on his way back to the house, he asked me to stay with Eliza until he was back. I'd also phoned work but even to my own ears the explanation of my absence had sounded fabricated and Simon gave a heavy resigned sigh as he said he'd expect me in tomorrow.

When I came back Eliza sat on one of the orange chairs with a pair of crutches propped up next to her and a bandage around her foot. Jerome sat in the chair right next to her, his shin bandaged up too. The two of them were chatting and smiling, torsos turned toward each other. Eliza reached up and tucked the lose hair that hung in Jerome's face behind his ear. Jerome blushed. Eliza fluttered her eyelids. I smiled to myself.

A nurse told me that fundamentally Ada was going to be fine. The nurse explained that Ada was a little dazed and confused. She'd broken her wrist and bruised her hip when she'd landed on the tarmac. She would find walking tricky for a while and they weren't too happy with how the bones in her arm were laying; she might need an operation, only time would tell. They were going to keep her in overnight, to keep an eye on her. I wanted to see Ada, but she was asleep. I could come back the next day and take her home. Then the nurse added with a smile that meant her job was nearly done that Jerome hadn't broken anything and both he and Eliza were ready to go home. Would I like her to call a taxi?

To suddenly have responsibility for three people was laughable when I could barely look after myself. I was sure there was a better candidate for the job than me. But there was no one else looking for that role and I found myself promising to return to pick up Ada tomorrow before I climbed in the back of a taxi with my niece and my neighbour.

When we returned to Redferne Lane Noah and Sam were at Redferne House. For a moment I wondered why she was at the house until I remembered that she was their cleaner.

'Let's be off then,' Sam said to Jerome.

He'd already sat himself down at the kitchen table showing Eliza something on his phone. He looked up at Sam.

'Now,' Sam said.

Jerome rolled his eyes, then turned back to Eliza. 'See you soon, yeah?

She bestowed a glorious smile upon him and said in a breathy voice, 'Yeah, see you.'

He glanced at me and gave me a nod.

Noah took the seat Jerome had vacated before he and Sam had even left the house and took Eliza's hand. 'Are you alright my darling?'

She looked up at him with wide eyes. 'My ankle is a bit sore Daddy.'

'Oh darling, of course it is, come on, let's get you into onto the sofa so you can put your foot up,' Noah said, helping Eliza up.

I was surplus to requirement and after calling a soft goodbye I let myself out.

As I walked down the lane I felt deflated and tears prickled at my eyes. Once inside the house I sat on the sofa and smoked a cigarette unsure what else to do.

I started at the knock on the door. For a fleeting moment I thought it might be Torin, but it was Sam.

'Jerome tells me you were right nice to him at the hospital today,' she said. She wore her ASDA uniform. Jerome stood behind her, looking at his feet. His injured leg now covered in black jeans.

'So I wanted to come and thank you for looking out for my boy. It takes a right good person to show kindness to a neighbour and I thank you,' Sam continued. She spoke fast, her words almost merged into one. I had to listen hard to understand her.

'Oh, well, it was no trouble. I'm glad Jerome is okay.'

'Stupid boy can't stay out of trouble.'

'It wasn't his fault.'

'Ain't never his fault,' Sam scoffed.

'Really, he was just in the wrong place at the wrong time,' I tried to explain. 'It was an accident, just one of those things.'

'Well, I'm sure you're right, but Jerome is often in the wrong place, doing the wrong thing, at the wrong time. Christ knows how a little old lady managed to rip half a leg off his trousers.'

'I told you, it was the wheel Mum …' Jerome started, but with a glare over her shoulder, Sam had silenced him.

'Is the old dear alright?' Sam said.

'I think she'll be fine.'

'I'll send Jerome down to apologise then.'

'She's not home yet, she's spending the night in the hospital, just for observation.'

'Right, well, he'll come down tomorrow then.'

'I'm sure he doesn't need to ...'

'I think he does.'

'Okay.'

'Well, I came to thank you and I have, so now I'll let you get on.' Sam nodded making her flamboyant gold earrings dance.

'Thanks for coming by.' I called as they retreated to my gate.

Jerome looked back at me and nodded like his mum had, but maybe from him there was a hint of a smile too.

May 2011

The bells of the Cathedral were ringing as Dad took a stream of photos of Ezra and me. The tall spire was behind us and a hazy blue sky in the background. We were laughing as we pretended we'd just got married in the Cathedral and not City Hall opposite.

A warm wind drifted along bringing with it small clouds of dandelion seeds. The white specs of fluff kissed our clothes, hair and skin and left a delicate white carpet on the pavement. Ezra and I lifted our hands to feel the seeds brush past.

Mum, Dad, Josie and Eliza threw confetti. Some caught on the fabric of my dress, some in my hair. The tiny paper horseshoes and hearts mingled in the air with more dandelion seeds. The floor round us was covered with white fluff and paper shapes in pastel colours as they threw more and more confetti.

It felt dreamlike in the hazy light as though it wasn't quite real.

Noah took a picture of Mum and Dad with me and Ezra. Ezra and I were covered in confetti and fluff, dressed in clothes I knew my parents disapproved of. My parents flanked us, both neatly dressed; Dad in a dark suit and Mum in a floral dress and matching fascinator. Ezra stood in black jeans and a shirt and I wore a pale blue dress I'd got from a charity shop because Ezra said it matched my eyes. We both wore trainers.

Ezra and I could not stop smiling. Mum and Dad looked as though they found the disorganised nature of our wedding day a trial. They'd cancelled a trip to Devon they told me at least three times before I changed my name. It was such short notice; they'd told me more than once.

However much we denied it Mum and Dad were convinced the hasty nature of our wedding was because it was of the shotgun variety. But once Ezra had proposed we just wanted to get married without months of preparation and huge amounts of money spent.

Josie and Eliza threw more confetti, filling the air with little shapes again. Ezra wiped his hands on his jeans trying to get some of the confetti off, laughing as more stuck to him.

Eliza ran trying to catch confetti and dandelion seeds, her pretty pink dress swishing around her knees. Noah put his arm around me and kissed my cheek.

'You're really one of the family now. Good girl,' he said, as Josie took a picture of Ezra and me with his eldest brother.

Noah swapped places with his wife and another photograph was taken. Josie had her hands resting upon her huge belly, her pretty yellow dress stretched to the maximum; the baby due only weeks away. Her swollen feet barely fitted into her Birkenstocks. But she smiled almost as broadly as Ezra and me.

'Ezra, Torin?' Noah said, 'One of us brothers?'

I relinquished my new husband for a moment and watched as Ezra stood between his brothers while Dad took photos of them. Noah looked like he'd stepped out of the smart/casual pages of a gentleman's clothing catalogue posing with one hand on his hip in his cream linen jacket and jeans. Whereas Torin wore fitted black jeans, a plaid button-down shirt and a mantel of weariness. The smiles he drew did not once meet his eyes yet he did his best to hide it.

'Now let's go and get pissed,' Noah said.

Mum gave an audible tut and looked away from the Redferne's. I knew she liked Ezra well enough but she was baffled by the rest of his family.

The breeze blew again and with it came another swath of dandelion seeds. I let them kiss my face then watched them drift by.

'A moment Gracie?' I heard Torin say.

Behind him I saw that everyone else had drifted away to the restaurant at a swanky hotel, where Mum and Dad had insisted we have a meal and had made reservations on our behalf.

Torin and I looked at each other, serious, just for a second. The white dandelion rain fell on us and I had a glimpse of what might have been. One fleeting moment of 'what if?'

Torin plucked a piece of confetti from my hair and dropped it to the floor.

'Beautiful,' he said. He took another from my hair and let that fall too. He sighed. And smiled. 'Look after him, hey?'

I nodded. There were no other possibilities. Everything had turned out exactly the way it should have.

He placed a brief kiss on my cheek. 'Congratulations,' he said, with finality in his tone, already stepping away from me.

'You're going?'

'Aye,' he said. 'I've a plane to catch. Work.'

'Can't you stay for the meal? For a drink at least?'

'I should have been there yesterday. But I wanted be here today.'

I couldn't hide the hurt that he was not staying to celebrate with Ezra and me.

Torin pulled an envelope from the pocket of his shirt and pressed it into my hand.

'See you soon Gracie Redferne,' he said. He touched my cheek with his finger.

Not even on my wedding day could I quash what one touch from Torin provoked. Perhaps it was best he left.

I watched Torin walk away over the carpet of bruised confetti and dandelion seeds, a silhouette in the golden light. I knew he wouldn't look back.

When Torin was long out of sight, I looked down at the envelope, feeling something lumpy inside. I opened it and pulled out a worn leather bracelet that had once been mine. Some of the tiny silver beads were missing, but I'd have known it anywhere. The thongs that secured it had a kink where they'd been tied around a larger wrist than my own. I slipped in on my wrist and secured it, having to wrap the thongs around twice to make it secure, but the kink was still visible.

'Wife?' Ezra said, suddenly next to me.

I turned to him with a smile.

'He said goodbye?' Ezra asked and for a moment I thought he understood everything that had passed. Then I blinked and saw no such understanding in his eyes.

'Are you coming?' he asked.

'Yes,' I told my husband and slipped my arm into his and let him lead me away.

October 2014

Simon perched on the edge of my faux wood desk, his trousers hitched up and taut across his groin. I'd overheard some of the other girls in the office talking about Simon and his ever tight trousers. If I'd been a different person I might have told them about this moment over coffee in the staff kitchen, or wheeled my swivel chair over to my colleague and whispered in a giggle about Simon's trouser package. In reality, I wouldn't say anything to anyone, I'd drink coffee alone and try to catch up on the workload Simon had just placed on my desk.

'So Grace,' Simon said. 'If you could input these new client details and then file these,' he patted a pile of paper the size of a breeze block. 'I was hoping you might have them done by the end of today,' he sounded apologetic, 'we're a bit behind you see. You would have had yesterday…'

'It's fine,' I said, trying to smile up at him. 'I'll get it done.'

'Great,' he said. He shifted a little closer and reached over to put his hand on mine. 'I'm really pleased you're here today Grace. After our chat on Friday I was concerned I might have upset you?'

I looked at my computer screen. 'No,' I said, removing my hand from under his and pulling both of my hands up into my sleeves of my top. 'Not at all.'

'Good, that's good,' he sounded relieved. He clasped his hands together and cleared his throat. 'A few of us are going for a drink after work, perhaps you'd like to come?'

'Oh, I can't, I have to pick up my neighbour from hospital. You know, after the accident yesterday.' I glanced up at him before looking back at my computer screen.

'Of course,' he said. 'How is she?'

'She'll be fine soon enough I think,' I said.

'Good. Great.' He cleared his throat again. 'You'll have come for a drink next time then?'

'Sure,' I said, thinking it unlikely that I would ever go for a drink with him or any of these people I worked with. 'So, I should probably get on with this lot.' I tapped the pile of paper he'd stacked on my desk.

Once Simon had gone back to his office I began the mind numbing task of inputting the client details. Now and then, I looked up and caught Simon watching me from various points in the office; the kitchen doorway, his office, the water cooler. Each time he gave me an encouraging smile before returning to whatever it was he was doing.

I felt as though he'd set me challenge he actually wanted me achieve. I appreciated that he was encouraging me to be better at my job, like he saw something in me I failed to see myself. And it helped me want to finish this task he'd set me. If not for myself or the company, then just for him.

When numbers and client details began swimming in front of my eyes I spent twenty minutes under the concrete steps beside the office chain smoking and watching the rain fall. Then I returned to the office, determined to complete Simon's tasks. I wanted to please Simon.

It was gone five when I'd finished the client list and scooped up the stack of filing. I knew Simon was right behind me as I made my way to the bank of filing cabinets at the far end of the office. I didn't say anything when he started helping me but I gave him a smile. We worked silently for nearly an hour, moving between the stacks, opening and closing the metal drawers.

'You get off if you like Grace,' Simon said, having picked up the last of the filing and cradling it in his arm. 'I'll finish up. I'm sure your neighbour is expecting you.'

'Thank you,' I said, looking up at him and noticing for the first time that his eyes were a tranquil pale green like the ocean on a summers day.

'My pleasure Grace.'

I smiled, glad he seemed pleased with my efforts, pleased that I seemed to have done something right.

'See you tomorrow,' he said.

As soon as I left the office I felt a wave of exhaustion wash over me. I'd have liked to go straight home, drink something and lie down. But I went to the hospital and tried not to cry when I saw Ada sat in a wheelchair, ready to go. She looked like a little frail bird, folded up under a hospital blanket. After a quick chat with the doctor I was left in charge of Ada. I felt woefully inadequate and hesitated at the automatic doors sure that someone was about to realise that they couldn't let Ada leave with me. But summoning the last dregs of energy, I helped Ada from the wheelchair to the waiting taxi and said in the jolliest voice I could muster, 'Let's get you home, shall we?'

Ada was quiet in the taxi back to Redferne Lane. I think she dozed, and I was half glad to have a moment to gather myself and then terrified as I pondered what came next. As my chest contracted and my breath became short I reached into my bag and popped a little white pill from the foil and swallowed it with saliva. When the taxi pulled up by the bridge at the bottom of Redferne Lane I'd begun to feel the calming influence of my little white pill. Ada lifted her head, blinking, and I told her we were home.

I supported Ada with my arm around her waist as she took the twenty paces to her front door. Every step Ada took seemed to cause her pain. The doctor had assured both myself and Ada that nothing more than her wrist was broken but she had bruised her hip and knee and walking was slow and made Ada grunt and gasp. We fumbled with the front door key in the dark and I was terrified that any moment Ada would topple over. By the time I'd manoeuvred her inside and to her chair she was pale and shaking. I made Ada a cup of tea and encouraged her to eat a biscuit. While she sipped her tea, the colour returned to her cheeks, and she stopped shaking, but my heart still hammered in my chest.

Ada had been sent home with a bag full of medication. I sorted through it, reading the dosage of each label and gave Ada what was required for this evening, then put what she needed to take first thing in the morning into a chipped blue eggcup.

I dropped the eggcup when there was a knock at the door. Swearing to myself I left the pills on the floor as I saw Ada attempting to get up to answer the door.

I let Jerome in. He was full of smiles, carrying a bunch of pink carnations and went straight to Ada and gave her a big kiss on the cheek. She lit up like a firework, her teeth on show as she smiled.

As I grovelled on the floor trying to find all the tablets I'd dropped Jerome chatted to Ada as though they'd been friends for years. The air of anxiety I'd brought home from the hospital along with Ada disappeared.

It was only just past nine but Ada said she would like to go to bed. Jerome left with a promise to return tomorrow.

I wondered if he meant to keep his promise. For a moment I thought I might leave myself but I released it was unlikely Ada could manage the stairs alone. So between us we made the challenging climb up the stairs. She gripped the banister, and I held her and semi-lifted her up each step.

Once in her bedroom she struggled to even lower herself to sit on the edge of the bed unaided.

'Ada?'

'Yes dear?'

'I'll do whatever you need me to do, okay?'

'That's very kind of you.'

I hesitated. 'You might need to tell me what you want me to do.'

She looked up at me and gave me a small smile and nod.

'I think I need to get into my nightie,' she said. 'It's over on the chair.'

I'm not sure which of us was more uncomfortable with the situation. In an unspoken agreement we both acted as though it was not unusual or embarrassing for either of us. As I helped Ada undress she chatted about the woman that had been in the bed next to her in the hospital whom she'd taken a dislike to. Somehow the sound of her voice made it easier to see Ada naked. Her words distracted me from the huge purple bruise on her hip, her swollen knee, her small drooped breasts and the loose skin than hung off her thin muscles.

Ada seemed childlike as I slipped the pretty floral nightie over her head. She sat for a moment as I folded her clothes and placed them on the chair where her nightie had been. I never folded my own clothes but Ada's house was so ordered and tidy I felt obliged to maintain it as best I could. I knew what was coming next and as I took Ada to the bathroom we were both silent. I helped her sit and left the room for a moment.

Waiting on the landing I traced the flowers on the carpet with my toe. The pearly green wall paper next to the bathroom door was peeling. I heard Ada call my name and went back into the bathroom.

When Ada was in bed I tucked her pastel pink cellular blanket over her. The satin edging matched her nightie.

'Thank you dear,' she said, not for the first time during the past few hours.

I forced another smile. All I wanted to do was inhale thirty cigarettes while I downed a bottle of wine but I had no intention of leaving until she was finally settled for the night.

'You're a good girl,' Ada said.

I chuckled at her misconception. 'Are you comfortable?'

'Yes dear.'

'So I'll come by first thing in the morning okay?' I said.

She nodded.

'Night,' I said and turned off her bedroom light.

I went downstairs, leaving the landing light on and left Ada's house. Without bothering to turn on the lights in my house I went straight to the fridge and extracted the wine. Filling the nearest mug, I went back into the living room and sank down on my sofa. The wine was cold and beautiful. I lit a cigarette and tried to clear my thoughts of Ada. But a myriad of 'what ifs' ran through my mind.

My heart beat faster and my chest felt tight. I swallowed a little white pill.

But I knew my thoughts would still churn until dawn.

Picking up the crochet blanket from my sofa, I draped it around my shoulders. I grabbed the bottle of wine, slipped back out into Redferne Lane and went two doors down.

As quietly as I could I let myself back into Ada's. Concerned she would think I was a burglar I tiptoed up the stairs to tell her it was just me. But as I looked in on her she was already asleep, just as I'd left her.

Returning downstairs, I sat on her sofa in the dark, pulled my blanket close around me, took a swig of wine and lit a cigarette.

I woke up to find Jerome looking down at me.

'What are you doing?' I asked, sitting up, instantly annoyed with him.

'What are *you* doing?'

'What does it look like?'

'Are you always this charming first thing in the morning?' he asked with a grin that further irritated me.

'How did you get in?'

'Door was on the latch,' he said, with a shrug.

I didn't remember leaving the door on the latch but then I often didn't remember things that I'd done.

I went into the kitchen, needing to move away from Jerome for a moment so I could calm down and become a touch more rational.

'She's not up yet then?' Jerome asked, from the doorway.

'Obviously not.' I filled the old enamel kettle and went to put it on the range when I realised the range was cold. I hadn't thought to light it the night before.

Jerome watched as I knelt in front of the great black beast and opened the door, before making a little pyramid of fire with thin kindling I found in a neat bundle beside the coal bucket. After loading a small amount of coal in I closed the door to the range hoping I'd done it right.

Jerome was still watching me when I returned to the living room wondering if I should just go back to my own house and boil a kettle. Ada's coffee table was still littered with my detritus of the previous evening. I cleared the table of the wine bottle, ashtray and my cigarettes. I folded my crochet blanket and tucked it behind the sofa then realised Jerome was no longer in the room.

'Go girl,' he said, from the hallway.

Out in the hallway Jerome stood at the bottom of the stairs, grinning and watching Ada as she made her way unaided downstairs. She was fully dressed and her hair combed.

'Good morning,' she said, in triumph, as she reached the bottom.

Jerome took her arm as she wobbled and showered her with more praise.

They passed me and went into the living room. While I counted down backwards from ten, I could hear Jerome joking with Ada as he settled her into her chair.

Back in the living room I explained about the range and offered to go back to my house to make Ada tea and toast. She thanked me and I slipped home.

When I returned with a tray of tea, toast and a jug full of hot water, I could hear Ada and Jerome talking and laughing. Ada and I never talked or laughed like that together and the stab of jealousy was overwhelming. I was close to throwing the tray of tea and toast on the floor and flouncing out into the lane in a tantrum. But after a couple of deep breaths, I pulled on a smile and took the tray into the living room. I was rewarded with such a genuine smile from Ada that I forgot my jealousy and sat beside Jerome on the sofa.

After her breakfast, Ada made her way back upstairs to use the bathroom. As I made to assist her she'd kindly told me she would manage alone. So instead I cleared the breakfast things and retreated to the kitchen with the last of the hot water in the jug. Jerome came in as I started to wash up. He opened the range and threw in coal in a haphazard fashion.

'Be careful, you'll put it out,' I snapped.

'No I won't.'

'You will if you just throw it in like that.'

He slammed the door of the range closed.

'Careful,' I warned again, turning to him, scowling.

'Or what?'

'What do you mean, or what?'

We faced each other.

'Why are you having a go at me?' Jerome said, through tight lips.

'Why are you even here?' I said.

'Why are *you* here?' He threw back at me.

'She's not your responsibility,' I pointed out.

'She ain't yours neither.'

I stumbled on my words for a moment as though recoiling from a slap to the cheek.

Jerome and I glared at each other but the air of confrontation began to deflate.

'I like her,' I said softly now, all my aggression gone. 'She can't manage on her own.'

'Well I like her too,' Jerome said, although he still spoke with a fragment of animosity. 'And I know she needs help, that's why I'm here.'

I swallowed and nodded.

Jerome gave me a small nod back.

He picked up a tea towel and dried up as I resumed washing-up. I heard Ada coming slowly down the stairs and back into the living room. As I finished up in the kitchen Jerome went through to speak to Ada. I could hear them talking about horse racing that was on TV later today. It sounded as though they were planning to watch it together. I hovered in the doorway unable to join the conversation. Both Jerome and Ada were animated as they talked about horses with unlikely, if not ridiculous, names and their corresponding jockeys; it was a complete unknown to me.

Unsure of my role I went out of the front door and stood in the lane, leaning against Ada's front wall. I'd used the excuse of wanting a cigarette, even though Ada wouldn't have minded if I'd smoked inside.

The crows were chattering at the top of the beech trees on the other side of the lane. The leaves had begun to turn orange, as though fire was slowly spreading through the branches. A solitary leaf floated to the ground. Soon all of the leaves would be amber and fall, covering the lane.

'Good morning.'

I looked up to find Torin before me.

I flung myself at him and wrapped my arms around his neck, surprising us both.

He laughed, putting his arms around me too. 'Well, I'm pleased to see you too Gracie,' he said.

I untangled myself from him, embarrassed, and muttered a hello, looking at our feet.

'You alright?' he asked.

I looked up, 'Yeah, fine.'

'What are you doing?' he asked. 'Where were you last night? I came to see you but you weren't home.'

'I slept on Ada's sofa.'

'Of course, Josie mentioned the collision. Apparently Eliza's been milking it for it's worth,' he gave me a smile of collusion. 'How's Ada?'

'Not too bad, but in need of a little support.'

We regarded one another for a moment. Torin's hair was a little damp and had rolled into tiny tight curls just above his ear. He was only wearing black jeans and a plaid shirt but he looked well-kept and in order. In contrast I was still wearing yesterday's clothes and I felt wonky and dishevelled; I probably didn't smell great either.

'So I came to see if you were free today?' he said, with a smile that showed his teeth.

'I need to get some shopping for Ada and…'

Torin cut me off, 'I'll help you.'

'You don't need to.'

'I want to,' he said. 'What else do you need to do today?'

I hadn't thought beyond what Ada needed and judging by her companionship with Jerome, I was surplus to requirement.

'Not much,' I said.

'Great, then I'll come and get you in an hour or so and we can start with some lunch. You look like you could do with feeding up a little,' he said and before I could reply he'd begun walking back up the lane.

'What's her story then?' Torin asked.

I glanced at Torin, surprised that he wanted to play this old game of ours. He gave me a spirited grin and it was all the encouragement I needed. I looked towards the woman he'd indicated with a subtle nod. She was tall with thick chin length hair the colour of wholemeal bread, that gave her a triangular appearance. She wore draped clothing, in shades of green, that gave no indication to her shape beneath. She kept glancing at her phone and fiddling with her wedding ring.

'She's waiting for her pimp,' I said.

Torin gave a low laugh that appeared to begin deep in his chest before it bubbled from his lips.

'Her pimp has a new client for her. An eighteen-year-old millionaire, who made his fortune on a mobile phone app.' I continued. 'The young man isn't interested in girls his own age, as he finds them immature. He's still a virgin and wants a mature woman to show him the ways of the world.'

'Christ, I'd forgotten what a twisted little mind you have,' Torin said, shaking his head at me, but still chuckling.

'They'll be in here in a minute,' I said.

We both drank from our pints, then Torin made a spluttering sound. He spilt a little of his pint down his shirt and placed the glass on the table, wiping his mouth with the back of his hand.

'Check it out,' he said.

I looked over to see a two men joining the woman. One was indeed a young man, dressed in pale chinos and a blue blazer like he'd just come from a regatta. The other man was older and wore a battered leather jacket and slicked back hair. He appeared to be introducing the younger man to the woman.

Torin and I collapsed into childish giggles.

'So what happens next?' I asked, barely able to contain my mirth.

'They're…' Torin stopped as a laugh overtook him. 'They're going to the Travelodge on the bypass…'

We laughed so much; my face hurt and my stomach muscled ached. When finally, the giggles began to subside, I looked at Torin and recognised the flood of pleasure his company gave me. But with that realisation my mood suddenly plummeted as I felt all that I had lost.

'What's the matter?' Torin asked.

I shook my head. 'Nothing. I'm just tired,' I said, pulling the smile back on my face. 'Ada's sofa is really uncomfortable. I didn't sleep well.'

'You do look tired.'

I nodded. Tired didn't come close to the exhaustion I felt these days. My one night on Ada's sofa was just a drop in the ocean.

'Is that all?' he asked.

I didn't answer but looked at his dark eyes as they searched my face for an answer.

'How's work?' Torin tried.

'Shite,' I said, with a small smile.

'That bad?'

'I don't know. No,' I said. 'It's not that bad. It's just…' I sighed. 'I need a cigarette.'

Torin came outside with me into the pub garden. The sky was grey and heavy, promising rain. A young couple with multiple piercings and tattoos sat engrossed in one another on the only wooden bench available. So Torin and I stood with our backs against the wall and smoked in silence, watching the couple who had eyes for nothing but each other.

'What's their story?' Torin asked, with an expectant smile.

'They're in love,' I said bluntly, and felt as though someone was punching a hole in my chest. 'They're happy.' I went back inside and began to gather my stuff.

'Wait up Gracie, I'll come with you,' Torin said.

'You don't have to.'

'I know but I want to.'

We crossed town without speaking, conversation was impossible as we wove between people and pushchairs. It seemed as though everyone had a small child holding their hand or a babe in arms pressed against them in a sling. Torin broke the silence when we turned from town toward the railway bridge at the bottom of Redferne Lane.

'So correct me if I'm wrong but we were having a nice time right?' he said.

I nodded.

'Lunch was good, the beer was lovely, we were even having quite a laugh, yes?'

'Yes.'

'So what changed?'

'I was just suddenly reminded of what I don't have anymore.'

'Are we talking about Ezra?'

I shrugged. Of course I was talking about Ezra but it was more than that. I'd lost Torin too, only here he was, taking me out for lunch and making me laugh, just like old times.

'Are we ever going to talk about Ezra?' Torin asked.

'What's there to say?'

'I don't know, you tell me.'

Again, I shrugged. Ezra was gone. It was shite but there was nothing I could do about it.

We came under the bridge onto Redferne Lane then stopped outside my house. I was tempted to ask Torin in but I didn't want to talk about Ezra. And I didn't want to think about how much Torin had meant to me once upon a time. How much he still meant to me.

'Shall I come down and see you in the week?' Torin said.

'If you like.'

'Would you like me to?' I could hear the irritation in his voice.

I looked up at Torin. 'Yes, please.'

'Take care then, alright?'

'And you,' I said and went inside.

April 2011

Torin was waiting at the station to collect us. He wrapped one arm around Ezra and his other around me as we walked to his car. I couldn't believe how familiar he smelt and how comforting it was to see him. And he looked well, so much better than when we'd seen him last, despite the unforgiving weather that surrounded us.

In Bristol, the snowdrops had already come and gone; the daffodils were in bud. The further north we travelled the less greenery there was, the small white flowers of hawthorn had yet to adorn the naked branches. Beyond the windows of the train there were desolate brown fields patch-worked beside fallow green ones and thick hided cattle grazed on bales of pale yellow hay. When we finally reached Torin's house frost still lay on the ground and crows gathered in the skeletons of trees. It didn't feel like spring.

Out of the blue Torin had invited Ezra and me to his house in Scotland. It was the house he'd grown up in, the house that had belonged to his father. A gothic Victorian building, like something out of a 19th century novel, where the heroine might throw herself out of the top window when spurned by her lover. Dark wooden panelling, heavy furniture and cobwebs decorated the place. There was more shadow than light inside and a chill to match, with the lack of central heating. But somehow Torin made up for the cold and dark; with his manner and his laughter, he lit up the rooms of the house with radiant warmth.

Both Ezra and I were surprised to find a woman already at Torin's house. I assumed she was his girlfriend. Torin threw us her name, Lyn; then walked past her into the kitchen, leaving Ezra and I to make our own introductions to this woman.

Lyn must have been heading toward her forties, tall and willowy, with pale blue eyes that looked cruel even when she smiled. She was the Snow Queen; one minute she might offer Turkish Delight and the next she might have us locked up in the cellar. I disliked her instantly.

The four of us sat at the large kitchen table and had coffee with a splash of brandy, to warm us Torin said. Lyn smiled a lot as though trying to gain favour. Torin ignored her. Ezra and I kept exchanging bemused looks.

Torin cooked a meal that evening. He'd always been a good cook. There was nothing fancy about the roast chicken and potatoes and the dark green kale he prepared for us, but it tasted good. Lyn may have thought differently, as she hardly ate a thing, just nibbled a thin slice of breast meat. She muttered something about butter and wouldn't have a serving of the kale on her plate. When Torin brought out a bowl of trifle, she excused herself from the table. Not long after, Torin followed Lyn upstairs. Moments later we heard their raised voices but not the actual words. Ezra and I sat drinking wine until we could no longer hear them arguing before we went upstairs to bed.

The following morning when Torin, Ezra and I sat sipping coffee around the kitchen table we saw Lyn walk out of the front door with a suitcase and climb into a waiting taxi.

Torin didn't even say goodbye to her.

I did not feel I could ask what was going on and nor it seemed did Ezra.

Shortly after Lyn's departure Torin suggested a walk. Glancing at the vile weather beyond the windows I was reluctant to leave the house. But Torin insisted and dragged us out, promising that if we went high enough we'd be able to see over the cloud. The frost from the previous day had thawed only for freezing rain that was blown sideways by a foul wind to take its place. More than once Torin told me how beautiful it was, but I struggled to see anything through the mist that descended, wrapping the hilltop in its embrace.

After twenty minutes of walking uphill in the driving rain, Ezra and I turned back and returned to the house. But Torin continued up into the mist muttering to himself.

'What's going on?' I asked Ezra as we traipsed back down.

'I have no idea.'

'Did you know about Lyn?'

'I knew there was someone. Possibly someone serious.'

'They're serious?' I was surprised.

'Well as serious as Torin as ever been about anyone I think.'

'Do you think they've split up?'

'I don't know. But I'm guessing they have.'

When we got back to Torin's house, soaking wet and a little unsure of how the weekend might progress, Ezra and I retreated to our room and spent the day keeping each other warm in bed.

When we re-emerged in the early evening and shuffled into the kitchen, we found Torin cooking. We'd not heard him return.

'We thought you'd got lost?' Ezra said.

'Hardly,' Torin said. He poured dark amber Scotch into glasses and slid one to each of us.

'Have you heard from Lyn?' Ezra asked, after he'd taken a glug.

'No.'

Ezra and I glanced at each other.

'What did you do to upset her?' Ezra asked.

'I was kidding myself that she was something special. Turns out she wasn't.'

'Cryptic as ever,' Ezra said.

'Aye, well you don't really want to know the ins and outs do you?'

'I wouldn't mind, you know, if you needed to share?' Ezra was grinning, eyeing his brother. 'If you need a hug?'

'Fuck off,' Torin snapped, but there was no venom in his tone.

Ezra laughed, glancing at me, and I smiled back. But I could see all was not well with Torin and I wished Ezra had been kinder.

'Best drink up, only way to keep warm in this God forsaken place.' Torin lifted his glass in a silent toast.

I sipped cautiously, dreading the burn in my throat and chest. I was surprised to find I liked the feel of the liquid warming me from the inside.

We moved on to wine while we ate around the kitchen table, a welcome fire crackling in the large hearth. I imagined a robust house keeper, turning a hog on a spit in that fireplace, wiping her hard working hands on her apron.

Well past midnight, Ezra staggered to his feet. 'Bed time for me I think. You coming Grace?'

'Lightweight,' Torin muttered, then looked up at me. 'You'll not leave me to drink alone, will you Gracie?'

'It is getting late,' I said.

'Why don't you stay up and keep the old man company?' Ezra stroked my back with affection.

'I don't know.'

'Stay up,' Ezra said, and poured more whiskey into my glass. He gave me a fond smile and a kiss on the cheek, and for Torin he issued a warning, 'Don't get her too drunk old man, or you'll have me to deal with in the morning.'

'I'll look after her, don't you worry boy,' Torin threw back.

Torin and I looked at one another while we heard Ezra walk up the stairs. The ghost of the past snuck into the room and even though I thought we'd put it all behind us, suddenly there was just a little something in Torin's eyes. And probably mine too.

'So…' Torin said.

'So?'

'Ezra seems happy?'

'Yes.'

'And you?'

I nodded.

Torin nodded too then turned his face away and looked toward the hearth. We did not speak but sat before the fire, listening to crackle and spit of the burning wood and the wind howling outside calling eerie cold sounds down the chimney.

'You'll marry him,' Torin stated. I noticed him fiddle with the bracelet on his wrist; black leather with tiny silver beads.

'I don't know.' I laughed. Ezra and I hadn't discussed marriage.

'He hasn't asked you?'

'No, but I don't mind.'

'You should. He's a fool not to put a ring on your finger,' Torin said, 'or some bloke with a tattoo will come and steal you away.'

I laughed again, but his comment made me nervous. 'I don't need to be married to Ezra to know I don't want anyone else. I'm his, ring or not.'

'Oh aye, I know you are, and that boy is yours.' He smiled. 'You're perfect for one another.'

It was odd to hear those words from Torin.

'So, what about you? What about you and Lyn?' I asked, wanting to steer the conversation away from Ezra and me.

'Ach, Gracie my dear, there is no more me and Lyn.'

'I'm sorry.'

'No you're not,' he said and emitted one of his loud laughs, 'and nor am I. Not really. She was a harridan sent to vex me.'

'What happened?' I couldn't help but laugh at his turn of phrase.

'I don't know,' he shrugged. But I guess he just didn't want to tell me.

'Were you serious about her?'

He looked up, 'Serious enough. But she wasn't who I thought she was, she wasn't what I wanted her to be. I thought I could make do but somehow bringing her here made me realise I couldn't. When I thought about her meeting Ezra,' he hesitated, 'meeting you, I knew I couldn't be with her.'

'Do you love her?'

'No.' He paused. 'But I think you knew that already Gracie.' I'd forgotten the way he could look at me. I'd forgotten how it made me feel.

'I should go to bed.' I said, standing up.

'Don't do that,' he said, looking up at me. 'I'm sorry.'

I frowned at him.

'I would really appreciate your company tonight. I could do with a friend. You might just save me from drowning in self-pity.'

I nodded and sat down again. Friends. Torin and I could be friends.

I was still a little hungover when Ezra and I returned to Bristol and walked back to our flat from the station late in the evening. Orange streetlights back-lit the rainy night; it had not stopped raining since we'd left Scotland. We didn't meet another soul on the way home, just trudged silently, getting soaked.

Then beside a large signpost near the roundabout, Ezra stopped.

I stopped too.

He took my hands in his and knelt down on one knee. He was smiling, almost giggling.

'Ezra? What are you doing?' I asked, looking down at him kneeling on the wet pavement.

'Marry me Grace?' he said. I was sure I heard the curl of a Scottish burr unfurling in those three words like he'd brought the accent back with him on the train. He sounded just like Torin.

'Seriously?'

'Seriously.' He pulled a small navy velvet box from his coat pocket and flipped open the lid. Inside was a delicate gold ring set with a sapphire and two small diamonds.

'Where'd you get that?'

'Torin. It belonged to our great-grandmother.'

'Did he tell you to ask me?' I thought back to our conversation the night before.

'Not told me as such, just, you know, he said you wanted to get married.'

'I never said that.'

'Don't you want to get married?' The fear in his voice that he'd got it really wrong was so evident I would have walked down the aisle that second.

I knelt down in rain to join him and took his hands.

'Of course I want to marry you Ezra. I want to spend the rest of my life with you.'

October 2014

Jerome knelt in front of Ada's hearth blowing into the glowing embers. His fingers prints had left greasy smudges all over her brass tongs. Ada was in the same place I'd left her the evening before; ensconced in her comfy pastel pink velvet chair, the cast surrounding her broken wrist resting on the arm and her slippered feet on the matching footstool.

'That's it, just keep blowing and the flames will come. Then you can put a bit more wood on,' Ada said.

Jerome looked out of place in her house, kneeling on the rose patterned carpet, the shire horses above him on the mantel piece. But he'd come over to her house every day since she'd come home from hospital. And Ada obviously liked him.

He'd had his hair cut. Gone was the tangled mop and now his hair was clean and cut into a modern floppy fringed sort of thing he flicked out of his eyes every few seconds. It suited him.

It was nice to see that the range and the fire in the living room were still lit and the house felt warm. Autumn was setting in and it wouldn't be long before it disrobed into winter. Strong winds had buffeted the bus all the way home from work. I was chilled to my core and had expected to find Ada's house cold and unwelcoming. But it was not, thanks to Jerome. I had to admit that without Jerome I would have struggled to look after Ada. He came round after school, filling the hours until I arrived after work. Plus, Jerome was so easy with Ada in a way I wasn't sure I would ever be.

'Jerome mended my bike.' Ada gave a wide smile.

'Really?' I looked at the youth dressed in his school uniform. It wasn't only his hair that had changed; there was something altogether different about him. I wondered if it had anything do with my niece. I'd seen them walking to school this morning; Jerome was carrying her bag.

'He wanted to surprise me,' Ada said. 'He did it all himself.'

'That's kind of you Jerome,' I said.

He looked up at me. 'I wanted to mend it. Mum said it was the least I could do. It's out the front now. I put it away after I showed Mrs West.'

'You must call me Ada,' she said.

Jerome smiled.

It was very considerate of him but I wasn't certain if Ada would ever be able to ride her bike again. The hospital had phoned to tell Ada she would need a minor operation on her wrist as the bones weren't properly aligned. It would only be an overnight stay. But more convalescing and I was concerned that Ada may not ever be able to cope on her own again, let alone ride her bike. I wasn't sure she would ever go back to being the way she was. She seemed so fragile.

Although she was a little better than when she'd first come home from hospital there was still a lot she couldn't do. With her broken wrist and bruised hip she couldn't light the range herself. Ada couldn't cook or clean. She couldn't shop and she got tired standing up for more than a few minutes at a time. And walking was hard. She could just about make it to the bathroom upstairs but the trip exhausted her. I was pleased to help her. And Jerome helped a lot too, but I wasn't sure what the future held for Ada.

'How's your young man?' Ada asked.

'What?'

'That handsome man with the lovely voice and big hands?'

'Torin?' I asked, but I knew it was who she meant.

'Yes.'

'He's not my young man.' I pointed out.

She let out one of her odd nasal laughs. 'I saw the way he looks at you.'

'He's Ezra's brother,' I said, feeling myself flush.

She made a noise and waved her cast to dismiss the fact as irrelevant. I could see Jerome smirking to himself.

I went into the kitchen to hide my burning cheeks. Ada hadn't liked the idea of it, but I'd got her a new kettle, a little electric one that held just enough water to fill her small teapot and wasn't too heavy to pick up. I'd also bought her a toaster. We'd spent half an hour making toast, so she was used to it and trusted that it wouldn't burn her house down.

When I went back into the living room Jerome and Ada were watching the horse racing on the television. I stood with the floral tray in my hands and watched them. Jerome sat forward on Ada's settee, jigging like he was riding a horse himself and muttering at the screen as if he could make the horses go faster by sheer will alone. Ada's mutterings were louder as she geed the racers on. She cheered as a horse crossed the finish line.

'I told you he'd win,' she said to Jerome.

'I can't believe it, he was on at like 50/1,' Jerome said, and pushed his hair out of his face again.

'You owe me a cigarette,' Ada said, with a toothy grin.

'That I do.' Jerome reached into the pocket of his school trousers and flicked open a gold packet and offered Ada a cigarette.

What should I say? Should I tell Jerome he shouldn't smoke? Should I be telling Ada off for betting with a child and encouraging him to smoke? Was he even still a child at fifteen? I ended up not saying anything. I put the tray on the table and asked if there was anything else Ada needed.

'No dear, you get on home if you need to.'

So I said goodbye and went home to my dark, cold and empty house where the only thing waiting for me was a bottle of wine.

The wind kept throwing the rain at the window, rattling the old glass as though trying to get inside. I sank all the way under the surface of the bath; the water was hot and instantly made me a feel just a little better. Resurfacing, I picked up my glass of wine and took a hearty sip, trying to let the tensions of the day and week seep out of my bones. I'd got soaked coming home from work. Ada's living room light was on as I passed and I glanced in her window, through the net curtains and saw the outline of Jerome moving about the room. I hoped he was making her smile. He was good at that. I could not face going in to Ada's this evening; I was drenched and cold and work was doing my head in.

Simon was always so nice to me despite the fact that I was consistently useless. He'd asked me into his office this morning and he'd been kind as he told me I'd made loads of mistakes with the invitations for an event in December. It had set back the printing and therefore the invites would not go out on schedule. He should have been pissed off with me, I wish he had been, but instead he'd made me coffee and talked me through every mistake with infinite patience. His kindness made me feel terrible. And I knew everyone else in the office probably resented that he was nice to me.

I heard my front door open and Torin's unmistakable voice calling my name. I stepped out of the bath and grabbed a towel.

I reached the top of the stairs and he was already on the third step coming up.

'Torin,' I cautioned. Cold air from outside ran up the stairs and slipped beneath my towel making me shiver.

He stopped, eyeing the towel that barely covered my modesty.

'Sorry,' he said, not bothering to hide his smirk.

He was well groomed, dressed in a shirt and smart jacket with his hair coiffed in a rakish manner. It was somewhat disarming that he looked so attractive.

'I've brought dinner. You like Chinese right?' He smiled and lifted the white carrier bag in his hand. 'And I got us a couple bottles of that shite white stuff you drink. Mind, I also got some red in case you might want to drink something else?' He lifted his other arm and the bottles in a blue carrier bag clanked against one another.

'I wasn't expecting you.' I felt my towel coming lose. Drips were rolling down my back.

'Aye, but I'm always a nice surprise, right?' he said, throwing me another grin.

I tried to adjust my towel without exposing any more of myself.

'So?' Torin said. 'Are you going to join me?'

He looked up at me and I looked down at him.

A pearl of water rolled down my thigh.

Goosebumps covered my skin.

'For Christ's sake put some clothes on Gracie,' he said and backed down the stairs and went into the living room.

As I got dry and dressed I could hear him moving around downstairs. It was comforting to hear him in my house. When Torin had lived with Ezra and me I'd always been able to tell who was in which room just from the sounds of their movements. Ezra had been concise in his actions, economical and practical. Torin was a fiddler, so many of his acts seemingly unnecessary and yet I'd always enjoyed watching Torin and his constant movements.

Coming back down the stairs I paused on the threshold of my living room.

The room had been cleared of dirty mugs and other crockery. The wood burner was lit, the main light was off and the table lamps softened the room with warm yellow light, making it rounded and cosy, the corners in shadow. Not only did my living room look different, but it smelt different too. There was the aromatic scent of the food but I could also smell Torin. It wasn't aftershave or deodorant but something intrinsically male that wafted through my house. It was unsettling, but I'd be lying if I said it was unpleasant.

'Nice of you to dress for dinner,' he said.

I couldn't help but smile.

Torin had laid out the foil cartons, plates and glasses on the coffee table.

'This looks great. Thank you.' I sat down beside him on the sofa.

'This is kind of an apology, for not coming around during the week as I'd said I would,' he explained.

'It's fine Torin, you didn't have to do this,' I said. But every evening I had half hoped he would turn up and when he hadn't I'd berated myself for my sulky behaviour the weekend before; no wonder he didn't want to see me if all I did was sulk.

'How was work?' he said, holding out a glass of wine.

'I don't want to talk about it,' I said, as I accepted the glass.

'That bad?'

'Not bad, just killing me a little each day with mundanity.' The wine tasted good.

'So quit?'

'I can't.'

'Why? Do you need the money?' Torin shifted his body toward me and regarded me with a puzzled expression.

'Money's not an issue. Ezra was very organised about life insurance.'

'Of course he was. He always was a sensible boy.'

We sat quiet for a moment and I realised it was a long time since I'd said Ezra's name out loud.

Torin was still looking at me as though I was a cryptic crossword.

'So why can't you quit?' He asked.

'I really don't want to talk about it.'

'You always were good at ignoring things.'

A barbed retort was on my lips but I swallowed it down with a sip of wine. 'Don't start on me Torin. I just don't want to think about it right now okay?'

'Alright Gracie,' he conceded. 'Then maybe we should eat?'

Every morsel I put in my mouth tasted amazing. I hadn't realised how hungry I was.

As we ate Torin talked. Life at Redferne House was a little taxing; Torin was not used to living in the hub of a family home. Noah was stressed and often shouting, Josie was pregnant and snappy for no apparent reason, Barty and

Godfrey were noisy and untidy and Eliza was sullen and difficult. Jerome had been spending a fair amount of time up at the house, talking in whispers on the sofa with Eliza. I liked the idea of Eliza and Jerome together. It made me smile. But I think it made Torin uncomfortable.

We talked a little of Ada; she was going back into hospital next week for the operation on her wrist. She would only be in overnight. We had acquired a wheelchair for her, although we had yet to take her out in it, waiting for fairer weather, but it offered possibilities. After she was home again I hoped to take her for an outing.

'I almost forgot, I have an invitation for you. From Josie and Noah.' Torin pulled a creamy envelope from his pocket and held it towards me. 'They're having a joint party for Noah and Eliza, although I think she'd rather be doing something else to celebrate her sixteenth birthday.'

'Right.' I said, taking the envelope.

'And Josie wants to know if you'd like to go shopping?' he said.

'What for?'

'For a dress, for the party? I said you would.'

'Why would you say that?'

'Because I thought you might find it fun?'

I gave Torin a look. He knew I was not one for clothes shopping.

'I'll tell her you were overjoyed at the idea then?' Torin said, raising his eyebrows.

'I don't like shopping.'

'I know.' Torin gave a laugh. 'But Josie wants to bond with you.'

I sighed.

'Besides, you need something to wear to the party. You can't wear one of Ezra's old T-shirts.'

I didn't reply because anything I would have said would have been spiky or rude. And Torin was right. I both loathed and delighted in the way Torin spoke truths to me. He'd always known me, understood me, right from the very moment we'd met.

Changing the subject, Torin talked about his house in Scotland. He talked of going home.

'You know, it is a beautiful place this time of year, all the autumn colours…' he trailed off and took a long sip of wine. He wiped his mouth on the back of his hand and rubbed his hairy jaw, making a crackling noise. 'You should come up and stay with me Gracie?' He threw me a quick glance. 'I know you don't like to fly but we could take the sleeper train. And the Scottish air would do you good.'

'Is it any better than Somerset air?'

'Oh aye, cleaner and colder too, better for your lungs,' he paused, 'and your mind. Perhaps you'd do well to leave this place. For a time at least.'

'I'll think about it.' I said. Maybe he was right, maybe I should leave, but I didn't want to. And I didn't think that going to Torin's house in the depths of Scotland was a good idea.

'So, Gracie, can I tempt you?' Torin asked.

'Sorry?' Was he still talking about visiting his house?

'With some red?' he asked, holding up a bottle.

'Oh, no, thanks, I'll stick to white.'

'As you like it.' He bent forward and poured more wine.

I'd only just noticed we were drinking from glasses. They hadn't been used since Ezra and I moved; Mum had given them to us the Christmas before Ezra died. He'd hated them, called them hippie chic; funny blue hand blown things, you needed two hands to hold, as the glass was so thick.

'Where did you find these?' I asked Torin.

'In your kitchen,' he replied narrowing his eyes, like maybe it was a trick question. 'Were they missing?'

'No, I'd just forgotten about them. I haven't seen them for ages.'

'What do you normally drink wine from then?'

I shrugged, 'A mug?'

Torin laughed. A hearty belly chuckle. A sound that bounced off the walls of my home and filled it with a warmth ordinarily absent.

'Christ, you are the most uncouth wee lady.'

'Have you only just noticed?' I smiled.

'Oh no, I saw you for what you were long years ago,' he said, with something in his eyes that crept beyond affection. Torin looked away. 'It's late, I should let you get to bed,' he said abruptly.

'I'm not tired.' I hesitated before I said, 'Maybe we could watch a film or something?'

'Alright,' Torin said and went to look through the DVD's but I stopped him. They were all films I'd watched with Ezra. I would not watch them again; especially not with Torin.

'Let's watch something neither of us have ever seen?' I said.

We found a film we thought was a zombie movie, but it turned out was a love story between a zombie boy and a human girl. I was not ready for Torin to leave when the movie ended so I suggested we watch another. Torin did not respond with words only took the TV control and flicked through the list of films. He chose a film about a guitarist in the 1960's telling me he'd wanted to see this for some time.

I was tired and could feel my eye lids getting heavy. I knew I shouldn't but I couldn't stop myself from resting my head against Torin's arm when my eyes could no longer stay open. He did not push me away only adjusted himself so it was more comfortable for the both of us.

June 2010

My dress made a noise every time I moved, from all the little beads on the fringed hem. The silk stroked my skin like a lover. My hair was twisted up in an elaborate bun thing on the side of my head, secured with crystal headed pins and I wore a headband to match the dress with a six-inch feather that stuck straight up and danced when I moved. And the shoes were made from a pale green silk fabric, embroidered with flowers in silver thread, with a thin strap and a delicate silver buckle. I even had beautiful ivory underwear and stockings; I'd never felt so pretty and feminine. Even though I barely knew her, I liked Josie immensely for choosing this outfit for me; a thank you gift for the wedding invitations I'd done for her and Noah.

'You look beautiful,' Ezra whispered in my ear, as we stood toward the back of the crowd as Noah made a short speech.

I glanced at Ezra wondering for a moment if he was teasing me or not.

He smiled as though he realised I doubted his sincerity. 'You really do look amazing. Truly, truly amazing.'

I blushed. 'Thank you.' I smiled and let my eyes wander down and back up the length of him in his simple off-white suit, creamy shirt and red and white striped tie.

'You look pretty hot yourself.'

He grinned. 'You think?'

I nodded.

Ezra placed his hand on the small of my back and rubbed the bare skin, revealed by the low cut of the dress, with his thumb.

The air was hazy from the warm summer day and the sky was decorated with romantic wisps of cloud. I smelt the honeysuckle growing over the wall that ran the length of the garden at Redferne House.

The guests raised their glasses in a toast to the happy couple.

Surrounded by smiles, I smiled too as Noah kissed Josie, the new Mrs Redferne, all the while relishing the soft caress of Ezra's fingers on my skin.

I had seen little of Ezra since the previous day. The women, (myself, Josie, her mother and her two bridesmaids, both single women in their thirties) had been at Redferne House for the evening before the wedding. We'd had a light supper of salmon and salad. A beautician had come to the house, and we'd worn face packs, had our nails manicured, and every unruly hair waxed or plucked away. There'd been no alcohol involved. I'd been nervous about it for weeks, having only met Josie twice before, but actually it'd been fun and I'd discovered I liked Josie. I hoped in time we'd become friends.

Ezra had been with his brothers at a hotel in town. I doubted they'd done anything but drink wine and eat fine food. I'd only seen Ezra again once we'd arrived at the registry office in town.

Whether by design or coincidence I didn't know, but the registry office was housed in a lovely art deco building; white with curved edges and fine metal work. Ezra was sat in the front row with Noah and Torin. Noah was resplendent in a fine linen suit and a straw boater that suited his easy laid-back gait. Torin was fully attired in a cream and pale green pin striped suit, waistcoat and all. His hair slicked back. He should have looked good, but he was thin and gaunt. I knew he'd been ill, but I hadn't expected him to look so rough.

Josie came in on her father's arm wearing a golden yellow silk dress. Layers of delicate lace swam about her knees, a sun in gold thread bursting from the low waist and across her abdomen. No veil but a cream cloche hat with her golden curls spilling out underneath.

The ceremony had been sweet and light. We'd all walked back from town under the railway bridge and on to Redferne Lane. We passed the cottages on the right and carried on up to Redferne House itself. The large garden was in full bloom and decorated with cream ribbons hung from the trees that wafted in the warm breeze. Tables covered in lacy cloths were dotted about and a small marquee held a bar and trestle tables laden with food. The air was warm and relaxed, filled with light chatter and laughter. We'd eaten a large tea where I'd been sat between two elderly ladies I'd never met before, while Ezra was three tables away chatting with a gaggle of young ladies. I might have been jealous if he hadn't been throwing me glances and secret smiles all afternoon.

'Hmm, I've missed you,' Ezra said, turning to face me as the chatter of the other guests around us started up again now the speeches had finished.

'I've missed you too,' I said. I was so glad to know that the words were true.

A jazz band, set under an elegant canopy at the end of the garden played dance tunes.

'Dance with me?' Ezra said, still caressing my back with his fingers.

The band played as the hours of light stretched out, fooling us all into thinking it was not late; a faint paleness to the summer sky was still visible. But the solstice had us tricked and Queen Mab was about, weaving her magic. The consumption of Champagne increased and behaviour loosened.

Still giggling we left the dance floor. Ezra grabbed a couple more glasses of Champagne and steered me towards the table Torin was already sat at, smoking a cigarette and watching us. His smile didn't quite reach his eyes, but he was polite and gracious as we sat down. It unsettled me as I'd expected some acerbic comment from him. I'd expected awkwardness between us. Yet I was surprised that somehow the three of us slipped into being as though the past couple of years had not occurred. I remembered how well we got along and how much I missed the friendship the three of us had.

Ezra talked of Torin coming to stay with us before he left the country again but Torin shook his head, telling his brother there wouldn't be time.

'How long are you staying?' Ezra asked, his voice dripping with disappointment.

'A few days,' Torin shrugged.

'What? I thought you were staying a few weeks at least?'

Torin gave a tired smile. 'I've got a lot of work on. I can't afford any more time off.'

'Of course. Have you had to miss much since you've been ill?'

'Aye, a fair bit.' Torin shifted in his chair, looking away from Ezra and me.

Ezra glanced at me, then continued talking to Torin. 'So the business is good?'

'Aye,' Torin said, turning back. 'Really good. Although I'd like to get a bit more work back in this country.'

'That would be good. We miss you,' Ezra said, as we saw Josie approach.

She wore a lazy smile along with her pretty dress and walked with a slight wobble. 'So which of my new brother's is going to dance with me?' she said, her words a little slurred.

Ezra got to his feet, 'I'd be honoured.'

Josie hooked her hand into the crook of Ezra's arm. They walked to the raised floor, Ezra took her in his arms like the perfect gentlemen and they danced to a pacey tune.

Torin and I looked at each other and the past hung between us again. But everything was different now. We both knew that.

Torin looked so frail and thin, so unlike himself and it was more than just the way he looked that had changed. He still laughed a lot but there was a hollow ring to his laughter. But I saw the difference the most in his eyes, he could not quite hide a look of defeat.

I suddenly felt awkward sitting with just Torin and looked away from him. All around the women were wearing drop waist, knee length dresses. Their haired adorned with either a feather and headband or a cloche hat. They held fancy clutch bags with hands clad in elbow-length gloves and their necks draped in long beaded necklaces. The men were a sea of white and cream summer suits, sporting brogues and the odd foppish handkerchief or tie adding a splash of colour.

'It's like wandering into a Merchant Ivory production, right?' Torin remarked. 'Helena Bonham-Carter is going to pop out from behind a scone in a minute. Whatever possessed my brother to do this?'

'Josie?' I said, smiling, finally able to look back at him.

Torin made a noise in the back of his throat. 'Aye, Josie. She's a good woman.'

'Even though she's made us dress up like this?'

'Aye, even though she's made us dress up.' He looked over at me. 'It suits you.'

I rolled my eyes.

'You never could take a compliment.'

Torin and I shared look.

'It's good to see you Gracie,' he said.

'It's good to see you too.' I admitted.

'You're looking well.' He said. 'Ezra too. The both of you are looking right together again.'

I nodded and couldn't stop my smile. Ezra and I were right again.

Torin nodded.

'I wish I could say you were looking well,' I said, taking in the dark circles under his eyes and the deathly pallor his skin.

'Aye,' Torin said, with a small laugh. 'I look like shite, I know.'

I didn't know the details of Torin's illness, only that he'd collapsed and been taken to hospital. Torin had shared little about the whole experience with anyone.

'Were you very ill?' I asked.

'I've never felt so rough.'

'How long were you in hospital?'

'A couple of days.' He paused. 'I don't remember much.'

'What was the matter?' Somehow I felt I shouldn't be asking.

He blinked slowly. 'I wasn't looking after myself.'

I was about to ask exactly what he meant but Torin looked beyond me and smiled, then raised his hand in greeting. I turned to see who he was smiling so warmly at. A pretty young woman in an emerald coloured dress was giving him a flirtatious wave. She had auburn hair that was pinned up with large turquoise feather combs. There was something of a lopsided peacock about her.

'Who's that?' I asked, turning back to Torin.

'Oh, just some girl I know,' he said, with a shrug.

'Some girl you've shagged,' I muttered, before I could stop myself.

He chuckled. 'Aye Gracie.'

I looked at him and wished I didn't care about who he slept with. It was not my concern. But it hurt.

'At least she's not your sister, right?' The smile he offered was kind and without malice. He picked his glass up and raised it. 'Cheers.'

'Good health,' I said, picking up my glass and touching it to his.

'Aye, good health and happiness.'

I drank and forgot my ridiculous jealousy.

'You'll dance with me?' Torin said, barely making it a question.

'Yes.'

We swayed to a gentle tune, one of my hands held in Torin's and my other resting on his shoulder. He held me so lightly that I could hardly feel his fingers on my hip. We talked little and it was just nice to be with him without it being odd, without me feeling as though we should hide anything. Ezra was dancing with a plump lady in a lemon yellow dress not far from us, Josie was swaying, holding hands with Eliza, Noah's daughter from a previous relationship and Noah himself was cutting some moves with Josie's mother, making her giggle like a teenage girl. And I smiled to myself, feeling as though everything was right in the world once more.

October 2014

Ada sat in the hospital bed, perky and alert, her wrist and forearm now covered in a neon pink cast. The operation had gone well; the bone was now set correctly. Yet it was clear to me that she wouldn't be self-sufficient for the foreseeable future.

'I've brought you a cup of tea,' I said, placing a white utilitarian cup and saucer down on the bedside cabinet.

'I'd rather have a cigarette,' she said, with a cheeky smile.

I returned her smile. 'You're not supposed to get out of bed today. I'll take you for one tomorrow?'

'Will I be able to go home tomorrow?'

'Maybe,' I said. 'It depends on your blood pressure.'

The nurse had told me that Ada's blood pressure was a bit high, she suggested that Ada should consider giving up smoking. She'd spoken to me as though I was Ada's granddaughter and I didn't put her right. I didn't know either of my grandmothers; my dad's mother died long before I was born and my mum's mother died when I was three. For the short time while I visited Ada it was nice to pretend we were related.

'I have chocolate biscuits. Those ones you like with the thick layer of chocolate on the bottom,' I said to Ada.

Ada gave a cackle and told me I was a good girl.

I wished I was the good girl she thought I was. I wished I hadn't had to swallow two little white pills just to enable me to get through the hospital doors without gasping for breath. I wished I wasn't fixated on buying a bottle of wine as soon as I left and wondering if this evening I may as well buy two.

Ada ate two biscuits, dipping them in her tea, as she chattered away about the nursing staff, the doctors and what she'd had for lunch. I did my best to smile and listen.

'Are you alright dear?' Ada asked.

'Yes, of course. I'm fine,' I replied in default mode.

She stretched out her good hand and squeezed my fingers, as though to prompt some honesty from me.

'Work is a bit challenging of late,' I said, thinking of Simon and his kindnesses despite the mistakes I seemed to make every day.

She gave me a smile of empathy. 'Why don't you go home and get a good night's sleep? Everything always seems so much better after a good sleep in your own bed, don't you think?'

'Yes.' I nodded. 'I think I'll do that.'

I came under the bridge onto Redferne Lane at the same time as a train rode over the top. The sound was huge and oppressive as though the entire train was in my head and running across my chest. I had to pause on the other side of the bridge as I felt suddenly faint. I looked at Ada's house opposite as I steadied myself with my palm against the rough bark of a tree. It took me a moment, but it dawned on me that the lights were on in Ada's living room when they should not have been.

I went in to her house and a thick haze of smoke and the distinctive smell of skunk weed billowed out of the sitting room. Through the fog I glanced Eliza elegantly sprawled on Ada's sofa and Jerome sat on the floor beside her, his arm resting on her leg, a joint smouldering between his fingers.

'What's going on?' I asked.

'We're just hanging out,' Jerome said, jumping to his feet with guilt fired speed. I saw the panic in his face.

'In Ada's house?'

He shrugged.

'Jerome?'

'There ain't nowhere we can go,' he said.

'To get stoned?' I could feel a colossal spike of anger rising.

'No, well yeah, but I mean we just wanted …' he flushed deep red, 'we just wanted hang out together.'

I understood exactly what they had just wanted to do.

'So you can shag my niece?' I said, barely able to keep my temper.

Jerome looked at me with animal eyes that glowed with venom. He too looked as though he could hardly contain his rage. And that only fuelled my anger.

'Are you going to answer me?' I paused. 'Do you think you can just come here and fuck her on the sofa then smoke a few spliffs?'

'You ain't my mum, you can't tell me what to do.' His tone told me I was spot on with my evaluation.

'No, I'm not your mother but I can tell you to get the fuck out of Ada's house. How dare you come in here?'

'Ada wouldn't mind.'

'How do you know? Have you asked her?' I tried to lower my voice.

Jerome clenched his teeth, his jaw jutting out; he was a firework about to explode.

'Look at the state of her,' I said with a softer tone, pointing at Eliza. 'For Christ sake she's a state.'

'You're a fine one to talk,' he threw at me full of venom.

I glared at him.

'She's alright, she's just sleeping,' Jerome said and now his tone was softer too as he looked at Eliza.

'What's Noah going to say?'

'Who cares what he thinks, he don't care what Eliza does. All they care about is the other kids. They don't know nothing about Eliza. They don't give a shit about her.'

'Is that what she told you?' I asked.

'Yeah.'

'Well it's not true, of course they care about her.' I knelt by my niece. 'Eliza?'

Her eyelids fluttered open like she was a Disney Princess and she smiled.

'Hello Grace.'

'Are you alright?'

'Yes,' she sighed.

I had to admit she looked as beautiful as ever. She had a pink blush to her cheeks and was positioned in an elegant pose. She stretched a little and sighed a pretty sound.

'Maybe it's time go home?' I suggested.

She nodded.

'I'll take her,' I told Jerome.

Jerome ignored me and followed us all the way up Redferne Lane. Just before we got to the wall of Redferne House Jerome put out his arm and stopped us. I was about to argue but Jerome pointed ahead. His mum was coming past the walled garden.

'Please Grace, don't let her see us?' he sounded scared, all of his bite and bravado gone.

There was probably no need for Sam to know what Jerome and Eliza had been up to, so we stopped, hidden by the trees and waited for Sam to pass.

Sam had come around the side of the walled garden, from the direction of garages. She walked past the gate and slipped into the meadow, taking the longer walk back to the cottages. It struck me as an odd time to be cleaning the house – once the children were in bed.

We continued on and I suggested Jerome waited outside the wall of Redferne House and he had the good sense not to disagree.

Eliza felt light as she leant against me. Such a delicate waist and fine boned wrists. I suddenly felt sorry for Jerome, despite my anger. She was the kind of girl that would steal his heart, wrap it up and then savagely break it. And when she'd finished with him she wouldn't even give it back, but keep his broken heart locked away so he'd never truly forget her.

But I couldn't blame her. She probably had no idea of the power she had and no more control over what would happen than Jerome did. No doubt she would not come out of this unscathed either. The both of them were young and vulnerable.

'Don't tell Daddy,' Eliza said, with a whisper of a voice that sounded like a wisp of silky gauze in the breeze.

'Tell him what exactly?' I asked, unsure which part of the evening she wished to hide from Noah.

'Don't tell him I was smoking.'

And what about being alone with Jerome, I thought, would she like me to tell Noah that? I couldn't help but wonder what they might have got up to on Ada's sofa; just kisses and cuddles or more?

'I won't say anything this time, but you've got to be careful okay?'

She nodded.

I looked at her pale face in the evening darkness and could still make out the glow in her cheeks.

'If you ever need to talk…' I began and was cut off as Noah opened the front door.

'I've told you before…' he stopped and frowned. 'Eliza? Where have you been?'

'She was with Jerome, I think they lost track time,' I said.

'Jerome?' Noah said, as though he didn't know who that was. He ushered his daughter into the house. And said 'Come in,' to me.

'I think she's a little tired,' I said, as Noah closed the huge door behind me.

'Are you alright poppet?' Noah asked.

'I don't think I'm very well Daddy,' she said, looking up at him with big doe eyes.

I had to stop myself from rolling my eyes.

'Come on then, let's get you up to bed,' Noah said.

I took that as my cue and announced my departure. Noah thanked me for delivering Eliza home then took his daughter upstairs.

Jerome was still waiting by the wall when I came out.

'Is she alright?'

I nodded. He apologised and started to say something else.

'You can't just go in to Ada's house okay?' I snapped.

He nodded. 'I know. I shouldn't have taken Eliza there.'

'And you shouldn't have got her wasted.'

'She wanted to.'

I blinked. 'Be careful Jerome,' I warned. 'Actions have consequences and you should remember that.'

I could see he wanted to rant at me, shout at me or tell me where to get off. But he took my words with gritted teeth. He gave me a curt nod and walked back towards the cottages at a pace I had no intention of trying to match.

The gate of the walled garden banged closed behind me and I turned to see Torin.

'I thought I heard your voice,' he said. 'Why didn't you stay and say hello?'

'I was just seeing Eliza home,' I said and then explained what I'd stumbled upon at Ada's house.

Torin laughed gently as I told him.

'I didn't know you were here,' I said, feeling that all the tensions from the day had begun to ease from me, just from seeing him.

'Aye, I'm here.' He looked at me with his head on one side.

I pulled my coat a little tighter around myself as the chill of the evening began to settle in my bones.

We both spoke at the same time. Then laughed.

'You first,' Torin said.

'I was just going to ask if you wanted to come down for a bit…'

Torin blinked slowly then said, 'Aye, Gracie, I'd like that.'

And as we walked down Redferne Lane, I couldn't quite remember why I'd felt this day had been so challenging.

The wind caressed my cheeks as I pushed Ada up to Redferne House in the wheelchair. Josie had asked us to come for food and some Halloween fun with the children. It was our first attempt at an outing and I was a little apprehensive. To quash the anxiety, I'd pressed out a couple of little white pills from a foil strip as I'd sat on the bus coming home. But Ada was excited, and she giggled like a school girl, telling me to push the wheelchair faster.

She'd come home the day after the operation, in fine spirits and we'd settled back into a routine of sorts. I shopped for her, cooked and cleaned. Jerome came by after school most days and made her smile. For now, it worked.

It was only Josie, Torin, Ada and the boys at Redferne House. Noah was away for the night on business somewhere and Eliza was staying over at a friend's house.

Ada sat in chair in the kitchen watching with a smile on her face as I carved Godfrey and Barty a pumpkin. I bobbed apples with them. Torin laughed at me as I came up wet faced and grinning with an apple between my teeth. Barty and Godfrey were impressed with that feat. And more impressed still as I ate an entire doughnut off a string without using my hands quicker than either Torin or Josie did.

Torin played with the boys having created a game out of throwing the apple cores back into the bowl of water. It made the boys squeal with delight with every splash. He looked content playing with his nephews and I found myself watching him, noticing the curl of his hair on the nape of his neck and the flex of tendons in his tattooed forearm as he moved.

Josie startled me with the offer of a glass of wine and I knew she'd caught me watching Torin. She didn't allude to it but instead asked me what I thought of a dress she'd seen online that she thought she might wear for Noah and Eliza's party. She assured me she would still accompany me shopping so I could buy a dress. Somehow, right then, I didn't mind the idea of shopping with her so much anymore. It was about time I had something new to wear. And Josie was nice. Being here with her and the boys was nice. Being with Torin was more than nice.

Ada was falling asleep at the kitchen table and Josie looked tired too. It was time to go home. Torin told Godfrey and Barty to run upstairs then he'd read them a story in a moment. As Josie helped Ada into her coat Torin came over.

'Goodnight Gracie,' he said and kissed my cheek, his hand on my hip.

The contact of his lips on my skin made my breath catch.

He straightened up and looked into my eyes. 'Maybe you'd like to go for a drink tomorrow?' His fingers still touched my hip.

I really wanted to go for a drink with him, but I hesitated. I knew Ada and Josie were watching us.

'Please?' he asked.

I nodded not trusting myself to speak.

I pushed Ada down Redferne Lane with a smile on my face. I'd had a nice time; a tonic to another week of work. The rain had stopped after days of stormy weather. The moon was full, lighting up the lane in silver. It was a quiet evening with no sign of spirits or sprites about; perhaps it was too early for the goblins and ghosts to venture out.

At Ada's house I helped her settled for the night and she had me pour her a glass of sherry and one for myself.

'He's a good man,' Ada said.

I knew she was talking about Torin.

'Yes,' I said.

She took a sip of her sherry. 'And rather handsome.'

I took a sip of sherry so I could ignore her last comment and almost spat it out again as it was so sweet. I managed to swallow and put the glass on the table.

'I met a handsome man after Patrick died,' Ada said, with a twinkle in her pale blue eyes.

'Really?' I smiled.

She gave a naughty giggle as she nodded. Then she told me about an affair she'd had. It had lasted for years. He was married. But she said she didn't mind, he'd been kind and gentle and loving. Her only sadness was that he'd always been careful that she would never have his child. She had loved him and he'd loved her too. She said that having feelings for another man had saved her. It didn't make her miss her husband any less but helped her to live.

After biding Ada goodnight, I closed the door to her cottage. At once I heard an unusual noise. At first I could not make out whether it was an animal in the bushes near to me or something else in town further away. But I realised quickly enough it was someone up on the railway track, on the bridge that crosses over the beginning of Redferne Lane.

Reluctantly I went toward the railway bridge, looking up, trying to make out who was on the track. But I couldn't see anything from the lane. I knew there was a gap in the fence on the left of the lane. It was easy enough to squeeze through and then only a little scramble up the bank to the track itself. I felt a wave of panic at being right next to the track as though a train might rush past at any second without prior warning. Yet I heard no sounds of an approaching train. But I could hear someone talking.

I was surprised to see it was Jerome on the other side of the track, perched on the end of a sleeper. He was gesticulating and talking as though in deep conversation with someone, but he was quite alone.

I called his name. He did not respond. I tried again and still he did not appear to hear me. As though crossing a road I looked both up and down the track before carefully stepping over the rail. The large gravel stones poked at the soles of my feet through my trainers. My heart raced and my mouth was dry.

Jerome still did not seem to notice me and for a moment I was angry. I touched his arm, harder than I intended because he was pissing me off. He leapt to his feet and made to grab me, his hand moving towards my throat. But he was slow and clumsy and I pushed him hard. He fell backward, tripped on the rail and fell across the track.

'Get up,' I said, when he just lay across the track looking up at the sky.

He still did not stir. I checked up and down the track again, full of fear at an oncoming train I still could not hear. Sure that no train was coming for the moment I bent over, took Jerome's hands and managed to get him to his feet and off the track. Feeling safer again, I launched into a rant about his stupidity. But I do not think he was of a mind to hear or comprehend. He was utterly wasted. I softened my voice, put my arm around him, guided him down the bank and back onto the safety of Redferne Lane.

I banged on his front door and bit my lip as Jerome swayed next to me, wondering if it was such a good idea to let Sam see Jerome like this. I was grateful when Sam did not come to the door. I didn't knock again but took him into my house.

As soon as I opened my front door Jerome vomited on my doormat. I managed to get him to my kitchen sink before he threw up again.

I hoped that at least some of whatever he'd taken was now in my sink or on my doormat.

He was shaking and pale as I sat him on my sofa with a bowl in his lap, in case he might not have entirely emptied his stomach. His pupils were as large as the full moon outside, but black and dead instead of light.

I made him sweet tea and left him to sip it while I put my doormat in the wheelie bin and rinsed the sink. I lit a fire in the wood burner and then poured myself a glass of wine, just a little one, to quell the racing of my pulse and thoughts.

I began to feel less rattled by the experience and Jerome too appeared to be coming out of the depths of shitfacedness.

He groaned, and I thought he was going to puke again, but he only rubbed his face and swore under his breath. He looked over at me, frowning and said my name as a question.

'I found you on the railway track,' I told him.

He groaned again and rubbed his face once more.

'How are you feeling?'

He looked up at me again. 'Stupid.' Then he closed eyes and leant back against the sofa.

Jerome stayed that way for quite a time and I thought he must have fallen asleep. I got myself another drink and stood in the doorway smoking a cigarette looking up to the moon. It felt as though it should be four in the morning but it was only just past ten.

Jerome came into the kitchen; he was unsteady on his feet and stumbled into the table. He looked unwell and exhausted, his face tinged slightly green. He asked me for a cigarette. I wasn't sure it was the best idea, but he seemed used to making his own decisions and mistakes so I handed him the tobacco pouch.

I watched him fumble with the papers and tobacco for a minute before I offered to make it for him.

'Thanks,' he mumbled and came to sit on my back doorstep.

I sat beside him and we smoked in the silvery moonlight.

'It's my birthday,' Jerome said, after a long silence.

'Happy Birthday,' I said, automatically.

'Thanks.'

'Did the celebrations get a bit out of hand?'

'Took a load of shrooms at a party, someone had made a brew. I don't remember much. Not sure how I got to the railway track.' He spoke in a slurred whisper.

'You alright?'

He gave a small laugh, 'Think I'm still tripping out a bit.'

'Probably.' I offered a small smile.

He returned it.

I sat with Jerome on my back doorstep while he came down. He sipped more sweet tea, I drank more wine, and we smoked cigarettes as the moon crossed the night sky. And we talked. Mostly Jerome talked about Eliza and how much he liked her. She'd been at the party too although Jerome said he didn't think she'd had any of the mushroom tea. I doubted Noah and Josie knew about the party.

I did not care to look at the clock when Jerome finally thought he might be able to sleep and slipped out of my house and into his own.

January 2010

In previous years we might have only just gone to bed, with our ears ringing and the beginnings of an almighty hangover. But last night we'd seen in the New Year with a bottle of Champagne, watching Jools Holland's Hootenanny, in our new bed, in our new flat. We'd made love and turned out the lights, listening to fireworks still going off around the city. Now lounging in bed after a solid night of sleep Ezra and I were debating which of us was going out into the pouring rain to buy supplies.

Ezra had a rare day off, a day when he'd promised he would turn his phone off, not open his laptop and give me his undivided attention. A day we'd decided we would do nothing more than lay in bed, watch movies and eat junk food. A day where we were both making the effort to rekindle our relationship.

I drew the short straw; while I ventured out into the foul weather Ezra stayed home making coffee and keeping our bed warm. He promised he'd make my trip out worth my while, and I left our house wondering what bedroom delights I could look forward to.

Hood up against the rain and a smirk on my lips, I walked the deserted streets toward the nearest shop. I wasn't looking where I was going, and I walked right into him.

'Christ woman, watch where you're going!'

I'd know that voice anywhere.

I pulled my hood down as I looked up at Torin's face.

'Gracie?' He stepped back and ran a hand over his wet hair.

He was ashen faced and wore dark circles under his eyes. His pupils took over almost all of his irises and he swayed like a branch in the wind.

The rain hammered down on us, plastering my hair to my head.

'Happy New Year,' I said.

'Aye, right Happy New Year.' Torin laughed.

He was wasted; his eyes rolling and his jaw clenched in a rush.

'You had a good night then?' I asked.

He ran a hand over his head again and chuckled. 'Aye, a bit messy.' As he pushed back his hair from his face I noticed the tails of his bracelet were coming loose and some of the little silver beads were missing. I wanted to say something, so he didn't lose it but I couldn't.

He blinked and swayed slowly as though he suddenly had no idea who I was, what I was saying or who he was himself.

'What are you doing here Torin?' A few streets away from our new flat in Bristol was the last place I would have expected him; Ezra thought he was in Canada.

'Staying with a friend,' he mumbled.

'A girl?'

'Aye, a girl, Gracie.' He gave a sordid laugh.

I frowned at him as my initial surprise at seeing him disappeared.

'Where have you been Torin?' I couldn't keep the hurt from my voice. Neither Ezra nor I had heard from Torin in months.

'Have you missed me Gracie?' He stepped forward and went to touch my face.

'Don't.' I pushed his hand away.

He staggered, smirking. I could smell the alcohol on his breath.

'Does Ezra know you're here?'

'No.'

'Are you going to come and see us?' I asked, but I already knew the answer.

He shook his head, 'I don't think so.'

'Ezra would want to see you.'

'I can't see him,' he said and stumbled a little away from me.

'But he's your brother.'

'Aye. And he's your boyfriend.'

We stood looking at each other. For a moment I saw tenderness in his eyes but then he wobbled and blinked.

'I need to get back. There's a naked woman waiting for me to do bad things to her,' he said and grinned.

Stung, I started walking, making sure my shoulder hit against him as I passed.

I heard him call my name through the falling rain but I didn't turn.

He grabbed my wrist and span me round to face him. 'I'm sorry. Forgive me Gracie? I'm a bad man. You know I'm a bad man. Don't be angry with me?'

I saw the look of anguish on his face and my anger dissolved a little.

'Where have you been Torin?' I asked again. 'You just left, no one's heard from you for months.'

'What else was I meant to do?'

I didn't have an answer.

He smoothed his thumb over the inside of my wrist. 'No good would have come of me staying anywhere near you.'

'Couldn't you have at least said goodbye?'

'It's better this way, it's better if you hate me just a little.'

'I don't hate you,' I said.

'You should.'

'I can't.'

Torin pulled me into a hug. I had not let myself remember how my head rested against his heart when he held me.

'Goodbye Gracie.' He kissed my forehead, releasing me and turned away. He didn't look back, and the rain made his outline fuzzy long before he was out of my sight.

I walked on to the shop. Only I couldn't remember one single thing I was there for. I finally left the shop with a white carrier bag full of things I had no idea if we'd wanted or not. Trudging through the rain, I made myself think about Ezra waiting in our bed, in our new flat. Our home. Our fresh start. I thought about how we were happier now. I thought about how we were going to spend the day in bed watching movies and eating junk food, drinking Champagne and making love. And I reminded myself that this is what I wanted. Ezra was what I wanted.

November 2014

Torin was at my door in his work clothes; black utility trousers with knee pads and many pockets and a matching jacket with a small logo on the breast. His knees were dusty and his jacket was speckled with white paint.

'I'm sorry I'm late,' his said, his breath clouding with every word. He seemed tense, his brow furrowed. 'I've had a mare of a day.'

'It's fine,' I replied, feeling the chill of the evening air creeping past my legs and into my house. The temperature had dropped from the previous day as though nature had decided that autumn had now truly arrived.

I wasn't even aware that Torin was late. I didn't know what the time was. After Jerome had left yesterday I'd had one of those nights when thoughts wrestle with one another and sleep is played out in a tangle of odd dreams. Most had been a mash-up of Jerome's antics and the Halloween games I'd played at Redferne House. But the chaste kiss Torin had placed on my cheek yesterday had been a recurring element. And then I'd had a vivid dream of Torin and me tangling between the sheets, that was anything but chaste.

'I've just come straight from work and as you can see I'm not ready to go,' he sighed, and rubbed his palm against his beard. 'I would have called you but I realised I don't have your number. How do I not have your number?'

'I don't know,' I mumbled, as an image from my dream flashed into my thoughts and made me blush.

'Me either.'

He seemed on edge.

'You could just come as you are?' I suggested. Perhaps a drink would do him good.

'But I'm filthy,' Torin said.

As I spoke I pulled my coat from the post of the bannister, smiling. 'I've always known you were filthy Torin.'

A small smile broke onto his face and I felt inordinately pleased that I'd put it there.

'Come on, let's just go for a drink and you can tell me about your shitty day,' I said.

'If you insist,' Torin said.

I fell into step beside Torin and he began telling me about the new job he'd started, just in town; a multi-stage for a festival in the town. The job was technically challenging and the local team he'd hired weren't as experienced as they'd claimed. He was passionate in a way I'd not witnessed before. Every now and then he suggested that what he was talking about must be boring but with only a murmur of encouragement from me he continued. I was surprised that I knew so little of what Torin did on a day-to-day basis.

We went to a local pub that Torin had visited before. It was a drinkers' pub, no food on sale beyond crisps and nuts. Real ales, proper cider and Polish lager on tap and a small selection of spirits was all that was stocked behind the small bar. The décor was an eclectic mix of antique and kitsch, ecclesiastical and pagan with highlights of Farrow and Ball paint on the walls.

Torin brought us pints of cider, assuring me I'd like it, despite my reservations at its urine like appearance. We sat on mismatched chairs at a table made from the cast iron stand of an old sewing machine table; it still had a foot pedal. The first thing he did after he'd taken a long swig of his pint was to take my phone and tap in his number, and then he called it, making sure my number was on his phone too. And then we talked. By the time we'd finished our first drinks I'd been fully introduced to the intricacies of the events staging industry. After the second pint Torin's shoulders had finally lost the tension that had held them aloft and his face had relaxed back into his familiar smile.

We went outside for a cigarette and the air was icy, the sky above, crystal clear. I felt the chill creeping into my bones as we stood in the cold. We lent side by side against the wall of the pub and as we smoked I told Torin of Jerome's shenanigans of the night before.

Torin shook his head with a wry smile. 'Well, he can't feel too bad as he's been up at the house all day. When I popped back to the house this afternoon, to pick up some tools, I caught them canoodling on the sofa.'

'Canoodling?' I sniggered at his choice of word.

Torin inhaled and then blew a smoke ring. 'Aye, canoodling. They can't leave each other alone.' Torin chuckled. 'Christ, do you remember what it was like when you first fell in love?'

'Yes Torin, I do,' I mumbled. Perhaps he had no idea who I'd first fallen in love with. I didn't know who his first love was.

'All you want to do is fuck them, even if you fucked them ten minutes before,' he continued, oblivious.

I took a couple of deep drags of my cigarette and looked at a crack in the concrete floor, needing to look anywhere but at Torin right then. My head was a gooey tangle of cider and nicotine and erotic dreams and young love. And with

Torin beside me, the warmth of him permeating my every pore, I knew I could no longer deny that something in me had switched back on. I longed for sensations I'd not experienced for such a time. I'd forgotten they existed, until Torin had come back. And it was more than one feeling; it was a heady, traitorous mix of emotions I'd thought I had no need to feel anymore. I did not want to feel those things for Torin and yet I relished being with him and felt such warmth toward him.

'I hope he doesn't get his fingers too badly burnt,' Torin said.

'Why would he get his fingers burnt?' I asked. I could see a small pulse racing in his neck, just above the tip of his tattoo.

'Because that's what women do. Especially beautiful women.' Torin licked his lips, then smirked at me.

'Pretty boys can be heart breakers too,' I said, as Torin dropped his cigarette to the floor and extinguished it with the chunky toe of his work boot.

'You think Jerome is pretty?'

'Handsome, yes,' I said, with a smile at the tone of contempt in Torin's voice.

'Christ, you don't fancy him do you?' Torin said, with distaste.

'Behave yourself, he's like half my age. He's a child.' I laughed.

'Hardly a child.'

'He's still very young.' I dropped my cigarette butt and watched it smoulder for a second.

'I wouldn't blame you, you know, if you went there. You're a woman with needs.'

'Oi,' I said, and landed a playful slap on Torin's arm.

'Ouch!' Torin exclaimed.

'That didn't hurt.' I grinned. 'But this will.' I wacked him as hard as I could; the palm of my hand on his bicep.

'Ow!' He rubbed his arm, then tapped my forearm with the back of his hand.

'That was rubbish,' I said and hit him again.

He slapped my arm, harder this time. It smarted.

I jabbed him in the ribs with my fingertips and laid another slap on his arm before I took a couple of steps back towards the pub door.

Yet he moved so much faster than me. I blinked, and he'd grabbed me. Somehow he'd gotten both of my wrists in one of his hands and started poking the side of my abdomen with his fingers. I shrieked and struggled, laughing, then stamped on Torin's foot. He let go, and I felt myself free for a second before he had one of my hands in his, twisting me around so I had my back to him. I pushed back against him hard, with all the force I could muster and perhaps because he wasn't expecting it he stumbled and released me again. I turned to face him and we sparred; a slap, a block, a feint to the left, a jab in the ribs to the right, all the while giggling.

'Truce,' he said laughing, once he had hold of both of my wrists again.

'Truce,' I said, out of breath, with cheeks warm from the exertion.

'I'd forgotten how feisty you could be,' he said, slightly breathless himself.

Blood rushed around my veins and my heart beat, full of life. And I knew I hadn't felt like this in such a long time.

I struggled to get my wrists free.

'Calm?' Torin questioned, his eyes playful.

I smiled and nodded.

Still grinning, he narrowed his eyes as though assessing whether he could trust me to behave. But then his smile changed and we were just looking at each other. From the shadows in the dark of his eyes I knew he was holding back while still relishing the intimacy we shared. I wasn't sure how long we could carry on before one of us forgot how to behave and I slid my wrist from his grasp.

'Shall we get another drink?' I asked, already heading back inside.

We went upstairs and played pool in the games room, until I couldn't stand to lose another game. Then we lent against the wall on the long landing, as there was nowhere left to sit, sipping yet another pint and talking of nothing of consequence. We watched those that passed us and made up their stories as we'd done many times before. Torin made me laugh, and I delighted in the slight ache in my cheeks. I had not felt so relaxed with another person for so long. I'd forgotten how it felt to enjoy another's company so much and how someone else can make you a better version of yourself, a far better version.

We were the last to leave the pub, somewhat drunk and merry. Outside it was cold and we each buttoned up our coats against the sharp wind. I pulled my hat down low and my scarf up high so little more than my eyes were exposed. The moon was waning and wispy clouds drifted past dulling the light. Torin draped his arm around my shoulders, casually, as though the gesture meant nothing. But I was so aware of the weight of his limb around me and the gentle clasp of his fingers on the top of my arm. And I revelled in the warmth his body emitted as he walked close beside me.

We were outside my house before I was ready to be home. We stopped in the lane and Torin dropped his arm from my shoulder.

'I've had a lovely evening Gracie,' Torin said, standing before me. 'Thank you.' He edged my hat up a centimetre then eased my scarf down until it slipped beneath my chin.

'So have I. Thank you.'

'My pleasure.'

A different man and woman might have kissed then, but Torin blinked and I looked away. We both spoke at once. Then we both laughed, a little awkward, a little nervous.

'I was just going to say goodnight,' Torin said, with a wonky smile.

I'd been about to ask him to come inside but I was glad we'd talked over each other and I hadn't spoken the words. It was right that this lovely evening finish just like this.

'Yes, goodnight,' I said.

He gazed at me. His smile grew more lopsided. Torin lent forward and pressed a soft kiss upon my lips. He did not pull away immediately but lingered.

I could feel his beard against my lips. His breath mingled with mine.

Torin stepped back just a little, just far enough, so that we were no longer touching.

'You should go inside,' Torin said. 'It's cold.'

I nodded. 'See you soon?' I reached out and placed my gloved hand to his beard.

'Aye Gracie, I'll see you soon.' He mirrored my gesture, but he wore no glove and I felt the heat of his fingers on my cold cheek.

He lifted his fingers from my face and gave me a gentle shove towards my door. 'In you go now.'

He waited in the lane until I went inside and closed the door.

Jerome stood on the threshold to my house. He wore the white shirt and red and blue striped tie of St Marys. But he also wore a red hoody, black trainers and black jeans I assumed were not school uniform. He pulled his bottom lip against his teeth and frowned at my feet.

'Come in,' I said and made a sweeping gesture with my hand, that held my glass of wine. I'd just got home from work and it hadn't been a great day.

Jerome ducked his head as he came through the low doorway and paused.

I watched Jerome's eyes flick about the room. He took in my laptop on the coffee table, a couple of notebooks and a collection of coffee mugs. A pile of DVD's stacked precariously on the floor. Shelves housing all sorts of books and things and stuff and the shabby grey sofa with the multi-coloured blanket thrown over the back.

'How's it going?' I asked. I hadn't seen him since his birthday although I'd heard Sam shouting at him at various points over the weekend.

'Alright.' He flicked his long fringe, offering me a look of his face before the hair flopped back over his eyes. He cleared his throat. 'So I just wanted to come and say thank you. You've been well nice to me, at the hospital and the other night and that.' Slipping the strap from his shoulder, he slung his bag in front of him and unzipped it. He pulled out a box a Milk Tray and held them toward me. 'These are for you.'

'Jerome that's really kind of you. Thank you.' I said and accepted the chocolates. I was astounded. And touched by his gesture.

'I'm sorry about the other night.' He talked to my flagstones. 'I ain't never been so wasted.' He flicked his hair again. 'I'm never doing that shite again.'

I smiled inwardly in recognition of the sentiment and knew it was more than likely he'd give a repeat performance of overindulgence sooner rather than later, if my own behaviour was anything to go by.

We exchanged a few words about Ada and as the conversation drew to a natural close I expected him to leave. But he didn't. Instead, he sat down on the sofa and picked up one of my old sketch books.

'I was right lucky the other night,' Jerome began. 'Mum weren't home. She didn't come back all night. So she didn't see what state I was in.' He frowned looking down at my sketch book. 'I reckon she's seeing someone.'

'That's nice?'

'So long as he ain't like the last wanker she was shagging.' He continued to leaf through one of the sketch books that were full of pictures of Ezra. Sketches I'd done when I was falling in love with him.

'These is well good.' He said, before I'd worked out the right way of telling him to put down my sketch book without being rude.

I forced a smile and thanked Jerome.

'You want to see some of mine?' Without waiting for an answer Jerome took out a ring bound sketch book from his bag, the corners softened and bent with use. 'I've seen you, you know, drawing, when I look in the window.'

'You look in my windows?' I asked, a touch freaked out.

'I'm not perving, just you know, I look in when I'm passing. I like to see what you're doing.'

I dreaded to think what else he might have witnessed but decided to let it pass. I sat down beside him, placed the Milk Tray on the table and flicked through his sketch book. The first page held a drawing of an old lady. Then the second, third and fourth pages too. They were all in soft pencil lines; gentle grey strokes over the thick creamy paper.

'Is this your Grandmother?'

'Sort of,' he said, with a shrug. 'That's Betty. She was Mum's foster mum. My real Gran died when Mum was little and Mum didn't have anyone else and so she lived with Betty. And when I came along, me and Mum lived with Betty. My dad didn't want nothing to do with me, so I've never known any different.'

I smiled at the affection in Jerome's voice.

'She's dead now.'

'I'm sorry.'

'She was old.' He shrugged.

I knew that defensive tone he used, and I knew how to bat away pity better than most.

I turned another page of his sketch book.

'She had a stroke,' Jerome said, after a minute, when I'd thought the subject was probably closed. 'Pissed herself in her chair.'

I didn't say anything, just looked at him so he knew I was listening. Sometimes that's all you need.

'I found her when I came home from school. She must have been there all day. She was already cold. She looked all funny and it stank.'

'I'm really sorry Jerome,' I said. 'That must have been quite a shock.'

'Yeah.' He paused. 'I like drawing her. From photos. So I don't forget her.'

No wonder he'd taken such a shine to Ada, she was a substitute.

I looked down and turned another page of his sketch book. To my surprise there was a near perfect image of Eliza. I looked up at Jerome. He rubbed his hair with his hand then ran his fingers over his mouth and just stared at me with his vivid blue eyes.

I turned the pages of his sketch book and found image after image of my niece. She was as beautiful through his lines as she was in the flesh. Her silvery blond hair sketched in fluid waves in his light style. His pencil had captured a true essence of her.

'I like drawing her,' he said, like a confession.

Smiling at him, I said, 'Yes, I can see, you've drawn her very well.'

I looked down at the pictures again and turned to the next page. In that drawing Eliza was all but naked, posed like a Pre Raphaelite nude, with only an artfully placed drape of cloth to cover her.

'Shit, you ain't meant to see that,' he said, and made to grab the sketch book.

'Wait,' I said, pulling it out of his reach, 'this is good.' I looked up at the picture as I held it as far away from him as I could.

'Stop, give it back.'

I stood up while turning the next page to find another semi naked picture of Eliza. I couldn't help smiling. I felt like I'd just found an unknown John William Waterhouse.

'Hey, whoa, slow down, these are amazing Jerome, you should show everyone.'

'But then she won't never speak to me.' His cheeks were flaming red.

'What do you mean?'

'She made me promise no one would see. If her Dad finds out…'

'Don't worry, I won't tell,' I reassured him. I could just see Noah freaking out over something like this.

'You won't?'

'No. There's nothing wrong with drawing pictures like this as long as Eliza is happy for you to?'

He gave a smile that alluded to their private moments.

'But Jerome?'

'Yeah?'

'Be careful, okay?'

'Sure,' he said in a dismissive tone as though there was nothing for him to be careful about.

'Do you take art at school?' I asked, moving the conversation on.

'Yeah,' he hesitated. 'And I want to go to art college but Mum reckons it's a waste of time. She says my drawing won't pay the rent.'

'You should go to college if that's what you want,' I said. 'And there are ways of making a living from your art.'

'You try telling Mum that,' he scoffed, took his sketch book from and hands and snapped it shut.

February 2009

'You can't make this all better with a dozen red roses,' I said, already turning to walk away. It was cold, and I wished we hadn't come out for a meal.

'You're just going to throw me that line and turn your back?' Ezra all but shouted. People in the street turned to look at us.

'I'm tired Ezra. I just want to go home.' And I wanted to cry.

He followed me, pulling his coat tight around himself as though it were armour, as though he might need the protection.

We passed couple after couple enjoying the most romantic evening of the year. They carried oversized teddy bears or bouquets and held hands. The final couple we passed kissed passionately in the middle of the road as though they desired each other so much they couldn't wait until they'd made it to the safety of the pavement on the other side.

I had not kissed Ezra like that for so long. If I was honest it was even before Ezra's indiscretion; I was pretty certain the wane in our passions had coincided with Torin coming to stay. But he was not the reason Ezra and I did not kiss anymore, let alone with traffic stopping passion. I was sure it was not because of Torin. Yet I struggled to find other reasons that made sense of what was wrong between me and Ezra.

I hailed a taxi. Ezra gave me a questioning frown; we rarely caught a taxi, preferring to walk. But I was so tired of the evening, so tired of the rift between Ezra and me, and cold, really cold.

On our return home, I went to the kitchen and poured a large glass of whiskey, not even bothering to take my coat off. I knocked it back and poured another, steadying myself with one hand on the counter.

'Are you going to get drunk again?' Ezra asked, standing on the threshold to the room in his woollen overcoat and smart long-toed shoes; his suit and tie visible beneath.

'Yes.' I drank the next shot down and poured again.

Ezra rubbed his face with both of his hands. 'How long are you going to keep doing this?'

I didn't know the answer.

'Getting off your head every night is not exactly helping.'

I shrugged.

We'd visited the conversations over and over again, but it made no difference what we said anymore. The simple fact was that I could not let it go. I would not go back to the way things had been. Not yet. Maybe never. I loved Ezra, but I was so fed up with thinking about what he'd done, what I'd done, what we'd both said, what we hadn't said.

'Will you at least pour me one then?' Ezra asked, coming into the kitchen.

He rarely drank whiskey, preferring wine or ale.

He took a glass from the cupboard and held it up. 'I may as well join you, right?'

'If you like,' I said, and poured him a shot.

He drank his shot down, grimaced and held out his glass again. 'Maybe it'll help?'

'You think?' I asked.

'Nothing else seems to make a difference. Cheers.'

It felt like a dig. It felt as though he was beginning to blame me for the situation we found ourselves in.

'Can't you just back off?' I asked. 'Do you have to keep pushing? I can't just make myself feel okay with all this.'

'I'm not pushing you Grace.'

'You are.'

'What, taking you out for dinner and buying you flowers is pushing you?'

'On Valentine's day? Yes, it is. It's not like we've ever done Valentine's day and now things are shite you pull out a dozen red roses and take me to dinner and suddenly expect that it'll mend everything?'

'I don't expect it to mend everything. I just hoped it would give us an opportunity to have a nice time, to be a couple. To have fun. Perhaps if you hadn't been shooting me daggers all evening it might actually have been romantic,' Ezra said.

I swallowed the contents of my glass and refilled it. Ezra followed suit and held his glass out to be refilled as well.

'Why is this all my fault now?' I asked.

'It's not.'

'Then why are you constantly having a go at me?'

He looked at me with a hard frown that made his eyes thick black and cold; shark like. He washed the look off his face by downing the thumb of amber in his glass.

'I screwed up,' Ezra said. 'You know that. I know that. My entire bloody family knows it. And I'm sorry. I'm really fucking sorry. But I think you know as well as I do that I wouldn't have done it if things with you and me were okay.'

I didn't think it was a good idea to speak. I did not like what he was implying, and I knew he had more to say. I anesthetised myself with the contents of my glass.

'When exactly are you going to start admitting that this is about far more than what I did?' He paused. 'Grace?'

I shook my head, turned my face away and stepped back.

'Don't turn away from me,' Ezra said, in a low voice, simmering with anger.

I took my time turning my head back to look at him.

'What about you Grace?' I was surprised by the look on his face; there was fear in amongst the anger. 'When are you going to admit to what you've done?'

I was woozy with drink; my heart pounded and the fear from Ezra spread to me.

'I know there's been someone,' Ezra said, with a hurt tone.

I frowned.

We looked at each as though properly for the first time in months.

'Are you still in love with him?' Ezra asked, as though he was slicing open his own chest to reveal his heart.

'What are you talking about?' I said back, just as softly. 'There isn't anyone.'

'Am I crazy? Is there really no one?'

'No.'

'No? I mean I wouldn't blame you? I just need to know Grace?'

I clenched my jaw, pressing my teeth together as hard I could. I couldn't speak.

'All those times you turned over at night I thought it must be because there was someone else…?' Ezra waited, looking at me, imploring. 'I mean it's ridiculous but if he wasn't my brother I'd have wondered about you and Torin? All those times I came back to find you asleep against his shoulder? But I mean that really is crazy, right? Jesus, am I just fucking crazy?'

'What exactly is it you think I've done?' I questioned.

He shook his head.

I could tell Ezra everything. But in so many ways there was nothing to tell. And no good would come of saying anything. I knew if I told him even a slice of it, Ezra and I would definitely be over. Not only that but what of Ezra's relationship with Torin? I wouldn't tell Ezra anything. I couldn't.

I refilled our glasses, downed my own and with glass and bottle in hands went from the kitchen through to the living room. Depositing the bottle on the table, I knelt in front of the pretty fireplace. The fire I made was haphazard and looked as though it had little chance of creating much heat but I found I did not care and sank back onto the sofa, leaving my coat on.

I was half way through a cigarette when Ezra came into the room. He went straight to the hearth and began to resurrect the ailing fire. The flames licked a log with the promise of filling the room with heat.

Ezra turned to me. 'I'm sorry.'

I nodded.

'I didn't mean that, about Torin.' He gave an anguished laugh and shook his head. 'I'm clutching at straws. Jesus, he's my brother, right?' He came to kneel before me. 'I just don't want to lose you Grace.'

I knew there was an untruth in there. He did want to ask about Torin. He did suspect something.

'I can't do flowers and dinner right now, okay?' I said. And I would not talk of Torin.

Ezra nodded.

'I don't know how this is going to turn out,' I said. 'I know I don't want to leave and yet I'm not sure how to stay either. Because if we can't be more than we are now I don't think either of us can stay.'

'Surely we have to try, right?' The desperation in Ezra's voice broke my heart.

I nodded.

'That's all I was trying to do tonight. I just wanted to show you that I love you and I want to be with you.'

I took his hands, and I was shocked by how unfamiliar they felt.

'I'm sorry Ezra,' I said, as tears rolled down my cheeks. 'It's just so hard.'

He nodded and then for the first time in months I let him hold me.

November 2014

I went straight up the lane after work with the sinking sensation I was holding up proceedings. Eliza let me in, told me she hated living in the house and went upstairs. In the kitchen Josie was arguing with Godfrey and Barty insisting they would not be allowed to go outside to watch the fireworks until they put their clothes back on. Godfrey was entirely naked and Barty just wore socks. Every time Josie insisted they should get dressed they sang a tuneless song that's lyrics consisted only of the words 'willy' and 'bum'. She gave me a tight smile before she continued trying to dress the boys.

Torin sat at the table still in his work clothes a fresh glass of red wine in his hand and a clenched jaw. He stood, went to the fridge, poured a glass of white wine and handed it to me. I started to ask him if he was okay when Godfrey and Barty began another chorus of the willy-bum song.

Torin gave a slight nod of his head, mimed smoking with his fingers, then ushered me out of the kitchen. I could feel Torin's hand on my lower back as we stepped out of the house and into the garden, protective and caring, perhaps a little proprietary. But I liked it, I more than liked it.

'It's doing my head in here,' Torin said. 'I think I might have to find somewhere else to stay.'

'You could stay at mine?' I said, before I'd even considered what I was saying.

He smirked at me and held my eyes for a moment until I looked away unable to stop the flush in my cheeks. 'Here,' he said holding a packet toward me, one cigarette elevated above the others.

We smoked standing in front of the unlit bonfire. It was a majestic pile of pallets, off cuts of two-by-four, and random shaped pieces of ply. Crowning the mound was a former dining room chair that now only had three legs, no longer benefitted from a seat cushion and was missing an upright from the back. And upon seat sat the Redferne Guy. Apparently he was an effigy of James Redferne from centuries back that had Catholic sympathies in what was primarily a Protestant family. He'd almost lost the entire Redferne fortune, including the house, in some scandal, hence the ghoulish effigy.

'So I meant to ask the other night, but I was so wrapped up in my own shite that I didn't. How's work?' Torin said.

'Hmm, it could be worse.'

Torin was looking at me but I didn't look at him because I knew he's see how bad it really was. I was making so many mistakes and Simon continued to be kind and patient. Today I'd put the wrong addresses on nearly a hundred invoices. After Simon had perched on the edge of my desk and pointed out my error in that calm voice he uses, I'd realised that he must be checking everything I do otherwise no one would have noticed the mistakes. I'd had to hide in the toilet for half an hour. Long enough for my tears to abate and the little white pill to begin easing the tension in my chest, allowing me to breathe properly again.

'But it could be better?' Torin asked.

'Everyone hates their job, right?' I quipped. 'How's it going with this new job of yours?'

'Aye, it's a little better, I've brought down a team of my people to oversee the locals and that's helped a load and now I've got my head around some aspects I'm pretty happy with the way things are going. And by the way Gracie, you're wrong, not everyone hates their job. I don't. Noah doesn't and I like to think my team like what they do.' Torin turned to face me as he spoke, his arms crossed over his chest. 'Why don't you do something else?'

'Like what?'

'Rocket scientist? Brain surgeon? Stripper?'

'Funny.'

Torin was about to say something else when the back door opened and Barty and Godfrey came out, followed by Josie. The boys were wrapped up in winter coats, hats and gloves but it did nothing to slow their movements and within second they were running around the unlit bonfire shrieking something I couldn't decipher. But their exuberance made me smile. Josie moved slowly, often sighing, one hand at the small of her back, the other low beneath her bump, as though she was supporting the baby inside her.

Eliza came out with a mask of teenage injustice.

'Christ, I thought she might have got over it by now,' Torin said.

'What?'

'Noah told her she couldn't invite Jerome.'

'Why?'

'Family only.' Torin said. 'Noah has taken a dislike to the boy. Which, I might add, he fails to understand will only make the boy more attractive to the girl. Forbidden fruit. We all want what we can't have, right?'

'But Eliza likes Jerome anyway, it doesn't matter what Noah thinks, surely?'

'Who knows the workings of a teenage girl's mind? Or any female come to that. I certainly don't. You women are a complete mystery.'

'Oh and you're crystal clear to understand.'

'I am.'

'You are not.'

He looked at me, his head on one side.

'Have you heard from Noah?' Josie asked Torin, as she came towards us.

'No,' Torin said, pulling his phone from his pocket. 'You want me to call him?'

'Well, you can but every time I've tried, it just goes to answer phone.' She sighed and shifted her weight from one foot to the other, resting in her hip. 'He promised he'd be here, Torin.' I could hear how let down she felt by Noah's absence.

'Aye, I know, I'll call him.'

I stood with Josie as Torin walked off a little. I couldn't imagine how it felt to carry a child inside you. How it might be to feel that extra weight, to grow so much bigger than you were, to know that another whole human was growing inside you. In equal parts I was both amazed and appalled at the notion. I half wanted that for myself and yet was terrified by the idea too.

'How are you feeling?' I asked Josie.

'Oh, I'm fine, just a bit tired.' She sighed again and moved her weight from hip to hip. 'Godfrey, don't do that darling.'

I looked over to the boys where Godfrey was poking his brother with a plank of wood he'd pulled from the bonfire.

'So, we're shopping tomorrow?' I asked.

'Yes, yes, how exciting.'

'Yes.'

There was a silence which I knew I should have filled but I couldn't think how.

Then I noticed Eliza crouched beside the pile of wood.

'Eliza?' I said.

She ignored me and I saw the flare of a match. She held it forward and immediately flames leapt through the pile of wood. The smell of petrol fumes filled the air. The bonfire was ablaze.

'Godfrey, Barty, come here,' I said, leaping toward the boys. I took each of them by the hand and all but lifted them by their arms out of the immediate vicinity of the fire and back towards Josie. The boys giggled and demanded I do it again and I was relieved that they found their journey to safety a fun game and were not worried by the actions of their sister.

'Oh my God,' Josie exclaimed. 'Eliza whatever are you doing?'

'Why should we wait when he can't even be bother to be here for family?' she spat the last word as though it was poison.

Torin returned, announcing Noah was on his way.

The fire licked its way hungrily through the pile and the speed with which it caught made Eliza stumble back a few steps. She stuffed her hands into her pockets and gazed into the flames, ignoring the rest of us.

Josie tried to hold the boys close to her, but they wriggled free, so I went again and pulled them back by grabbing each child by the arm. Torin joined me in the task of keeping the two boys far enough back from the fire and Josie looked on, muttering profanities under her breath.

After a time, Josie managed to coax the boys inside for a moment on the promise of toffee apples. Eliza sat on a bench away from Torin and me, leaving us by the bonfire. It had burned down a little now, the effigy long gone. Orange flames curled over and back across the charred wood. The smell was delicious, almost edible.

'Should we go and sit with Eliza?' I asked.

'I think she's made it pretty obvious she'd rather not be disturbed.'

I glanced over to our niece remembering the many hours I'd spent alone as a teenager hating everyone and everything. Torin was probably right, I'd only offend her further if I tried to talk to her.

Twenty minutes or more passed before Noah finally turned up, flushed and blathering excuses of traffic and office politics. He expressed his disappointment that we hadn't waited for him before lighting the bonfire and Josie explained in clipped tones that the children had been waiting a long time. He produced a large box of fireworks and, in a slight huff, went off down the garden to set them up. Eliza skulked up the garden in his wake, despite Josie advising her otherwise.

Torin and I supervised Godfrey and Barty with sparklers. I was terrified one of them was going to hold the hot end or jab someone else with it. The four of us traced temporary patterns in the dark and as the last one was extinguished in the bucket of water, the first rocket flew into the sky and exploded into a starburst of pinks and greens. And finally Barty and Godfrey stood still.

Josie stood with her boys and Torin stood close to me, closer than was necessary. Half way through the display, he turned to me, his face illuminated in the green light of a firework and said, 'Pretty, so very pretty.'

We gazed at one another for a moment until a loud bang made me jump and Barty started crying. Torin scooped Barty up and held him on his hip telling his nephew not to be scared.

As the bonfire burned low, Eliza announced she was going out. Both Josie and Noah started to protest but before either one of them could make themselves heard she was gone, slamming the door behind her.

Noah asked Torin if he'd like a drink. Josie gave Noah a look, she then threw the look to Torin and Torin declined his brother's offer.

'The boys need to go to bed,' Josie said to Noah.

'Yes, yes, of course, come on boys, Daddy's going to put you to bed tonight.'

Both of the boys at once began to moan. They wanted mummy.

A flash of hurt crossed Noah's face before anger over took.

'No,' he all but shouted, 'Daddy is taking you to bed. Daddy is going to read a story. And you are both bloody well going to like it.'

'Noah,' Josie said, in a gasp. 'Don't.'

'For God's sake,' Noah roared.

And then Josie, Barty and Godfrey were all crying.

I mumbled something and made my departure and I wasn't surprised but delighted that Torin followed me.

'Christ, I need a drink,' Torin said, as soon as we'd passed through the wooden gate and out onto Redferne Lane.

I gave a small laugh. 'I've got a bottle of wine at mine?'

'Just the one?'

'There might be two?'

'Then I'm all yours.'

Mine? What would it mean if he was mine?

He gave a laugh and snuck his arm around my waist. 'Fuck, are families always so grim? Why do people even have kids if that's how it is?'

I smiled. 'I'm sure there's more to it than nights like this. Something deeper, more fundamental, something more basic, more biological.'

'Wow, that's deep Gracie,' Torin said, pulling me just a fraction closer to him.

'Hardly.'

'No, really, it's getting to the root of things. I think so many folks have babies just because they can and they don't even think if they should. I'm a prime example of that. My parents should never have had me, it was only laziness and lust that produced me.'

'What about love?' I asked.

'Aye, maybe love too. But that's not enough.'

'Isn't it?'

'No.' He said abruptly, then he laughed again. 'Christ, I don't know, maybe it is. Maybe it's all you need.'

We were at my door. I moved beyond the gate to the front door.

'So are coming in?' I asked as Torin hesitated in the lane.

He blinked, 'Maybe I should head back, see if I can defuse the situation?'

I felt a jolt of disappointment. 'Yeah, maybe.'

'But I'll see you Saturday, for the party?'

'Yes, of course.'

We stood looking at one another in the cold and dark.

He closed the gap between us with a couple of steps. I felt his hand on the back of my head, his fingers slipping into the wisps of my hair. Then a kiss on my cheek. He stayed close to me for a moment longer. I could smell him and longed to press my face into his neck and really inhale the essence of him. But he withdrew. And before I was ready he was stepping backward into the lane.

'See you on Saturday,' he called, with a raised hand, already walking away.

December 2008

The sound of the front door opening startled me.

'Ezra?'

I looked up expectantly at the living room door. But it was Torin, not Ezra.

'Hope I'm not disturbing you? I'm on my way back to Scotland. I've been staying down at the house with Noah, so I thought I'd come and see you before I head back north.'

I hadn't seen or heard from Torin since September when he'd left so abruptly. Again. And like he always did, he'd just turned up, bad penny style.

He was all smiles and a jolly demeanour, but I could tell he already knew. Torin walked over toward me, he frowned when he clocked the vodka bottle in my hand.

'Are you alright Gracie?'

'Not really.'

'What's going on?' Torin perched on the sofa next to me, his elbow resting on his knees and his hands clasped. He smelt of the cold outside as though he'd brought the winter night inside with him.

'Like you don't know,' I scoffed.

'Just tell me, huh?'

'Ezra shagged a girl from his office at the Christmas party. He's left me. I haven't seen him for over a week. He said he needed some time to think. But I'm sure you already knew that.' Tears formed in my eyes as I spoke the words.

'Aye, I did.' His breath clouded in the air as he spoke.

I hadn't yet had the boiler fixed and house had been freezing all week. The living room was dressed up ready for Christmas with a large dark needled tree Ezra and I had bought together, before he'd felt the need to put his dick into another woman. The mantel piece was draped with silver tinsel and white fairy lights twinkled as though they were stars in the night sky. The room should have been cosy and happy with festive expectation, but instead it felt cold and desolate.

I took a swig from the bottle of vodka.

'Are you sure that's a good plan?' Torin asked.

'I don't want to think about it anymore. This will help.'

'Well, it might for a few hours.'

'You can join me if you like?' I said, offering him the bottle.

He drank, grimaced and passed the bottle back. I took another swig and shuddered.

We sat in silence. The odd car passed the house outside with a gentle shush and the wind shook the window pane. The subtle sounds of Bristol beyond my window made sure it was never silent in the house. I drank again.

Torin got up and knelt in front of the hearth. He was wearing a thick overcoat and tan leather boots; he looked smarter than usual.

'Have you spoken to Ezra?' I asked.

I suspected Ezra was staying with Noah at Redferne House although I did not know for sure.

Torin nodded, his attention still on the fire he was nursing to life. 'Aye, I've been with him all week.'

'How is he?'

Torin looked at me. 'Messy.'

'Good.' I drank again.

'Slow down, hey?' Torin came over and took the bottle out of my hands and placed it on the table. He sat back beside me. 'Talk to me?'

'What should I say?'

'Just tell me everything Gracie.'

I couldn't tell Torin everything. I couldn't tell him that since he'd moved out three months ago, the cracks in my relationship with Ezra had become gaping holes. I couldn't tell Torin that I'd felt his departure so acutely it was as though someone had died.

Shifting my body to face him and tucking my feet up on the sofa, I said, 'She's not even pretty Torin. He said he didn't even like her. Did he tell you that? Why would he shag a girl he doesn't even like?'

'I don't know.'

'He said he was drunk, and it just happened. But you don't just accidently stick your dick into someone you don't even like just because you're drunk. Do you?'

'You know things can happen when you're pissed. You know that as well as I do.'

'Are you making excuses for him?'

'No. All I'm saying is that you take what he says as what he means.'

'It's my fault,' I said, knowing I had to start being honest.

'It's not your fault Gracie.'

We looked at each other for a moment but Torin was wrong, it was my fault. I'd been turning away from Ezra's advances for months now.

I sighed. 'What if he doesn't want to be with me anymore?'

'I'm sure he does,' Torin said. 'This is a blip. A minor hiccup. These things happen in relationships sometimes. In time you'll both have forgotten that Ezra was an idiot and you'll be all happy every after again.'

'A hiccup? He had sex with someone else,' I said, with a bubble of anger rising in my blood.

'Aye but it's not like he loves her. You'll get over it.'

'Fuck you Torin and fuck him too.' I let rip with the full scorned woman rant. My voice rose, the obscenities came thick and fast and Torin took my words as though he was the one that deserved them.

'Angry Gracie is kind of scary,' Torin said, once I'd run out of steam.

'I don't really hate him.'

'I know,' Torin said.

He put his arm around my shoulders and said soft words of comfort into my hair as I leant my head against him. It felt nice to held by Torin.

I missed being held. I missed Ezra. I kept wanting Ezra to hold me and tell me it was all going to be okay but he was the one that had made it all such a mess.

I inhaled. Torin smelt nice. I curled into him as close as I could. And he held me firm against him with his arms tight around me.

'I know he regrets it,' Torin said, after we'd been sat in each other's arms for a beautifully long time. He tucked my hair behind my ear and stroked my shoulder. 'I don't think he's himself at the moment. He's super stressed about work and well …' he let the idea of something more linger in the air.

'What?' I asked, sitting back, Torin's hand fell against my thigh. My knee was resting against his leg.

'Did I screw things up between you?' Torin asked.

'What do you mean?'

'Things between us …' He didn't need to finish the sentence; we both knew what he was referring to.

'Is that why you suddenly left? Did you think I'd fallen in love with you?' I mocked.

'We weren't behaving as we should have been Gracie.'

'We didn't do anything.'

'That's why I left, so we wouldn't do anything. Because we would have. Sooner or later. You know that.' He paused. 'He seems to think that maybe you're seeing someone?' Torin ventured.

'I'm not. You know I'm not.'

'Perhaps there's someone on your mind?'

'And who might that be Torin?'

I noticed the bracelet on Torin's left wrist; black leather with tiny silver beads. I ran my fingers over it. Torin sighed. I felt the hairs on my arm stand on end and raised my eyes to Torin's. The way he was looking at me was not platonic. I felt the heat rise between my legs without hesitation.

The look we shared said everything.

And then we were kissing.

I leant against him and ran my hand over his beard, over his neck and pushed my fingers into his hair. He was holding me against him, his hands spanning my back. Torin pushed me back on the sofa and fell between my legs. His breathing changed as he reached his hand under my top. He slid it across my stomach and up to my breast. I couldn't think of anything except how amazing his fingers felt on my skin. I moved my hips and rubbed against his groin. We kissed and moved together, holding each other tight.

Torin pulled away but stayed kneeling between my legs. 'For Christ's sake. This was not part of the plan Gracie.'

'No? This isn't why you came here?' I asked, sitting up to face him.

'No,' he said, and ran a hand over his hair.

'Did Ezra send you?'

Torin shook his head as he adjusted himself in his trousers.

'Does he know you're here?'

'No.'

'Then why did you come?'

'I wanted to see if you were alright.'

'I'm not alright. This is not alright.' I untangled myself from him, picked up the vodka bottle from the table and took one swig after another.

'Steady on.'

'Fuck you.' I said and drank more.

We'd spent the entire year he'd lived with Ezra and me acting as though we were just good friends. But it was a pretence we'd both played along with. And now, at the first opportunity we were kissing and dry humping like teenagers.

'Seriously, slow down, you'll only make yourself ill.' He took the bottle out of my hand.

'I don't care,' I said, and snatched the bottle back.

'Gracie,' he started.

'Don't Torin. I can't believe you've come here and we've…' I gave a small cry of frustration at my stupidity. 'What I am going to do?'

'I don't know.'

I gave another cry and stood up, trying to distance myself from him further. My head span from alcohol. I was wasted. I blinked and tried to stop the room from spinning.

'Of course you don't know, because it's not your problem. You can just leave, like you always do and I'll clear up the mess you've left behind,' I said, feeling belligerent with alcohol.

He got to his feet and stood before me. 'I don't have to go…' he said, but I heard the uncertainty in his voice.

'What, you're going to stay? And then what? We finish what we just started? What about Ezra?' I spat the words at him because I already knew he would leave.

He looked at me. 'What do you want Gracie?' He spoke with such tenderness.

I shook my head. 'You need to go.'

'But…'

'Just go Torin,' I said and sat back down on the sofa with my back to him.

'If that's what you want,' he said, and left the room on quiet feet.

A moment later I heard the front door close.

I picked up the vodka bottle and downed the rest in one go.

I felt him holding my arms, shaking me. Heard him saying my name. Saw him when I opened my eyes.

'Grace?' Ezra said. 'Can you hear me? What have you taken? Tell me?'

I blinked a few times.

Ezra had the phone against his ear and was asking for an ambulance.

'Whoa,' I said, sitting up as fast as I could and grabbed the phone from his hand and cut it off. 'I don't need an ambulance.'

He looked terrible. Pale and drawn.

My head throbbed and my mouth felt as though it was lined with old carpet. I rubbed my face with my hands and realised there was vomit by my feet. I made a noise of revulsion as I guessed it was the contents of my stomach.

'Seriously Grace, if you've taken something I should take you to hospital even if you feel alright.'

'It was only vodka.' I told him trying to convey with my voice how much of an idiot I thought he was.

'I thought…' he sighed.

'No.' I got to my feet, stumbled from the room and went upstairs to shower. I looked as bad if not worse than Ezra did. Beneath the steaming water I scrubbed my skin in the shower but I couldn't erase the memory of Torin kissing me, of how it had felt with his hands on me. Half of me wanted to relive every moment of Torin's caresses and the other half of me wanted to forget he'd ever existed.

When I came back downstairs, the living room window was open, making the room freezing cold and the Christmas decorations sway. Ezra had cleared the room of vomit and the rest of the detritus from the night before. He sat on the edge of the sofa holding a cup of coffee between both of his hands. Another steaming mug sat on the coffee table and beside it was a glass of water and a packet of paracetamol.

'How are you feeling?' Ezra asked, watching me cross to the coffee table to collect his thoughtful gifts.

'Great,' I said and threw him a plastic smile.

I sat in the armchair as far away from Ezra as I could be while still being in the same room. I balanced my full mug on the arm of the chair, knowing it would irritate Ezra. Then I made a cigarette.

'You know you really shouldn't drink so much,' Ezra began.

'And you really shouldn't have shagged someone else,' I snapped.

He blinked his eyes and took a deep breath. 'You scared me Grace.'

'Why are you here?' I asked.

'This is our home,' he said.

'You left.'

'Because I thought we both needed a bit of space.'

'And now what?'

He swallowed. 'And now I'd like to come home. I'd like to stay here. With you.'

I hadn't been sure he'd come back and now he had I wasn't sure if it was the outcome I wanted.

'But…' I started and stopped with a sigh.

'What is it Grace?'

I shook my head.

'Can I stay?' he asked.

I inhaled.

Exhaled.

'Can we work this out?' he asked. I heard the fear in his voice.

'I don't know.' It wasn't the answer he wanted, I knew that. But it was honest.

He nodded. 'I am so sorry Grace. If I could turn back time…'

'Don't. You sound like an eighties power ballad.'

He gave a small smile.

I returned it as best I could.

'I love you Grace.'

I didn't hesitate when I replied because despite everything it was true; I did love Ezra. But I'd begun to realise that perhaps it wasn't enough just to love him.

November 2014

'It's been like spring today, not autumn,' Ada said, leaning on her walking stick and looking out of her kitchen window, over the meadow. 'All these showers and then bright sunshine.'

'Have you seen the rainbows?' I said, as I put a couple of plates away in the cupboard.

'Oh yes, so pretty aren't they?'

As I put away the rest of the washing-up we talked a little more about the weather. I heated up a tin of Campbell's condensed mushroom soup for Ada's lunch as we discussed domestic arrangements; things she needed done and things she wanted. She was getting better, but she still wasn't able to do much for herself. And it seemed more than just the physical impairments, she seemed to have lost confidence in herself and deferred all questions about her domestic arrangements to me. Jerome, of his own accord, still came every day and did whatever Ada asked him to and I did her shopping and cleaning but I was aware of the fragility of the situation. I wasn't sure how long Jerome would continue to come to Ada's. I doubted my own reliability too. And yet for now the three of us muddled along.

'You're off in a minute then dear?' Ada asked.

'Yes, when Josie gets here.'

The office was closed today while we were having a software update, so we were in sync with head office. I'd suggested to Josie that we could go shopping this afternoon, if she could find someone to have the boys. Grudgingly Noah had agreed to work from home.

'I thought you might like this, to go with your new dress,' Ada said and placed a royal blue velvet box into my hand. 'My mother gave it to me but I never had a daughter to pass it on to but I can give it to you. A thank you Grace, for everything you do for me.'

Inside, nestled against the creamy satin interior was a pendant of swirled gold holding a red stone. It was old-fashioned and not something I would have chosen but the sentiment was perfect. It was the sort of gesture I'd always secretly desired from my mother but had never been the recipient of. I thanked Ada with tears in my eyes. Ada gripped my hand and returned my watery smile.

Josie, Jerome and Eliza came to the door together and I think Ada was happy to let our moment pass without fuss. From Ada's reaction, I gathered it was not the first time Jerome and Eliza had come together. Ada was already directing my niece to the sideboard to get the playing cards.

'Well looks like we're no longer needed,' Josie said. 'Shall we?'

There was pretty autumn sunshine over the meadow, fine enchanting rain fell on the lane itself and just visible through the canopy of leaves a handsome rainbow. It was a lovely day. I only wished I could feel as enthusiastic about the shopping trip as I did about the weather. All morning I'd been filled with anxiety at the prospect of this outing with Josie. Had I not swallowed a little white pill I may well have struggled to even go through with the excursion.

As soon as we were on the lane Josie apologised for the previous day and I reassured her she did not need to but she said sorry once more before she changed the direction of the conversation. She chattered as we walked to the only decent clothes shop in town. I wished I could be more like her, so easy and bubbly and garrulous.

As we stepped inside the small outlet, the bell above the door clanged, announcing our entrance. I could smell the thick hessian flooring and it moved slightly under foot, like I was treading on something living.

'Good afternoon,' the shop lady said, in a warm singing tone. She had a 1950's thing going on; a full red skirt, pretty white blouse and a kerchief tied in her dark brown hair. She was one of those women that suited make-up too. I admired her thick eyeliner and cherry red lipstick.

'We're just looking for a nice dress for Grace, for a party. Do you mind if we have a little look around?' Josie said.

'Of course not, go ahead and just give me a shout if you need anything.'

I forced myself to look at the rail beside me and moved each coat hanger to view the clothes. It was the kind of shop where they stocked various labels and there was only one of each item on display. The clothes seemed to be arranged in some random order I couldn't fathom, dresses next to knitwear, next to trousers, beside a coat.

I went from the first rail, to the next, my despondency increasing. I didn't want to buy a dress and I didn't want to go to the party either.

'Seen anything?' Josie came toward me with an excited smile.

I shrugged.

Josie gave me an assessing look. 'You want something sexy,' she said, and kept moving her hands up and down her body, not actually touching herself but close enough. She gave another sigh and a little shimmy of her shoulders. 'But not slutty, you know? Something simple but stylish.'

She picked up the first thing beside her and held it up against me, tucking the coat hanger under my chin. 'What about this?'

It was a blue and white striped dress that had a nautical feel to it. It wasn't a bad dress, but it wasn't my sort of thing.

The shop lady was on her feet, coming out from behind the counter, as if she'd caught the scent of prey.

'You would definitely need that in a smaller size, you are so delightfully tiny,' the lady said. As she moved I could hear the swoosh of her skirt.

'Yes, it should fit here,' Josie placed her hand over her breast, 'and here,' then moved it to her hip.

'I was thinking of something less patterned,' I said, feeling like my voice had lost all volume.

The shop lady gasped and went over to another rail. 'What about this?' She held up a simple navy blue dress.

'It's nice.' I admitted.

'Then you must try it on,' Josie said. 'Come on.'

She goaded me into the curtained changing rooms. I stood staring at myself in the mirror. Torin was right, I did look like shite. I hated my hair short, and I looked pale and ill as though I never saw the light of day. And I was skinny and not in a good way, I looked like a starved prisoner. I definitely shouldn't wear stripes.

'Darling, how are you getting on?' Josie called over the curtain. 'I bet you look divine.'

I couldn't help smiling at my reflection. How nice it must be to feel divine. Perhaps it wouldn't hurt to just try the dress on, maybe then I might feel divine. I probably wouldn't look any worse than I did already.

As I struggled out of my coat and hung it up on a hook, I heard Josie and the shop woman talking about Josie's pregnancy. I considered trying the dress on over my jeans and top but I could already hear Josie telling me off for not doing it properly. Feeling cold and sweaty at the same time I peeled off my clothes. With a sigh of resolution, I put the dress on.

'Is the size alright?' the shop lady asked.

I hesitated, looking at myself in the mirror again. 'Yeah, I think so.'

The dress looked nice. Maybe not divine, but it turned me from skinny retch into a female of shape. Somehow I was feminine all of a sudden. I gave a little swish of the skirt and with it came a smile. The colour reminded me of a Wispa wrapper. Maybe I could still be a sweet treat for someone to unwrap, full of holes but a pleasant experience still.

'Darling, you are transformed,' Josie gasped, with her hands to her chest, when I came out of the changing room.

'You do look wonderful,' the shop lady said. She gave a little noise of excitement. 'These would look lovely with that dress.' She scooped up a pair of grey patent ballet flats and held them toward me, 'and what about this little red belt?' She turned to Josie, 'what do you think?'

The shop lady was good at her job. The shoes, the dress and the belt did look nice together. They looked nice on me. And I liked that they made me feel like someone else. I wasn't Grace Redferne in these clothes, I was, well, I don't know who I was, but I didn't feel like me for the first time in an age. And it was nice.

With my new dress, belt and shoes in a stiff cardboard bag, Josie then guided me into Boots.

'You need tights darling.'

She escorted me to the right aisle and picked up a couple of pairs, 'What about these?'

I wanted to tell her she wasn't my mother; I could buy tights myself.

So I picked up a pair of thin black tights that had a swirly pattern in the weave.

'Lovely,' Josie said, looking proud. 'Now, let's think personal grooming. Do you need to stock up on anything while we're here? There's nothing worse than hairs poking through your tights.'

She may as well have just told me I'd turned into a hairy beast with muff hair bursting from the bottom of my trouser leg. I had been less than regular about depilation but she didn't need to point it out.

I muttered something about razors and wandered off to what I thought might be the appropriate aisle.

I didn't bother saying anything when Josie slipped some mascara and moisturiser into the basket.

'Ooh look, Grace,' Josie said, on the way to the till and pointed at a range of hair accessories. 'This is just the same colour as your dress.' A little hairclip with a flower. 'It'll look so sweet just slipped in the side of your hair.' She placed it against my head.

When we'd exited the shop Josie paused, 'You know what?'

'No,' I said, wondering what she wanted to do to me now.

'We should go for a drink.'

'But…' I looked at her rounded stomach.

'Sometimes I think all of these rules when you're pregnant are so extreme, I mean one little glass of something nice isn't going hurt the baby.' She said, patting her abdomen, 'Besides he's almost cooked.'

We went into a cavernous cafe bar in the centre of town I'd never entered before. It was a modern place with an eclectic mix of faux paintings hung on chintzy wallpaper, not a matching table in sight and nineties rave tunes played in the background.

'I thought you might be all funny you know, about shopping,' Josie ventured when we'd almost finished our glasses of wine.

'I'm not much of a shopper.'

She gave me a sympathetic smile, 'It means a lot to me and Noah that you're coming to the party.'

I smiled back and finished my wine.

'Do you want another?' Josie asked, surprising me.

'Uh, yeah, if you like.'

She surprised me even more when she returned with a whole bottle.

'I'll just have a drop more,' she said and refilled my glass and then her own.

I'm sure it wasn't just the wine, but it was nice sitting in the warm bar with Josie. She was smiley and chatty and she laughed a lot. We talked about TV box sets and films. She liked to read and told me about books she'd read. We talked about Ada and a little about Eliza too.

Then suddenly she said, 'Sometimes I think Noah is having an affair.'

'What?' I was so surprised I couldn't think what else to say.

'I was pretty sure he was once before when I was pregnant with Godfrey but looking back I think I was probably just insecure, looking like a whale as I did.' She sounded ponderous as though she was just testing out the idea. 'But I found a receipt in his jacket from when he was away on business last month.' She laughed. 'I'm sure it was nothing, really. I mean it was just a receipt for dinner. They'd had Champagne. And when I gave it to him, he thanked me and told me he'd been looking for it, so he could claim expenses. He said it had just been dinner with a colleague. I'm being silly I know. Hormonal.'

I still didn't know what to say, and she moved on, launching into stories of her youth, long before children and Noah; tales of wild behaviour in foreign places. It was a side to Josie I had never known existed. I liked her all the more for it.

I should have been more aware; I should have stopped her. I should have made us leave, but I was rather enjoying myself, getting drunk, with a pretty new dress in a bag at my feet. I didn't notice how much she'd had to drink, assuming that I had consumed most of the bottle myself, but as we made to leave I realised that Josie was really drunk.

I walked her back up Redferne Lane to the house. She laughed and giggled and slurred her words the whole way back. Then as soon as she got through the door she threw up across the kitchen floor, at Noah's feet.

'My God you're drunk,' Noah roared at Josie while she retched. He rounded on me, 'What the fuck were you thinking, letting her get drunk?'

'I'm sorry, I didn't realise …' I stuttered.

'She's pregnant for God's sake.'

I apologised again.

'I think you'd better go.' Noah said, taking his wife by the arm and walking her across the kitchen.

I left feeling terrible, berating myself.

When I got home I threw the bag across the room hoping I could ruin the dress with the action. I swallowed two little pills with a swig of wine and took the rest of bottle to the sitting room, swigging it back between sobs.

⚜ ⚜ ⚜

'Once you have completed tutorials one to four there is a short questionnaire,' Simon announced across the office. 'Then the only thing left to do is have a drink at the bar on me.' He spoke the last words with a note of triumph knowing his words would make him popular.

Within minutes three of my colleagues pulled their coats on and gathered their things. I continued to trawl my way through to the end of tutorial three but the new software confused me and I was struggling to understand how to use it. I'd been late into work this morning, groggy and hungover after staying up stupidly late, drinking myself to oblivion to forget the Josie incident. So I missed the initial talk about the new software and started the tutorials long after everyone else had. I worked through when everyone else went next door to the bar for a boozy lunch but I was still behind. And I just didn't understand it.

Two more people left, wearing the excitement of Friday night. The lights at the far end of the office were turned off.

'How are you getting on Grace?' Simon asked, leaning on my desk with one hand splayed against the faux wood.

'Fine,' I said, on automatic.

'Almost done?'

I looked up at him. 'I'm just about to start tutorial four.'

He gave me a kind smile, 'It's a funny beast, this new software, tricky to get your head around, isn't it?'

I nodded.

'But once you do, it's great to use and you'll get the hang of it in no time.'

I sighed as I watched the last of my colleagues pull her coat on. She gave Simon and me a smile and said she'd see us in the bar next door.

'Come on, let's nail this,' Simon said, and pulled over the chair from the desk next to mine. He sat beside me and talked me through the final tutorial.

I could see the tendons in his hand flex as he clicked the mouse. He had long thin fingers with wide flat, neatly clipped nails. I already knew he didn't wear a wedding ring. The whole office knew he'd been single for well over a year. When his girlfriend had dumped him, he'd told us all at a meeting and apologised if he was in any way unreasonable in the coming weeks. He hadn't been. I'd never seen Simon be unreasonable.

The more Simon talked about the software, the less I understood, it was as though the more he explained the more complicated it seemed. My brain felt woolly and impenetrable. And Simon smelt nice.

I'd never noticed the way he smelt before, he wasn't one for flowery aftershave and nor did he ever have a stench of sweat some men always seem to carry. Right then there was something appealing about him. I wanted to lean a little closer and inhale rather than just catch traces of his scent. It wasn't helping me to concentrate on getting to grips with the new software.

We reached the end of the tutorial and Simon pulled up the questionnaire. He clicked in some boxes in a matter of seconds without even reading it out. He closed the programmes, shut down the computer and turned with a smile.

'All done Grace.'

'Thank you Simon,' I said, genuinely touched that he'd stayed to help me.

'Any time,' he said, looking pleased with himself. 'Now get your coat and come for a drink.' I was about to protest but he shook his head, 'No excuses this time, just one drink Grace?'

I couldn't refuse.

The bar was full of office types. Everyone seemed to be shouting, competing with the volume of house music that pumped through the speakers. Simon steered me to a group of leather sofas gathered around a low glass table where our colleagues sat. I could feel his hand placed on my lower back. And I was surprised to find I liked the connection.

Simon offered to get everyone a drink. He took orders and then turned to me, 'So, Grace, what can I get you?'

I floundered, somewhat overwhelmed by the noise and social situation.

'The cocktails are good. They do a lovely margarita?' he suggested.

'That sounds perfect, thank you.'

'Back in a sec.'

I sat on the empty sofa at the end of table. The others carried on their conversations, ignoring me. I wasn't offended. Over the past couple of years, they had all made an effort to get to know me, they'd all been nice but I'd never given an ounce of myself back. It wasn't because I didn't like them but it had been so difficult just keeping myself together after Ezra died. I didn't, perhaps couldn't, give anything of myself to anyone and now I was the outsider, the odd one and there seemed no way to remedy that. But I wasn't sure I even minded.

No one would notice if I got up and left. My whole life felt a little bit like that. I glanced over at Simon as he stood at the bar. He looked over and smiled. He'd unbuttoned his waistcoat and a few strands of hair had fallen over his eyes. He gave me a wave and brushed the hair from his face. Simon would notice if I left.

He came back from the bar with a tray of drinks and after distributing them he sat beside me.

'Cheers,' he said holding his cocktail glass up.

I clinked mine against his and sipped once then twice.

'Nice, huh?' he asked.

I nodded.

Simon told me about the climbing trip in Mexico he was planning. He was a keen climber and had scaled all sorts of faces, all over the world. It amazed me that I didn't know this about him. But really, I knew nothing about him. As he talked, I drank, relishing the hit of alcohol.

Simon offered to get me another drink, and I accepted. There was something different about Simon, outside of the office. I'd misjudged him all this time. Somehow the hue of his eyes seemed less insipid and now held something that intrigued me. The tone of his voice didn't seem quite so placid, here he was lively and interesting. Attractive.

'A different one for you this time, Grace,' Simon said, placing a pale pink cocktail with a twizzle of lime rind on the rim, in front of me. 'I think you'll like it.'

By the time Simon placed a third cocktail in front of me, most of our colleagues had left to go home, leaving only a guy that worked at the far end of the office from me and a girl that had just started with the company, whose name I had yet to find out. They looked as though they might leave together and Simon was shaking his head as he told me that office romances never worked out well.

Simon was going to visit his sister this weekend, he told me. She'd just had a baby and Simon was going to see his niece for the first time. I thought of Josie and inwardly cringed. Then Simon asked if I'd like another drink and I pushed Josie to the back of my mind.

We had another one or was it two more cocktails? Simon came back with shots of tequila too.

And then I felt a bit sick.

Simon disappeared and I couldn't remember where he'd gone. But I knew I needed to go outside. It was too noisy. Too busy. I really did feel sick.

I pushed my way past people to reach the door. Outside, I took deep breaths of the cold damp air. Seeking solitude and quiet I went down a thin alley beside the bar. Pressing my back against the wall I looked up. Above me, fine rain was illuminated in an orange halo around the street light. I took another deep breath; the nausea passed. I could hear the faint thud of music from inside the bar.

'There you are,' Simon said, coming toward me, one hand in his trouser pocket. 'What are you doing out here?'

'I wanted some air,' I mumbled.

'They have an area out the back you know,' he said, with a laugh. 'You didn't need to come and skulk in the alleyway.'

'Right,' I said, feeling another wave of nausea sweep over me.

'And probably not the best place to be alone at this time of night,' Simon said, standing too close to me.

'No, probably not.'

He looked at me with slightly bloodshot eyes and I knew he was about to make a move on me.

'Were you hoping I'd come and find you?' he asked, with a slight smile.

I made a noise as another wave of nausea trickled up my back, but Simon took it as sign of encouragement and smiled deeper.

'I mean there's always so many people around in the office…' he titled his head a little. 'You must have worked out that I like you…'

I sighed, quashing another wave of nausea.

He leant forward, hesitant, but I let him kiss me. I could do this. He lifted his face a moment and smiled before he swept in for a full open mouth snog. His lips were warm and the scent of him was still mildly appealing. His tongue and his arms were attempting to claim me. I didn't stop him. It was such a novelty to be desired. I liked it and I almost liked him.

He kissed down my neck and his hand slid up to my breast. I could feel his breath against my neck as his hand began to wander south, over my hip. He lifted my knee, pressing himself between my legs. He gave a little groan of desire and squeezed my breast.

I could tell him take me home. I could let him fuck me. I might even enjoy it; most likely he'd be eager to please.

'You've got such an amazing body Grace,' Simon said, as he moved his hips against me.

Another wave of nausea swept over me and this time the contents of my stomach decided it was time to leave. I just about managed to push Simon aside before I threw up on the pavement beside his smart shoes.

After his initial and understandable recoil, Simon was sweet and offered words of sympathy. Once I straightened up he went inside and got me a glass of water. I sat on some concrete steps a few metres away and waited for him to come back. And then he sat with me.

'I'm so sorry,' I said.

'It's fine,' he said, but I'd never heard him sound so despondent.

We watched a gang of young women leave the bar in a cloud of perfume and raucous giggles.

'How are you feeling?' Simon asked.

'A lot better, thanks.'

'Too much to drink? You're probably not used to drinking so much?'

I gave a small laugh at his misguided assumption.

'I'm sorry, I shouldn't have got you so drunk.'

'It's fine Simon.'

'I've ruined it.'

'No, I've had a nice evening.'

I heard him take a deep breath. I could sense he was looking at me. 'Would you like to come back to mine?'

'I don't think that's a good idea,' I said.

'Of course.' He nodded. 'Maybe when you're feeling better, we could go out?'

And all of a sudden it became very clear to me. 'I'm sorry Simon but I can't.'

He nodded. 'Is it still too soon? Since your husband?'

I could have quite liked Simon if I'd have given him a chance. But I told him he was right, it was too soon since Ezra had died. I lied and told Simon I wasn't ready to be with someone else.

There was a crackle as I pressed the plastic and the comforting metallic rustle as the foil split, birthing another little white pill onto the coffee table. I pushed the pill with my fingertip so it joined its comrade. I picked one up and placed it on my tongue. Filling my mouth with white wine I swallowed one, then the other, before going upstairs to get ready for the party.

I showered and shaved and plucked and pretended that I was excited to put on my new dress. I clipped the flower into my hair and stroked mascara onto my eyelashes as though it was something I did every Saturday night. By the time I placed the necklace Ada had given me around my neck I'd convinced myself that I would have lovely time at the party.

I was ready to go but I couldn't quite muster the ability to leave the house.

I opened another bottle of wine. Another little white pill sat in the palm of my hand, then slipped down my throat. For the first time that day I could let my thoughts dwell on the look on Noah's face when I'd brought Josie home drunk, without a punishing anxiety crushing the breath from my chest. I could ponder last night when I'd been close to letting Simon take me home, without hating myself. Finally, with my senses suitably numbed, I could face the thought of leaving the house, of walking up the lane and seeing Josie and Noah. And Torin.

I closed my eyes and let my thoughts drift and I wasn't surprised where they ended up.

The smell of outside mingled with something male. I turned my head and opened my eyes. Torin sat beside me on the sofa, as though summoned by my thoughts. His head was leant back, facing me, so he was looking right into my eyes.

'Hello Torin.' I was so pleased to see him. 'I was just thinking about you.'

'Hello Gracie.'

I sighed and smiled, enjoying his beautiful dark eyes.

'You started the party without me?' he said.

The bottle of wine was still in my hands.

'I think I've been misbehaving.' Even I could hear the slur in my words.

He gave a small laugh. 'What have you taken Gracie?'

'Nothing,' I lied, with a smile.

'Oh aye, nothing and something hey?'

'Leave me alone,' I said, without conviction as I managed to refocus on Torin's face.

'No.' He was smirking at me.

I found my eyes wandering over Torin; he wore a grey shirt, the hairs on his chest and his tattoo were visible between the undone buttons at his neck.

He looked really good.

'Alright Gracie?' I could hear the amusement in his voice.

I looked back at his face.

He held my eyes and his smile faded. He licked his lips.

Trying to catch my breath I turned away, rubbing my face as if I could wipe away the longing. I sat forward and took a swig of the lukewarm wine, then flopped back against the sofa cushions as the room moved in streaks of merged lights. I took another swig and braced myself for the head spin but it didn't come. In fact, as I sat up straighter I felt a touch more coherent and took another swig.

'Are you going to stop drinking that?' Torin asked.

I shook my head.

'Thought as much,' he said. He reached toward me and took the bottle from my hands.

I went to take the bottle back, but he grabbed my wrist with his other hand.

'What's all this in aid of?' Torin asked, lifting his knee onto the sofa and twisting his body to face me.

I was going to shrug and be quarrelsome but he shook his head at me. I felt his thumb on the thin skin of my inner wrist. His knee rested against my thigh.

'I don't know Torin,' I said.

His lips were dark pink and shiny from the lick of his tongue. His shirt sleeves were rolled up and my eyes were drawn to the tattoos all the way up his left arm. With my middle finger I touched the swirl of ink that reached down to the back of his hand. I traced the shaped up his forearm until it merged with the rest of the design.

'Beautiful,' I murmured, running my thumb back down another line of the tattoo that curled round to the inner side of his arm.

I heard Torin breathe, a little shallow but controlled.

My fingers moved down an inch or two, from his arm to his leg. I felt the solid muscle under my hand. I moved my palm up Torin's thigh.

'Don't.' Torin said, placing his hand on top of mine. I looked up, into his eyes and moved my hand further up his thigh. He did not let my hand quite reach his cock but close enough; I knew he was hard. He held my wrist in his hand, stopping my bad behaviour.

We sat staring at each other. I willed him to do whatever he wanted.

'Stop it Gracie. Don't look at me like that,' he said, then all but pushed me away so I fell back against the sofa.

He stood up with his back to me but I could tell he was adjusting himself in his trousers.

'You know where the door is,' I said. Before he could be the one walking out, I was throwing him out.

He turned to me, frowning. 'You don't have to be like that.'

I pulled my knees to my chest. 'You should go.'

'It's not as simple as just grabbing my cock. We can talk about this but now is not the time.'

'Please leave.'

'No.' He said, with a snarl. 'Not without you. We have a party to go to.'

'I'm not going.'

Torin gave a noisy exhale. 'Yes you are.'

'I don't want to go.'

'Fine, but you will.'

'Why do you even want to go?'

'It'll be fun?'

I shook my head and reached for the bottle on the table, I really didn't want to go to a party.

'Oh no, no more.' Torin moved the wine bottle out of my reach. 'These your shoes?' Torin said, kneeling on the floor in front of me.

I nodded.

He paused and looked at my face. He licked his thumb and wiped it under my left eye. 'You're smudged,' he said, as he wiped his finger along where his thumb had touched, to dry my skin.

The world seemed a soft and inviting place right then, with Torin right at the centre of it.

'Christ, you always were fucking trouble,' Torin muttered as he picked up a grey shoe in his hand, and held it toward me like I was Cinderella. Only I didn't want to go to the ball.

He lifted my foot and held it for a moment with his forefinger under my heel, then slipped it into the shoe. He took my left foot and slid the other shoe on, the back of it making a shushing sound as the leather moved against nylon. He smoothed my instep with his palm. For a second all I could feel was the warmth of Torin's hand on my foot. For that instant everything was perfect. Nothing else mattered. There was nothing else to feel. I wanted his hand to move up. I wanted to part my knees.

'Stop that,' he said, and placed my foot back on the floor.

'What?'

'All your feminine sighing.'

'I wasn't.'

'Whatever you say,' Torin said, standing. The spell was broken. He offered me a hand. 'Come on then and if you're a good girl I might even let you have another drink.'

'I'm not going.'

'Don't be a twat.'

'Did you just call me a twat?' I asked.

'Aye.'

A bubble of laughter burst from my lips. No one had ever called me a twat before.

'Fuck you, Torin.' I stood up, smoothed down the new dress and pretended my head wasn't feeling fuzzy.

He laughed back. 'That's my girl.' His eyes wandered down the length of me and slowly back up. 'Nice dress.'

I thought about thanking him for the compliment.

'Shame about your face.'

'What?'

'I don't know what you've taken but it ain't doing much for your complexion.'

Ignoring him, I grabbed a hoody that lay on the end of the sofa, and stuffed my arms into it, pulled the hood up and zipped it up to my chin. I stepped out of my shoes and padded out to the hallway and put my trainers on instead.

'Let's get this over with,' I muttered and opened the door.

I walked a meter in front of Torin all the way up Redferne Lane. My breath formed clouds in the cold air but I couldn't feel the chill. I paused as Sam came towards us. She was groomed to perfection, dressed in a slinky black dress that left nothing to the imagination. For a moment I thought she was crying, but she passed us throwing me a tight smile.

The sound of her high heels on the lane receded as Torin and I continued up to Redferne House. Torin opened the garden gate and held it to let me through.

'Eliza,' I said, as I saw her and Jerome sitting on the stone bench beside a bed of lavender. 'Happy Birthday.' I hugged her, smelt her sweet perfume and felt her soft hair under my palm.

'Put her down Gracie,' Torin said, pulling my arm.

'I'm just wishing my niece happy birthday.' I smiled at Eliza.

Eliza stepped back and gave me a broad smile. Jerome was chuckling.

'Great, now leave her alone and come inside,' Torin said, guiding me towards the front door.

'Have fun,' I called to Jerome and Eliza.

As soon as we went through the door I pushed away from Torin to greet Josie.

'Grace, so good to see you,' Josie said. 'The dress looks wonderful. You look wonderful.' She spoke with a smile and leant forward to kiss my cheek. Her lips brushed my skin and I felt the press of her rounded stomach against the flat contour of my own. She wore big gold dangly earrings that mingled with her butter blonde hair. She smelt of pretty perfume.

'Can I apologise for my behaviour the other night, it's not something I make a habit of?' Josie said, her face suddenly serious.

I gave her a kind smile. 'Forget it.'

'I want you to know that I don't hold you responsible in any way. It was all my own doing. I really am sorry.'

'No problem.'

'You must think I'm the most awful person in the world?'

'No.' I felt pretty entitled to that title myself. 'You're an amazing woman and a fabulous mother. And you look so pretty.'

She smiled at me.

I looked down her body; her bump looked even bigger. The black jersey fabric of her dress was stretched tight over her swollen belly. I put my hands on her. The tightness was surprising. I struggled to believe there was a baby inside her just an inch away from my hands.

Josie placed her hand on mine and the baby gave a kick.

'He's looking forward to meeting you. His auntie Grace.'

We both smiled, and it was enough that we both understood that everything was well between us; it was perhaps the best it had ever been.

'You've come with Torin?'

I knew she implied something with her smile and the way her eyes lit up.

I looked around the room. The house felt busy and alive with a rumble of chatter, laughter and music, crowded with people. I felt odd. For a moment I thought I might throw up, but it passed.

'I'm sure I saw him heading to the kitchen,' Josie said.

She squeezed my hand and moved away as I stood uncertain as to whether I wanted find Torin or not.

My head span and my vision blurred momentarily.

'Grace, lovely to see you,' Noah said, suddenly before me.

He sounded as though he meant it. Perhaps I was forgiven for getting Josie drunk. He smelt of ale and aftershave when he kissed my cheek, his skin smooth. He held me at arm's length, looked at me and grinned. I could not tell which of us was more drunk.

'Happy Birthday,' I said.

'Huh, yeah, forty-fucking-five, how is that even possible?'

I shrugged.

'And sweet sixteen for Eliza, huh?'

'Sweet?' I laughed.

The room tilted and Noah's face looked odd; his features seemed to blur like I was travelling past him in a fast car. But I could still feel his hands on the tops of my arms holding me in place.

I closed my eyes to stop the room from moving but the sensation continued inside my head, like my brain was turning inside my skull. I felt Noah's hands release me and swayed. My head stopped spinning, and I opened my eyes again.

'Alright Grace?' Noah sounded anxious. 'Shall I get you a drink of water?'

Noah put his hand on my lower back and guided me. We passed Josie. She held a hand on her swollen belly and I saw the stone in her engagement ring catch the light. I felt the engagement ring and wedding band that still adorned my left hand.

'Why don't you have a seat in here and I'll just pop into the kitchen and get you some water?'

He had me sit in the parlour. There was no one else in there. All I had to keep me company was a large upright piano, two burgundy velvet sofas, a huge gilt-edged mirror on the wall and a variety of lamps that gave off soft ambient light. I slumped back on the sofa and gave a loud sigh. Then I saw the art that hung opposite. It was a series of sketches of Bristol; the cathedral, the Arnolfini, Cabot Tower, the university building at the top of Park Street, Temple Meads station and Clifton Suspension Bridge. They were Ezra's. I'd watched him draw every single one of them. I never knew Noah had them. I hadn't even thought about those sketches since I'd followed Ezra round the city in those heady first months after we got together. And yet it felt like looking at pictures of home.

Stumbling to my feet I crossed the room, wanting to devour every stroke of graphite Ezra had laid on those six pieces of paper. I unhooked the frame from the wall, unfolded the clasps on the back and took the picture out. I placed the glass and wood on the piano lid and put my fingers on the lines of the cathedral feeling the slight indentation of the pencil on the paper. Ezra had touched these.

Holding the drawing to my face I inhaled, like I might catch a trace of Ezra.

'Grace?'

I turned and found Noah right behind me, watching, holding a glass of water.

'They're Ezra's,' I said, hugging the paper against me.

'Yes, I always thought they were rather good.'

I didn't want Noah to have those pictures. They should have been mine.

Torin appeared behind Noah.

'Alright?' Torin asked.

'We were just looking at Ezra's pictures,' Noah said.

'Oh aye?'

'He drew them at Uni,' I said, but even to my own ears the words were barely audible. 'Where did you get them?' I spoke louder, so loud it might almost have been a shout.

Noah took a step back from me, frowning. 'He gave them to me.'

He was lying, Ezra wouldn't have done that. Noah had taken them from me.

'Hey Gracie, why don't we get you a drink?' Torin said. He took the picture from me and handed it to Noah.

Noah held on to both the glass of water and the picture.

'But those are Ezra's…'

'Aye, and now they're Noah's,' Torin said, putting his arm around me. And he guided me out of the room through the inner hallway and back into the kitchen.

There were people talking all around us. It was too bright, too warm and too shiny. The windows were steamed up with condensation so I could no longer see the night outside. The kitchen smelt of baked goods and the worktops were laden with platters of pretty food. A huge creamy wheel of brie sat surrounded by grapes; only a thin triangle was missing from the whole.

'You should eat.'

I gave Torin a look.

'As I thought,' he said and manoeuvred me along to the drinks table. Then turned to face me, arms folded, scowling. 'Could you try and act less mental?' He was frowning; his black eyes shining.

'Fuck off.' I spoke quietly but with conviction. I picked up the nearest bottle of wine and poured some into a waiting glass, spilling some on the linen tablecloth; a dark patch formed beneath my glass.

'Can't you drink some water or something?'

'No.'

I lifted my glass and took a big gulp.

Torin gave a low laugh. 'Dear God you're a troublesome woman.' He picked up a bottle of red wine and poured himself a glass, then raised it at me. 'Well here's to you making a twat of yourself.'

I gulped the rest of my wine down, wiped my chin with my hand, picked up the bottle and turned away from Torin. I started for the French doors at such speed that I hit the glass with my forehead when the handle didn't turn as I'd expected. It hurt.

I left my face against the cool glass and my fingers on the handle, like I was a DVD on pause. I let the throb of pain run through me.

'You alright?' He spoke behind me, his breath on my neck. He put his hand on mine and pushed the handle down gently but also pulling just a little toward my abdomen. Ridiculously, the action aroused me. 'There's a knack to it,' he said, as he pushed the door open.

I felt Torin's hand on my wrist as though he was trying to stop me from going any further.

'Leave me alone.' I pulled away.

My body felt clammy as I stumbled into the conservatory. There were a few people playing pool on the swish new pool table in the centre of the room; Noah's birthday present. I heard the clock-pop sound of one ball hitting another and falling into a pocket. Other people sat on the mocha coloured sofas, talking in laughing voices that I couldn't pick out specific words from.

I sat on a chair away from everyone else and looked at the tiled floor through the holes in the wicker work of the empty chair next to me. I felt beads of sweat roll down my back and gather in the wire of my bra; hot and cold at the same time.

Torin sat down next to me.

I was angry with him, but I couldn't remember why. I shook my head as though it would help me remember what he'd done to upset me. Then I wished I hadn't as the room span. Torin's lips moved but the words that came out were stretched into sounds that made no sense. His face contorted, his features melting like wax down a candle. I closed my eyes for a moment hoping to stop his face melting. But with my eyes shut my brain felt like it was bobbing aimlessly in a huge ocean and being driven off course by the occasional large swell.

'Gracie?' Torin's voice was loud and clear like my head had just come out of water, and I opened my eyes. His face was back to how it should be.

I smiled, glad about something. Torin was wearing a nice shirt. I was sure I was angry with him but right then I couldn't think why I ever would be. He was so beautiful. His thick beard and dark black eyes. I loved looking into his eyes.

I was so glad he'd come back.

I'd really missed him.

I lay my head on one side to fully appreciate him.

I sat forward and kissed him.

Just lips on lips.

I put my hand on his neck, my fingers in his hair, and I kissed him, I really kissed him. Rushes flew down my spine as he kissed me back. Long deep kisses that involved every part of us both even though it was barely more than our lips that touched.

Torin suddenly pulled away as if someone had sounded an alarm.

I gasped; my head spinning like a carousel.

'Ach Gracie, what am I going to do with you?' Torin said, with a sigh, as he removed my hand that was still cradling his neck.

More kissing would be good. And then the rest.

'I think you should go home,' he said, standing up. Torin helped me to stand and slipped his arm around my waist as I felt my knees begin to give way. 'Let's go out the back way.'

With his arm still around me, Torin lead me out of the conservatory doors into the back garden. The cold air ran chilled fingers under my dress and made me shiver. Cloud covered the moon, and the garden was lit up by the lights from inside the house. As we reached the side of the house Torin and I stepped into thick darkness. I could still hear the muffled sounds of the party but I was very aware that we were alone.

'Torin?' I said, pausing and making him stop.

'You alright?' he asked, looking at me.

I took a step to face Torin and placed my palms against his chest.

'What are you doing?' he asked.

I slid my hand up and reached my fingers up to the back of Torin's neck and into his hair and pressed my body against his.

'Don't Gracie,' he said, but I could hear the sigh in his voice and feel the desire throbbing through him.

I laid my cheek against his chest. His hands gently held the tops of my arms. I smoothed his neck with my fingertips. I felt his thumb rub my shoulder.

'No Gracie,' he said and pushed me away. He took my hand and pulled me out from the darkness at the side of the house and into the knot garden at the front, illuminated from the lights inside.

I trailed behind Torin, all the way down Redferne Lane, having to concentrate to keep one foot stepping in front of the other. He opened my front door but didn't step inside.

'Aren't you coming in?' I asked.

'Not when you're like this,' he said as he gave me a gentle shove into my house. 'Do yourself a favour and just go to bed, alright?' He reached around me, said, 'Bye Grace.' I flinched once at his use of my proper name and twice when he closed my front door, shutting me in the house. Then I shouted some obscenities he wouldn't hear and picked up the wine bottle from the table.

I woke up on the sofa with a stiff neck, an arid mouth and Jerome frowning down at me.

'Morning,' he said, with a glance at his watch. 'Actually, it's afternoon.'

I groaned and struggled to sit up. 'What are you doing here?'

'Your back door was open. Came to get a cigarette? You mind?' He said as he took one from the packet on the table.

'Help yourself.'

'You look like you need coffee,' Jerome said, and went into my kitchen.

I sat on the sofa, feeling hollow, listening to him clattering around as I tried to wake up properly. My mouth felt as though I'd used paint stripper as mouthwash and my brain felt like it was being held in a clamp. My throat was raw and my stomach uneasy.

Jerome returned and placed two mugs on the table amongst the detritus of my bad habits.

'Does Eliza know her aunt's got a habit?' he asked, nodding toward the wine bottles, overflowing ashtray and empty foil pill strips.

'Don't.' I said putting my hand up. I didn't need his judgement.

'I'm not going to say anything, right?'

'Everyone drinks.'

'Yeah, but not every one's dropping pills, yeah?' He was smirking, highly amused.

'They're prescription.'

'Whatever.' He shrugged.

I wobbled on shaky legs into the kitchen and got a glass of water. I knew I'd feel better if I drank it but I could only manage a sip before I had to sit down at the table.

Jerome leant against the door frame like Torin often did. A sudden recollection of kissing Torin flashed into my mind and with it a tangle of emotions I couldn't decipher. 'I'm sorry Jerome. I'm not at my best right now,' I said, and scratched my scalp and rubbed my palms over my hair in the hope I could clear my thoughts a little.

He smiled, a true smile that went to his eyes and made them soften.

'I don't think bad of you. Everyone I know gets off on something. If it makes you feel any better, I'm not feeling too fresh after last night neither.'

'Did you have a good night with Eliza?'

'Yeah,' he said, with a grin that lit up his face. He shrugged, and a blush crept into his cheeks.

I smiled, and it made my head hurt.

Jerome busied himself lighting a cigarette. I attempted another sip of water. It went down a little easier.

'Ada's asking after you,' Jerome said. 'You haven't been round for a few days.'

'I'm sorry.' I'd forgotten about Ada.

'You don't need to apologise to me.' He gave a shrug as though he was indifferent.

'Is she okay?'

Jerome nodded. 'But she'd like to see you.' He inhaled, then blew out the smoke from the side of his mouth. 'She needs some shopping too.'

'I'll go round now,' I said.

'Have a shower first yeah?' Jerome said, with a smirk.

Ada acted as though nothing was amiss but I caught her throwing me anxious looks a couple of times. I discovered that in my neglect she and Jerome had muddled along but my absence was evident in the pile of dirty washing-up in the sink if nowhere else.

Ada wouldn't hear my apology but she did let me go and get her some shopping. In my guilt I brought her a bunch of pink roses and a coffee and walnut cake in addition to the list she'd given me. And when I returned I did the washing-up, made her a cup of tea and served her a slice of the cake on a pretty plate.

The sun had already dipped below the horizon when I left Ada's. I hesitated outside my house before I forced myself to carry on up Redferne Lane.

I was relieved when Josie answered the door and for a moment I thought I might get away with just speaking to her. She waved away my apology as I hovered on the doorstep reluctant to come inside.

'We all have a little bit too much to drink sometimes Grace,' she said, with a laugh, 'I should know. Besides, I didn't even notice if you were a bit worse for wear. Come on in won't you? We're just about to have tea.'

'I won't, but thanks.' I couldn't handle the prospect of sitting down at the Redferne kitchen table for tea and cake.

'Then you must come again soon? The boys would love it if you came? And I would too.'

'I will, I promise.'

'See you soon then Grace.'

I walked across the pea shingle, smelling lavender as my legs brushed the remaining flower heads.

I heard his footsteps as I opened the gate. It took some effort to turn and face him. He looked relaxed in a T-shirt and jeans, as though he'd been hanging out with his nephews all day, playing trains and being a wholesome individual. I felt dirty in comparison.

'How are you feeling today?' Torin asked.

'Like an idiot.' I managed to raise my eyes to his face as I apologised.

Torin rolled his eyes, like he was annoyed with my response. Or maybe he was just annoyed with the whole of me.

'I think you'd better have this back.' He held out a key attached to a red plastic fob. 'I should have given it back a long time ago.'

The key sat unwelcome in my palm, his body heat still held in the metal. I couldn't thank him for it.

There was a weighty pause when the air was heavy with things that wouldn't be said.

I turned my face away from him and stuffed the key into my pocket.

'I should go,' I muttered to the gravel beneath my feet, but I didn't move.

'You shouldn't take that shite you know.'

'What?'

'You shouldn't take those little white pills of yours, they're not doing you any favours,' he said, with such distaste I might have thought I was dog shit on his shoe.

'What would you know?'

'Quite a bit actually.'

'Really?' I said, filling with annoyance at his righteousness. 'How would you know anything about me when you haven't been here?'

'I don't need to have been here to see you're a fucking mess.'

'And you're surprised?'

'No, I just…' he sighed. 'I can't… We can't do this when you're so messed up.'

'Fuck you.'

'Really mature Grace.'

'Fuck you Torin.'

'Well fuck you too,' Torin threw back, then turned and started walking back to the house.

'That's right Torin, just walk away like you always do,' I shouted.

He turned, his jaw tight and walked back to me.

'When you're like this, some sense of self-preservation tells me that pursuing whatever is going on between you and me is not going to end well. So yes, I am walking away.'

'Why is this is always on your terms?'

'My terms?' Torin looked surprised.

'Yes, your terms. You always leaving when it suits you. The decisions are always yours. What about what I want?'

'My terms?' Torin shouted. He really shouted. And it scared me. 'I have no fucking terms. I never have.'

I shouted back. 'This has always been your decision.'

'My decision?' He inhaled, filled with rage. 'When you met my little brother, and stole his heart and blew his fucking mind, was that my decision?' He paused, waiting for an answer he wasn't going to get. 'No, I never wanted that. Never. You hear me? I did not want that. But I stood by year after year, after fucking year watching you with him, seeing how much he loved you. How much you loved him. And I wasn't ever going to stand in the way of that. I have walked away from you so many times because it's been the right thing to do. It hasn't been for me Grace. Believe me, it's never been for me.' Torin rubbed his face with his hand and took a deep breath before he said, 'I have taken great efforts to get over you Gracie. I can't do this again.'

He turned and walked back to the house.

September 2008

Torin was waiting outside my office again, sitting on the low wall of the building opposite, smoking a roll-up. My colleagues were laughing and chatting as they left for the pub. I gave them a wave and crossed the road.

'What are you doing here?' I asked Torin, with a smile.

'Waiting for you,' he said, with a flash of his eyes.

'Here I am.' I said, with a ta-da in my voice and did jazz hands.

'Aye, here you are.' He looked down the length of me and back up. 'Ezra called, he's still at work, said he wouldn't be home till late.' He let the words fall between us before he spoke again. 'I thought you might want to go for a drink?'

'That would be nice.'

It was not the first time Torin had met me from work and we'd gone for a drink. Ezra often seemed to be working late these days and the place where Torin was working was close to my office. He all but passed by on his way home, it made sense we'd head back to the house together.

Torin and I went to the same bar we'd been to before and sat at 'our' table. We could see out across Bristol docks and liked to talk about the people that passed the window; we made up stories about them as we got slowly drunk.

I came back from the bar with another pint. Once I'd sat down beside Torin again he raised his glass in a toast.

'Here's to you.'

'Me?'

'Aye, you.'

I frowned. 'Why?'

'I just want to toast my friend, is there a problem in that?' he asked with a quizzical smile.

'We're friends are we?'

'Aye Gracie, we're friends.'

'Who'd have thought it?'

'Aye, right.'

I thought back over the last year with Torin as our lodger. When Ezra had first told me he'd offered Torin our spare room, while he did a job in Bristol, I went nuts. Ezra and I had the biggest argument we've ever had but Ezra wouldn't back down and eventually I'd had to accept that Torin would be coming to live with us. And yet to my utter surprise, almost from the moment he moved in the three of us had had a great time. There was a lot of laughter and Torin was a far better cook than either me or Ezra. Somehow the three of us worked perfectly together.

'I'm glad you moved in with us Torin,' I said.

'Me too.'

'It shouldn't have worked.'

'Aye, it shouldn't.'

'It stopped you being rude to me.'

'I was never rude,' he protested. But we both knew that in the intervening years since Ezra and I had been together Torin had been nothing but horrible towards me.

'You were foul. Do you remember all those times you said I looked awful?'

He smirked. 'You know I didn't mean it.'

'And what about all those times you made me look stupid in front of your brothers?'

'I've never made you look stupid.'

'Do you remember that time you locked me out when we were all staying at Redferne House? Noah thought I'd locked myself out and when he let me back in he just shook his head at my stupidity.'

'Christ, I'd forgotten about that.' Torin laughed. 'Do you remember why I locked you out?'

'Because you were being mean.'

'No, because you called me a lecherous old pervert.'

I giggled. 'Oh, yes, I remember now. You are a lecherous old pervert. How old was that girl?'

He shook his head, smiling.

'What was her name? Candy?' I said.

'Cindy. And she was only a little younger than you.'

'Exactly. You lecherous old perv.' I elbowed Torin.

'Careful Gracie.'

'Or what?'

'Or I'll lock you out of the house and Noah isn't going to be there to let you in.'

I cuffed his arm with the back of my hand. Torin grabbed my wrist.

'You're feisty this evening, young lady.'

As he spoke I could feel the pad of his thumb against the inside of my wrist. I looked into his face and I found I knew every inch, from the lines about his eyes to the small scar on his cheek to tiny V of his hair line. My traitorous heart fluttered.

'Don't look at me like that Gracie,' Torin said, and released my wrist.

I turned away, took a deep breath and downed the last of my drink and muttered an explanation before going outside for a cigarette.

I exited beneath the air conditioning unit that belched out the smell of fried food and passed a group of rowdy young men gathered around a couple of wooden benches. Leaning against the far wall of the pub yard I asked myself what on earth I thought I was doing. I glanced at a young couple near me. They were cosied up against one another, oblivious to the world around them, looking into each other's eyes and talking in smiling whispers. I tried to think if Ezra and I used to be like that but I couldn't remember.

Torin came outside as I was making a second roll-up.

'Thought you might want another one,' Torin said, placing a fresh pint on a ledge beside me.

'Thanks,' I muttered.

Torin leant against the wall, his arm only a fraction from mine. He took my tobacco from the ledge without asking and made a cigarette. I handed him my lighter. I knew he'd blow a smoke ring with his first exhale. I watched it until it had dissipated in the evening air.

'You see that couple over there?' Torin said, with just the slightest indication of his head.

I looked across the yard and saw a short man in a pale peach coloured jacket standing in front of a large woman wearing a scarlet dress and platform boots. The man was talking and gesticulating with his hands as the woman listened while sipping her drink through a straw.

'What's their story?' Torin asked, looking at me with a grin.

'She has a rabbit fetish and makes him dress up in a bunny suit every Tuesday. She locks him in a cage and leaves him there all day while she's at work,' I told Torin.

He guffawed. 'Really?'

I widened my eyes at him.

'Fine, alright. Well, when she gets home, she dresses up as a fox, unlocks the cage then beats the living daylights out of him with a bunch of carrots,' Torin said.

I looked at him.

'What?' he asked.

'Well, it's a bit much isn't it?'

'You started it.'

We smiled at one another.

And we were back on safer territory.

We stayed at the pub until hunger beckoned and we left pausing at the falafel stall on the way home. Torin held the paper napkin containing the pitta bread to my mouth letting me take a bite before he took a bite himself. When I'd finished chewing he offered it to my lips once more. We sat side by side on the bus and tried to ignore the drunk man in a cheap suit talking to me. It was only when Torin put his arm around me and inclined his head in intimacy that the man turned away with an apology.

'Sorry,' Torin said, making to move his arm. But I rested my head against his chest and closed my eyes whispering a thank you. And Torin held me all the way home.

Ezra was still not back when Torin and I came into the cold dark house; our breath made clouds in the air as though we were still outside.

'Christ it's freezing in here,' Torin said, as he put a hand to the radiator in the hall. 'The heating's not on.'

'I hope the boiler isn't playing up again,' I said, going into the living room.

'I'll light a fire,' Torin said, following me in and kneeling before the hearth.

It was an ineffectual little fireplace, pretty, but not much good at heating the room. I'd spent many evenings looking at the pattern on the ceramic tiles on the cast iron surround. But I found my eyes drawn to Torin.

I liked how nimble his thick fingers were as he shaved off thin splints of wood with the axe for kindling. He placed them in a neat pyramid around a scrunch of newspaper. Then he lit the paper and sat back on his heels watching the tiny curl of flame. It stuttered and Torin leant forward to blow gently. The fire took, making the little pieces of wood crackle. Torin put a few larger bits on, waited to make sure the flames caught those pieces too then placed a pair of logs on the top.

He stood and came over to the sofa. I saw him hesitate, but I shifted over a fraction so he would sit beside me.

We put the TV on and watched something that was supposed to be funny. But I was tired and found my eyes closing. It felt like the most natural thing in the world to lean my head upon Torin's shoulder. He shifted to accommodate me better, putting his arm around me and I closed my eyes.

There had been a pale light behind the curtains as Ezra had kissed me goodbye a few hours ago, whispering he had to go back to work and that he'd see me tonight. I hadn't heard him come home last night.

The house was freezing as I went downstairs. I made a mental note to get someone to come and look at the boiler.

I'd filled the kettle before I noticed there was a bottle of wine on the kitchen table with an envelope propped up in front of it with mine and Ezra's name written on the front in Torin's looped scrawl.

In the envelope there was a wad of fifty-pound notes and a letter.

Dearest Ezra and Grace,

It's time I got out of your hair. I've stayed far longer than I ever thought I would – that speaks volumes of your hospitality. Thanks for putting up with me. I hope it's enough to cover my rent. See you soon.

Torin x

That was it; far more money than his rent and just a few lines to explain his sudden exit. I screwed up his stupid note, dropped it to the floor and stood on it.

I couldn't believe Torin would leave without saying goodbye.

November 2014

I pinched a sultana out of the teacake and flicked it towards a pretty mallard, paddling near the edge of the pond. The duck swallowed it down and looked back toward us waiting for more. I could feel Ada looking up at me from her position in the wheelchair.

'You look rather peaky dear,' she said.

'I'm alright,' I lied. I felt terrible and looked awful too. I should have been at work instead I was feeding ducks in the park with Ada.

'Jerome said you weren't yourself at the party.'

My stomach contracted at the thought of what Jerome may have witnessed.

'I haven't really been myself for a while,' I admitted.

Ada nodded and threw a piece of teacake to the ducks.

'I'm making a mess of things.'

She gave me a sympathetic smile.

'I had a fight with Torin,' I said and felt a stab of sorrow at the vicious words we'd thrown at each other.

'Perhaps you can make it up to him?' She said and adjusted the woollen blanket across her knees.

'I don't know if I can.'

'Some relationships will never be straight forward.'

I hesitated, thinking for a moment. 'Was it complicated with the man you met after Patrick?'

'Sometimes, yes. But we understood each other, and we understood the situation we were in,' Ada said. 'And most of the time everything was perfect.'

I struggled to believe that Ada's relationship with a married man had been perfect. No relationship was perfect.

Ada and I finished breaking up the teacakes and threw the last pieces to the ducks.

'Men aside,' Ada piped up, 'you have to look after yourself.'

'I'm not very good at that.'

She leant over and patted my hand. 'It takes practice.'

Despite the damp grey weather, we took the long walk around the pond; neither Ada nor I had anything to rush back to. We stopped at a bench that looked across towards the tennis courts. Ada lit up one of her favoured strong French cigarettes, I made a roll-up and we sat and smoked in companionable silence. I had a chill in my bones and felt as though I might never get warm again. Like the naked trees my outlook felt bleak. Even more so than before Torin had come back. Before he came back I hadn't been aware that my life was a mess but now I knew it was and it felt as though there was nothing to look forward to.

As though she was trying to distract me from my thoughts, Ada started talking about her husband and then about her lover. She hesitated when I asked his name. Then smiled when she told me his name had been Samuel. Their relationship had ended when he'd retired to France with his wife. He'd died some years ago now and even though they hadn't been lovers anymore they'd still been friends and he'd written to her until his death.

'Do you still miss him?' I asked.

'Yes, a little but really it's just the idea of him I miss.'

I wondered if the way I missed Ezra was akin to what Ada had just described. I'd become accustomed to waking up alone, used to living alone; going home to an empty house no longer crushed the breath out of me. It was a little surprising to realise I was used to life without Ezra.

'I've been thinking Grace,' Ada ventured.

'About?'

'Moving.'

'Moving?' I frowned. 'Moving where?'

'There are those places for people like me, for people that need help.'

'What, like a care home?' I asked.

'If that's what you want to call them.'

'But you don't need to do that. I help you Ada. And Jerome. You don't need to move.'

She smiled. 'You are both very kind and I am very grateful.' She patted my hand. 'But I'm not getting any younger and the both of you have lives of your own to lead.'

'You're part of my life.'

'And I'm delighted to hear you say so but I don't want to become a burden.' She put up her hand, palm towards me, to stop the disagreement that was about to leave my lips. 'I have some money put away and I want to use it to help myself. But I would like your help in finding somewhere.'

I hated the thought of Ada leaving Redferne Lane.

'Will you help me Grace?' Ada asked, with her pale eyes watching my face.

I swallowed. 'If that's what you want?'

She nodded.

'Then of course I will.'

Once I'd seen Ada home I could no longer avoid going home myself. My house was a mess; a perfect mirror of my mental state. There was only one black bin bag left in the cupboard under the sink and after I'd shaken it open I began to pick up the detritus that filled my house. I started with the empty cigarette packets on the coffee table, then tipped the contents of the ashtray into the bin. A sense of my environmental responsibility stopped me from chucking the wine bottles in the bin bag and I dragged the black recycling box in from outside. I dumped the bottles in the box not letting myself count the number on the coffee table and floor, knowing there were more in the kitchen, the bathroom and possibly my bedroom too.

My hand paused as I found a foil strip with two pills still in it. I knew the tears that were rolling down my cheeks would subside if I slipped them down my throat. But maybe that was the crux of it. Maybe it was about time I cried. Maybe it was about time I stopped hiding all this emotion under a blanket of medication.

Still holding onto the foil strip, I had to sit down. There was something hard, and I extracted my phone from beneath my arse cheek. I turned it on and it greeted me with a little musical hello.

There were three messages. I hoped they were from Torin but instead they were all from Simon. Each one increasingly more anxious, worried that I hated him, that I was avoiding him after Friday night. And the last message was spoken in a tone that implied he thought I may have done something stupid. He knew me better than I gave him credit for. Yet on hearing his messages, instead of feeling cared for, I felt even more unworthy as I hadn't given Simon a second thought since Friday night. Honestly, the fumble and puke with Simon on Friday night had paled into insignificance since my argument with Torin.

I wiped the tears from my face, took a deep breath and tried to do something right.

'Grace, I'm so glad you called,' Simon said, answering his phone after one ring.

'Hi Simon.'

'Are you alright?'

I couldn't answer that, so I said, 'Sorry I didn't come in today.'

'It's fine, no problem.' I could imagine him sitting in his desk chair, worrying the button on his waistcoat.

'No, I should have called. I just wasn't feeling great this morning.'

'Are you feeling better?'

'A bit,' I lied, as more tears rolled down my cheeks as I blinked.

He paused. 'Will you be in tomorrow?'

'Yes,' I said, running my fingers over the aluminium topping of the strip of pills still in my hand.

'Great.' He paused again. 'Grace?'

'Yes?'

'I'm really sorry about Friday night.'

'It's fine.'

'No, it's really not. I'm so, so sorry, I can't believe I acted as I did and…'

'Please Simon, it's fine. You don't need to apologise. I…' I faltered for a moment. 'I behaved badly.' And I didn't just mean with Simon. I'd been behaving badly for years.

Simon said sweet words, offering me forgiveness and comfort I didn't deserve. In the end I hung up because I couldn't take any more kindness from him. And I didn't want him to know I was unable to stop crying. I could have filled an ocean with the tears I spilt.

After I spoke to Simon I dropped the foil strip into the bin bag and before I could change my mind I called Dad and asked him not to write me anymore more prescriptions. He said he thought it was probably about time I stopped the medication; it was time I pulled myself together.

There were little white pills left in my bag that would sooth the tension in my chest. Instead, I settled for another cigarette, huddling beneath the concrete stairway opposite the doorway to the office kidding myself that I could still be on time for work.

I hoped to slip into the chair at my desk and pretend I'd been there all along. But as I pushed open the weighty glass door, feeling a little breathless, I was instantly aware that Simon was addressing the whole office. Everyone turned to look at me and Simon floundered, a touch fish out of water, our little fumble written all over his face. Too late he recovered himself. He greeted me eagerly with an indulgent smile and puppy dog eyes an employer should never indulge a late employee with. He moved to my desk, and all but pulled out my chair for me while my colleagues looked on with knowing looks.

Simon resumed talking to the office, and I gazed at my keyboard wishing I'd swallowed those little white pills residing in the bottom of my bag. I thought about the strip of pills I'd thrown in the bin last night and the one in my bathroom cabinet; it was more than possible there was another strip with one or two of my little friends left, hiding in the drawer beside the bed. I needed to get rid of them all.

'Grace?' Simon said, beside me, with the tone of someone who'd already spoken more than once.

I looked up.

He gave me a hesitant smile. 'You need to turn your computer on.'

Flicking my eyes to the left and then my right I saw everyone else was working while pretending they weren't listening and half looking at Simon and me.

I pressed the power button and heard the little purr of the computer starting up.

Simon placed a handout beside my keyboard. 'You probably missed the e-mail about the training today?' He didn't wait for an answer. 'We're just doing a couple more tutorials so we're really up to speed with this new software.'

I looked up at Simon and forced a smile. 'I'm sorry I was late.'

He shook his head. I wished he'd hide that look of affection in his eyes.

'I should get on,' I said, picking up the handout he'd given me, as though I knew exactly what I was doing.

Simon didn't move. He gave a little cough and leant close and pointed at the screen of the computer.

'You need to click on this,' he said and waited for me to follow his instruction. 'Then click this. Enter your usual username then the password that's on page six.'

I brushed aside my feelings of complete incompetence and thanked Simon. He retreated to his office but not before he'd slipped an envelope under my keyboard.

Working through the coffee break so I might avoid everyone else I pretended to make progress through the baffling software tutorial. When I was sure no one was watching me I opened the envelope and read the neat and ordered handwriting;

Dear Grace,

Sorry. Please forgive my abhorrent behaviour. I cannot emphasise enough that I have never acted in such a way towards a woman before and I will never forgive myself for my actions towards you on Friday evening. Can we start again?

Kindest regards,
Simon x

A knot of irritation tightened in my chest. Friday night was the one and only time I'd actually felt a grain of attraction towards Simon. He'd finally been a bit naughty and gotten me indecently drunk and felt me up outside a bar in a back street. That he was the one feeling intense remorse about his actions while I felt little more than mild embarrassment over my behaviour said a whole lot about the both of us.

Looking around the office I realised everyone was back at their desks. I went to the toilets and emptied every pill I'd found in my bag into the water and flushed them away before I was tempted to swallowed them. Then I snuck into the kitchen. With my back against the wall I noticed the local paper on the worktop opposite, open on the recruitment pages. I stepped across to scan the adverts and was surprised to see there were loads of different jobs out there. Jobs I'd never known even existed.

With a green biro I drew squares around adverts that held my attention for more than two seconds. Then crippling self-doubt flooded me as I realised how incompatible and under skilled I was for all of these jobs.

Crumpling the newspaper into a wonky ball, I chucked it across the kitchen only it didn't go far, just flopped at my feet. So I threw the pen. It ricocheted off the cupboard door and hit me in the temple.

I sunk to the floor, a failure.

It didn't take Simon long to find me and tears filled my eyes as soon as I saw the kindness in his. He sat beside me on the linoleum and I crumpled into his arms as soon as the first kind word left his lips. I wished I could like him as I felt him caress my back with the care of a lover. But I didn't care enough for Simon and as soon as I could quell the tears I extracted myself from his embrace.

'I can't do this anymore,' I said.

'You're having a really tough time.'

I shook my head. 'No, I mean, I can't work here anymore Simon.'

He frowned and rolled his lips together as though he couldn't allow words to spill from his mouth.

'I should have left months ago. You should have fired me months ago. I am the worst employee in the world.'

He shook his head.

'I am.' I sniffed and tried to take in some oxygen. 'I'm leaving Simon.'

He lifted his hand, and I let him wipe away the tears on my cheeks. 'You don't have to rush into this,' he said.

'Please stop being nice to me.'

He smiled. 'I like being nice to you Grace.'

And that was part of the problem. Simon would forever let me get away with being shite because, for some unfathomable reason he liked me.

I got up and Simon stood as well.

'Do you need me to put it in writing?' I asked. 'To make it formal?'

He waved his hands at me. 'Wait awhile Grace. Don't take this the wrong way but you don't seem to be in the best of minds to be making big decisions right now.'

'I need to start making some decisions.'

'At least give yourself a couple of weeks?' He paused. 'I'd really like you to stay.'

So I left knowing I wasn't coming back, but I promised Simon I'd at least consider staying. He told me he wouldn't accept my resignation if I didn't at least give myself two weeks to think about it; to think about what I was going to do next. And he had a point, it was about time I considered my future.

April 2007

'My manager is leaving,' I told Ezra, before I took a drag on my cigarette.

'No way, how come?' He said, looking up from his phone, his thumb paused above the buttons.

'She's got another job. More pay, better hours.'

'Good for her.'

'She's a bitch.'

Ezra laughed. 'True, but still, you know, it's good for her, right?'

I shrugged and inhaled again, trying to let the day and the week at the office leave my body. Ezra looked back at his phone, I suspected it would be several more hours until he wanted to leave the office behind. He still had his tie done up and jacket on, his shirt still tucked in.

The bar was full of people just like Ezra and me, twenty-somethings in office clothes that had just been released for the weekend, ready to party in Bristol's clubs and bars. The volume was rising with the alcohol consumption and the sun was only just nearing the horizon.

'Are they advertising for her replacement yet?' Ezra asked, his head still down.

'Yes.'

'You should apply,' Ezra said, as he placed his phone on the table beside his wine glass and looked up at me. His eyes looked dark, near black, in the ambient lighting of the bar.

'I don't think so,' I said, with a small laugh at his preposterous suggestion.

'Why not?'

'I'm not management material Ezra.'

'You could be.'

'I can barely organise myself, let alone an entire office.'

He gave me an indulgent smile and reached over to give my hand a little squeeze. 'Maybe.' He took a sip of wine. 'But what are you going to do? You know, long term?'

'I don't know,' I said with a small laugh.

My career, or lack of, was not what I wanted to be talking about on a Friday evening and so I tried to guide the conversation towards our plans for the weekend. For the first time in a while we had a free weekend, and I had ideas of visiting a gallery and maybe going to the cinema. Ezra quickly dispelled my plans, telling me he was going to the office tomorrow and then his phone rang. It must have been his project partner rather than his boss as Ezra swore a lot.

'Sorry,' Ezra said, after he'd put the phone back on the table ten long minutes later.

'You could turn it off?' I suggested.

'But work will probably call again.' He refilled our glasses from the bottle as he explained that the project deadline had been moved forward and therefore the whole team was having to work all hours.

'It's fine,' I said. From the moment I'd met Ezra I'd known he was focused and committed to his work.

'Are you saying it's fine, and it really is fine? Or are you saying it's fine and meaning it's really not fine?' Ezra asked, with his head on one side.

Before I could reply, his phone went off again.

I smiled and rolled my eyes as he answered.

As Ezra talked I pondered my solitary lie-in tomorrow and figured it might be nice to have the bed to myself for a change. I might get up at midday and go to the gallery on my own and then I could meet Ezra for dinner after he'd finished work.

'Right,' Ezra said, returning the phone to the table. 'All sorted.' He loosened his tie before he reached over and took my hand. 'You might not mind me working extra hours if you were focused on your career too?'

I took my hand out of his and picked up my wine glass. I considered being annoyed by his comment because it was such a Noah thing to say but I couldn't muster the animosity towards Ezra.

'Grace,' Ezra said, in a placatory tone.

I took another sip. 'I don't mind you working.'

'Uh, huh.'

'I don't,' I said, but I doubted myself a little.

Ezra took a cigarette out of my packet on the table. I watched as he lit it and was struck by the agile beauty of his hands. His nails were neatly shaped and clean. His fingers unblemished, the skin smooth and well kept. I glanced at my own hands and saw the ragged dirty nails, the ink stains and a graze on my left knuckles.

Ezra looked at me with his head on one side and gave me a wonky smile.

'What is it?' I asked, smiling back.

'Maybe it's time we thought about having a baby?' Ezra said.

'What?' I gasped.

He shrugged. 'I don't know, I've just been thinking about it recently and I quite like the idea of a little baby. Our little baby.' He reached over and took my hand again. He rubbed my knuckles with his thumb. 'What do you think?'

'I'm only twenty-three Ezra. I'm not thinking about babies yet.'

'But you have thought about it?' There was a slight pleading tone to his voice.

'No, not really. I mean I guess I always thought I would, one day.' I was frowning, and I struggled to lift it from my brow.

'Maybe one day could be soon?' Ezra suggested.

'What's the rush?' I reached for a cigarette.

'No rush. But if you're not all that career focused right now…'

'Who says I'm not career focused?' I interrupted.

Ezra smiled and widened his eyes.

'Jesus Ezra, you're so bloody…' I wasn't sure of the word I was looking for.

'Amazing?' he suggested.

I laughed. 'Why now?'

'Because I love you,' Ezra said.

'I love you too but that's not an answer.'

'Because that's what couples do Grace.' He rubbed my knuckles again.

'Do they?'

'Yes.'

I sighed and found my smile had fallen a little.

Ezra looked uneasy, and it suddenly felt too loud in the bar. 'Are you saying you don't want to have baby? Is this a commitment thing?' He asked.

It was easy to forget how insecure Ezra was sometimes, how he still doubted that I wanted to be with him, despite the three years we'd had together.

'No,' I reassured. 'We wouldn't have bought a house together if we weren't committed.'

'But?'

'But, I don't think we need to rush into having a baby, that's all.'

'That's all?'

'Yes.'

'But Grace, we will have children? One day?'

'Yes.'

'Promise?' He seemed so vulnerable, and I felt bad.

'Yes.'

'Good.' He squeezed my hand.

'You know what?' I said, slipping my foot out of my shoe.

'What?'

'In the meantime, we can practice, just so when we're ready we know we're definitely doing right,' I ran my foot up the inside of Ezra's calf and watched the insecurity in his eyes melt into desire.

November 2014

We almost didn't even get through the door. After seeing three other care homes that made both Ada and I want to slit our wrists we figured that Riverview would be just like them. Had it not been for the pub two doors down we'd have retreated back to Redferne Lane without even looking. But after Ada sighed and announced rather loudly, making the taxi driver sniggered, that she could murder a glass of sherry, we'd ended up in the grimy-looking pub sipping cheap sherry at just gone two in the afternoon.

'You've finally got a bit of colour in your cheeks,' Ada said after we'd ordered another sherry.

'Yeah, I haven't been well,' I said.

Since I'd quite work I'd been in bed shivering and sweating and hallucinating too. But I knew it was nothing to do with leaving my job but more to do with my body adjusting to the absence of my little white pills. I was almost grateful I'd felt so rough that I hadn't been able to get out of bed for two days because I just didn't have the energy to scour the house for any hidden little white pills. I didn't want to need them anymore. I told myself time and time again that I didn't need them and I think my body was beginning to get used to the idea.

'Feeling better?' Ada asked.

'Getting there,' I said.

Somewhat fortified after our third helping of sherry Ada and I figured we had nothing to lose from visiting Riverview. We had to pass the front door on our way back to Redferne Lane.

Ada elbowed me when she clocked the memorial table in the foyer, with a photograph of the recently deceased old lady that meant there was now a spare room.

'Just don't look, yeah?' I whispered.

'But that could be me next week,' Ada said, at full volume. She didn't do whispering.

'Yeah, well, I suppose it could.' I paused and smiled down at her. 'But only if you move in here.'

She cackled and slapped my thigh with her cast.

'Watch it,' I said, moving her wheelchair forward so she couldn't reach me any longer. 'Or you might break your arm.'

The sound of Ada cackling filled the foyer, and I wondered how long it might be before we were asked to leave. But I was pleasantly surprised by the greeting we received from the care worker that came out to meet us. She was a slim young woman with a heavy Eastern European accent and she rocked her nursey style uniform with panache. She smiled, introducing herself as Natalia directly to Ada, without one hint of condescension. Natalia swiped her pass across a sensor at the access doors. There was a beep and a click and then she pushed the door open, holding it so I could wheel Ada through before she shut the door, locking us in.

I'd expected the undercurrent of urine and disinfectant in the air like the other care homes but this place smelt only a little of boiled cabbage. And unlike the places we'd visited earlier, the decor of the room reminded me of Ada's living room, albeit on a larger scale. Plus, there was a flat screen TV and if I wasn't mistaken an Xbox.

Natalia showed us the communal facilities and I could tell by the smile on Ada's face she was interested. I liked that Riverview lacked an institutional feel and was cheery and homely too. There was proper carpet and real armchairs, not those faux leather, metal framed chairs that reminded me of health centre waiting rooms. The few residents in the communal area looked up from their board games and offered smiley greetings to Ada and not one of them gave off the air of death or dementia.

We visited the garden; a grassed square with a creamy gravelled path all the way around. The wheel chair managed the small stones of the gravel and Ada noted the convenient hand rails located around the garden, and the numerous benches. Natalia explained that it was a sensory garden; the planting was done to aid the feeling of tranquillity.

Next we visited what would be Ada's room. It reminded me of a budget hotel, at once clean and tidy, but a little bland. There was obviously a bed (I couldn't help but wonder if the previous occupant had died in that bed) and a wardrobe, along with a desk and chair and an en suite bathroom with hand rails just about everywhere you looked.

There was nothing wrong with the room. It was certainly more generous in size than an economy hotel room, but it lacked personality and yet Ada seemed delighted, making noises of approval as she looked around. She even heaved herself up out of the wheelchair and shuffled, clutching my arm so she could look out of the window; there was a charming view of the garden.

Half an hour later we were walking back to Redferne Lane and for perhaps the sixth time Ada told me how close Riverview was; only a ten-minute walk. Ada had the paperwork tucked into her cream handbag and I had no doubt that this was what she wanted. But I was glad I pushing her wheelchair and she couldn't see my face because then, as I had a little cry, she didn't notice and continued to chat about all things Riverview.

The chilly air calmed the jittery feeling and walking eased the anxiety in my chest. Whispering an apology Simon would never hear I slipped my letter of resignation into the post box and turned back for home. On the way I went into the only shop open this early and bought a roll of bin bags and some coffee. I'd realised after a long night tossing, turning, sweating and thinking that decisive action might be a way to combat the unease that flowed through my veins.

When I got home I went straight upstairs to the wardrobe. I lifted out all of Ezra's clothes and placed them on the bed. His suits went into a black bag straight away. Then too his shirts, ties and any attire remotely work related. I only hesitated when I came to the shirt he'd worn when we'd gotten married. The bottom button was still missing from where I'd ripped his shirt undone on our wedding night. But I couldn't remember him wearing it since we'd been married, so I folded it up and placed in the bin bag.

I moved to the chest of drawers and put his socks and underwear straight into black polythene. Ezra's T-shirts were the hardest thing to rid myself of; as though they still held some essence of him. But I put one after another into the bags and only kept his 'Queens of the Stone Age' T-shirt; he'd worn it when we first met.

I looked at the bed and realised that if I was ever going to have sex again, it would have to be in a different bed; my bed, not ours. It occurred to me there was more furniture I needed to be rid of and even the realisation was cathartic.

On the way to the kitchen to make a coffee, the cushions from the sofa and the throw on the armchair went into a bin bag. A dusty candlestick, trinkets from forgotten holidays all slid into the bag. A long dead houseplant went into another bag destined for landfill. I paused when I got to the photo of me and Ezra on Christmas Eve and I was so close to just dropping that into the bag too, but I stopped, running my thumb over Ezra's face to wipe away the film of dust. My shoulders dropped, and I placed the photo back on the now bare mantel piece, blinked a few tears away and swallowed the lump in my throat.

Back up in my bedroom I opened the ornate Chinese lacquer box that had been a wedding gift from Noah and Josie. We'd both kept our small amount of jewellery nestled inside the various decorated compartments; his on the right, mine on the left.

I slid open the right compartment. The two pairs of cuff links went straight to the charity shop pile. I picked up Ezra's wedding ring and rolled it between my fingers. They'd given it back to me with a few of his other effects. Now I had no idea what to do with it; I should have buried it with him. I put it back into his side of the Chinese box for now. I scooped out a gold chain I'd never seen him wear and placed in in the mounting pile of unwanted things. The beaded bracelet he'd worn all the time when we first met was the last thing in his side of the box. I slipped it on my wrist and smiled to myself as I remembered those first few months with Ezra; how he'd made me feel special and perfect.

As an afterthought I flicked open the compartment on the left and noted the tangle of silver chains and forgotten earrings that made up my collection of jewellery. At the bottom I glimpsed a leather bracelet with tiny silver beads.

I extracted it from the box and ran it through my fingers. It still held its shape as though it had only just been taken off Torin's wrist and the ties were still kinked. I draped it around my wrist, next to Ezra's bracelet and pinched the two together for a moment before I slipped the leather one into my pocket.

It was mid-afternoon by the time my bedroom was cleared of all things Ezra except the furniture, and the living room was piled with bin bags. I turned my attention to the area under the stairs, thinking it would be a quick job to just pull Ezra's old bike out. But I'd neglected to remember that there was two years' worth of stuff gathered around it.

There was the Henry Hoover I did not use. A collection of carrier bags. A tube of tennis balls. Two pairs of walking boots with old dried mud still attached to the soles. Ezra's coat was still lying over the bike seat, where he must have left it. I picked it up. It was cool under my fingers. I lifted it to my nose. There was just a trace of Ezra left in it. And it brought a lump to my throat. But after that first second I could only smell musty neglect and dust. I reached into the pocket. One held a used tissue and a Mars bar wrapper. The other, a shopping list and three pounds and sixty-seven pence in various coins.

I hung Ezra's coat over the banister and I was finally able to pull the bike out. As soon as I'd extracted it I wheeled it out of the house and went next door.

Sam answered wearing her coat and a look of disapproval when I told her I had a gift for Jerome. She peered over the wall and looked at the bike.

'I haven't got any money for that,' she said, as though she thought I was trying to have one over on her. She continued to do up the buttons on her cerise duffel coat.

'It's a gift.' I said again.

She looked at me, full of distrust, as though she thought I was grooming her son. 'I've got to go to work,' she said and glanced up the lane towards Redferne House.

I asked if Jerome was home. She hollered his name into the house and Jerome came to the door.

'I don't know what wool you've pulled over her eyes to make her so kind to you. Mind you say thank you.' Sam said to Jerome before she eased past me and started up the lane.

'What's going on?' Jerome asked, in a mumble.

'I have a present for you …' I trailed off as I took in the sight of Jerome. His eyes were dull and his lips turned down. 'What's the matter?'

'Eliza dumped me.'

'Oh no, I'm sorry,' I said and rubbed his arm, although I'd have liked to give him a hug.

'It's alright,' he said. 'She said it was getting too serious.'

It sounded like a lame excuse.

We looked at each other for a moment, both of us recognising that there wasn't much to be said.

'So you've got a present for me, have you?' Jerome said, trying to sound bright but not quite hitting the right tone.

'Yeah, come here, look, this is for you,' I said to Jerome, pulling him out of the gate and showing him Ezra's bike leant up against the wall.

'Seriously?' he said.

'Yeah.' I smiled.

'Was it your husbands?' he asked as he gave the brake handle a cursory squeeze.

'It was Ezra's, yes. But he doesn't need it anymore and I think it's time it had a new owner.' I ran my hand over the seat. Ezra's old beaded bracelet caught on the end and as I went to unhook it the elastic snapped, sending the beads falling to the floor. I gave a rueful laugh.

Jerome bent to pick up the beads but I told him not to worry. So he stood up, glanced at me, then looked back at the bike. 'It's a proper good one. You could get a good price for it.'

'I don't need the money. Besides, I couldn't sell it. But I would like you to have it. Think of it as a belated birthday present.'

He looked like he might say something more but Godfrey and Barty scooted past squealing hello. I looked up the lane to see Josie coming as quickly as her heavily pregnant state would allow. She waved to us then called to the boys to stop at the bridge.

'Is your mother home?' Josie asked Jerome when she'd reached us. 'I was sure she said she was coming up to the house this morning?'

'She just left,' Jerome said.

'Oh, how odd. She probably got started while I was wrestling the boys into coats. You know it's incredible, neither one of them wanted to put a coat on but they're the ones in tears when they're cold.' She started walking again. 'Must go, we're off to the park. Grace, you must come up for tea over the weekend,' she said, looking back.

I nodded, reluctant to commit with words, knowing a visit to Redferne House would most likely involve seeing Torin.

Josie waved, then waddled toward Barty and Godfrey, calling to the boys.

Jerome scanned the frame of Ezra's bike. He was close to it, running his fingers over the black rubber grips and the brake cables. Even though he was absorbed in looking at the bike I could see the aura of sadness still about him. I wondered if Eliza was sad or relieved now that she'd dumped him.

'I expect it needs a bit of work.' I said. 'But I thought you might enjoy doing it.'

He looked up at me. 'Are you sure about this?'

'Yes.'

Jerome hugged me.

I could feel the youthful leanness of his body, wiry and precise. I could sense the withheld strength in his muscles; what he chose to embrace me with was only a fraction of the power in him. I was glad he could hug me and it felt good and natural. I squeezed him back.

'Thanks Grace. Thank you so much. I'll take proper good care of it.'

'I don't know if you're interested but I've got some other things of Ezra's you might like? If it's not too weird?' I said.

Jerome came into my house and I could see him taking in the piles of stuff and bin bags. I showed him the clothes and DVD's and other things he might like and went to make coffee.

When I returned with two mugs, Jerome was wearing Ezra's old coat and holding the Christmas Eve photo I'd almost thrown out.

'Is this him?' Jerome asked.

The photo was taken after we'd gone up Glastonbury Tor on Christmas Eve three years before. It had been ferociously cold; an evil wind had turned our faces red. When we'd reached the top, we turned back down again almost straight away, finding no respite from the cold; the only corner of the tower that was shielded from the blowing gale was occupied by a dreadlocked young man playing a large drum with his palms. The sound had echoed against the ancient stones before being thrown away into the winds. Ezra and I had run back down the pathway, relieved when we got to the bottom. We'd gone into a pub not far along the road, hoping to find an open fire and mulled wine. We'd settled for cider and the sweaty warmth of drunken patchouli scented folk; tattooed, pierced and dreadlocked. An inebriated gent with several missing teeth and a Rasta coloured beanie hat had been making his beer money taking Polaroid photos. We'd wanted to get rid of him and handed over more coins than he asked, in return for the snap.

The photo was remarkably well taken, he'd centred the two of us perfectly, wisps of gold tinsel sat behind us against the exposed bricks. The dark wooden table with our half-finished pints before us, and our hands sat clasped together upon it. But the part I liked the most was the expressions both Ezra, and I were wearing; we were happy. And we knew how happy we were too.

'Yes, that's Ezra.' I said.

I watched Jerome, his blue eyes inquisitive, his lips already moving, like he was preparing them for the questions he was about to ask. I knew what he was going to say although not the exact words of course.

Jerome ran his tongue along the inside of his bottom lip, and frowned, before he looked up at me. 'Did he have cancer or something?'

I hesitated before I spoke, trying to calibrate my response. 'He wasn't ill. He was in an accident.' I paused. 'He used to cycle to work every day. On his way home, a lorry…' I stopped again. I knew what had happened to Ezra and to his body. There were ways to tell Jerome the same truth that didn't need to include certain particulars. I could shield him from some details that didn't change the outcome but made the reality less gruesome.

'A lorry knocked him off his bike,' I said.

'Harsh.' Jerome said, but from his tone I knew he wasn't finished. 'Did he like die on the road?'

'No, he died in the ambulance on the way to hospital.'

'Couldn't they save him?'

I shook my head. 'He was in quite a mess.'

Jerome looked at me expectantly like he wanted the full coroner's report.

'He went under the wheels. He had a lot of injuries.'

'He must have been proper mangled.'

'Yes, he was.' I found myself faintly smiling at Jerome's choice of words.

'Did you see him?' Jerome continued.

'Not until after.'

'When he was dead?'

'Yes.'

'What did he look like?'

I smiled again, finding his bluntness a tonic. 'Not quite like he should have.'

He narrowed his blue eyes at me. 'Why are you smiling?'

'Your lack of tact is refreshing.'

He looked down at the photo again for a moment. 'I'm sorry about your husband.'

I nodded.

'Do you miss him?'

'Yes.'

'He was right good looking. Not as fit as me, but still he was pretty buff.'

I laughed. 'I thought so.'

'You must have loved him a lot?'

'Yes. I still do. I hope I never stop loving him.' As I said the words, I knew they were true, whoever else I may also love.

And suddenly it was Jerome's complicated blue eyes that filled with liquid. He wiped them with the sleeve of his hoody. I saw a flash of the little boy he'd been not so long ago and the man he was soon to become.

'That's like the sweetest thing I think I've ever heard,' Jerome said, and handed me back the photograph.

It was cold and drizzling as I pushed Ada up Redferne Lane. I could only just see over her red umbrella and it inhibited all conversation. In a way I was glad because I had nothing positive to say. Ada had accepted the room at Riverview. Although I wasn't surprised it was all happening so quickly.

I was taking her to see Noah, so she could tell him she was moving. I couldn't stop thinking about the fact her family had lived in that cottage for over a hundred years and yet it had never belonged to them – it had always been the property of the Redferne's. It somehow seemed wrong that Ada didn't own it – at least she'd been able to save quite an amount over the years that made this move possible.

At the front door of Redferne House Ada struggled to her feet. I handed her the walking stick and stood poised ready to catch her should she fall. When we'd left her house she'd informed me she wanted to do this on her own, without the wheel chair or my help. She'd dressed up and done her hair and make-up too and I admired the way she was confronting the end of an era; with class and independence.

Josie opened the door and let us in, pulling Barty out of the way so Ada didn't trip over the child. Josie showed Ada into the drawing room so she and Noah might conduct their conversation in private. I wandered into the kitchen not sure who I might find.

There was only Eliza. She lifted her eyes as I entered. Her pale blonde hair was tied in a messy ponytail. She'd looked as though she'd been crying.

'Are you okay?' I asked.

'I'm fine,' she said, standing up and tucking her chair in with a bang. She stormed out of the kitchen her ponytail swinging.

I heard Josie snap at Eliza in the hallway and Eliza snarl back. Josie came into the kitchen with a look of exasperation.

'I don't know what's got into her at the moment,' Josie said. 'She's absolutely vile. You can't say anything to her.'

I was about to tell her that Eliza had broken up with Jerome but I stopped, figuring it wasn't my place to tell Josie.

'Anyway Grace let's have a cup of tea and you can tell me all about you.' She said, pulling a smile on to her face.

I told her I'd handed my notice in at work and she was full of ideas about what I might do now. She was bursting with enthusiasm for my prospects and wished I could imbibe a little of her positivity. At present all that seemed ahead of me was ridding myself of a lifetime of belongings.

We talked about Godfrey's birthday and I declined, as politely as I could, Josie's invitation to his party at the local soft-play centre. Instead I promised I would come later in the week to give him his gift.

Torin came into the kitchen with Godfrey and Barty hanging off either hand.

'Don't mean to intrude ladies,' he said with a smile, 'but I have two wee boys in need of nourishment.'

Josie made to get up, but Torin said, 'No, I can do it.' He tilted his head, wrinkled his nose and gave Josie an indulgent smile. 'If you tell me what to do, that is?'

Josie gave a smiling sigh as Torin deposited the boys at the table and listened as she began to give him instruction on what to cook for the boys. Not wishing to feel a spare part I got up and took the boys to wash their hands in the cloakroom. We returned to the kitchen, and I sat them back at the table, ready to eat.

Torin was still cooking their eggs, and it was difficult not to watch him. My heart ached to see him domesticated and seemingly happy; full of joy when I knew he was pissed off with me. I wished I could go and stand beside him and help, just so I could be near him, so I might know that I was forgiven. I wished I could be next to him and inhale the scent of him, feel the warmth from him; the things that reminded me I was alive. But mostly I yearned for his smile and just one look from his dark eyes and then I would know he cared for me still.

But I watched as he cooked the boy's eggs and soldiers, all the while entertaining them with banter and silly words and funny faces. He served them their eggs in novelty egg cups. He'd known the egg cups were in the very back of the drawer and cut up their soldiers in just the right way; different for Barty than for Godfrey. Without Josie having to say anything more he placed beakers of watered down apple juice before the boys.

Josie bathed him in smiles and he gave them back to her, and Barty and Godfrey in plenty. But I received not a look, let alone a smile and certainly no words from Torin. And I felt punished, truly punished and deservedly so.

When I heard the drawing room door open; I was on my feet and across the kitchen under the guise that Ada might need my support, but oh so grateful to leave the kitchen and Torin and domestic bliss behind.

Ada looked as emotional as I felt myself and I asked her, in a whisper, if she'd like to go home. I was relieved when she nodded and moved towards the front door without further discussion.

A few weeks ago I might have addressed my anxiety of the visit to Redferne House with a night involving a couple of little white pills washed down with a bottle of wine. But I was determined not to do that this evening. Having taken Ada home and settled her in for the evening I turned my attention to my life and the tasks I wanted to fulfil.

I arranged for a lorry to come next week and pick up my furniture and take the bags of clothes and other things. They were all going to a local charity that supported young people just starting out on their own. I liked the idea that Ezra's things would go to people with their lives ahead of them.

Now I knew what I was doing with all of this stuff it somehow made the process even easier and I made a start on clearing out the spare room. It still had boxes in the corner that Ezra and I hadn't unpacked when we'd moved in.

I looked out of the window at the dark evening outside and remembered how Ezra and I had thought this might become a room for our child. I wasn't sure if I mourned the loss of the family we'd thought we'd have or not. I'd wanted a family, a child. But I'd wanted it with Ezra and without him I wasn't sure if I wanted a child or not. I certainly couldn't look after one on my own – I could barely look after myself and was therefore grateful that we hadn't conceived.

I was startled by a knock on the door so late. Brushing the dust from my hands, I trotted down the stairs and was surprised to find Eliza at the door. She looked a mess with her pretty hair straggling around her face. Her beautiful eyes were red and puffy.

'Hello,' I smiled, pretending her visit wasn't out of place, as though this was not the first visit she had paid me.

'Can I come in?' she said, glancing up at me briefly before returning her eyes to the floor.

'Of course.'

We went into the living room but the sofa was piled with bin bags so I took her through to the kitchen.

'Are you moving?' she asked.

'No, just having a clear out.'

She nodded.

We sat at the kitchen table.

I offered her a drink, but she refused.

Eliza fiddled with a hair band she had around her wrist.

I resisted the urge to smoke.

'So?' I began.

She looked up and I could see secrets in her violet eyes.

As I looked at her, worry furrowed her brow, her lip wobbled and her eyes began to fill.

'What's the matter Eliza?'

She blinked the tears down her cheeks. 'I think I'm pregnant.'

I inhaled and bit back my initial freak out response with an exaggerated exhale. 'Have you done a test?' I asked.

She shook her head.

I knew there was an unopened packet of three pregnancy tests in my bathroom cupboard. They'd been there for two years, but I expected they would still tell us what we needed to know.

While Eliza went through the weeing on the stick procedure, she had me wait in the bathroom with her. We established that her period was over a week late, perhaps two. She and Jerome hadn't used a condom. On more than one occasion. And as we sat perched on the edge of my bath I was not surprised to see a little blue line appear.

I took Eliza back downstairs to the kitchen and made her a cup of tea and a piece of toast. My head was reeling. Eliza's probably was too, but I guessed she'd already had some time to think about her predicament. To reconcile herself with what she probably already knew was absolute. I had to look away from her as an unbidden jolt of jealousy tore through me then disappeared equally rapidly. And when I looked back all I saw was a child; Eliza looked so young.

'Please don't tell Daddy?' Eliza asked, as if to emphasise her youth.

'I don't know Eliza. Surely he's going to have to know, sooner or later?'

'No.' She gave me an imploring look. Then she burst into a full sob, putting her head in her hands. I placed my arm around her. She fell into me like a small child might hug its mother after a fall. I let her cry. I felt her slight body shuddering against mine and held her as securely as I could.

My heart broke for Eliza.

And yet I could not shake a wave of anger. At her. Jerome too. How could they have been so irresponsible?

It was then a thought struck me.

Once her tears had abated, I asked, 'Have you told Jerome?'

She shook her head.

'You need to tell him.'

'I don't need to tell anyone.' She filled with venom almost instantly. 'I don't want it,' she enunciated very clearly.

I sighed. 'You still need to tell Jerome.'

She shook her head again.

'Is that why you broke up with him?'

'I don't want it. And I don't want him either. Not now. Not now he's done this to me.'

I wanted to point out that she'd been part of it too but it would have served no purpose but to antagonise Eliza.

She looked at me, properly for the first time since she'd come into my house. With a steely look she said, 'I need to get rid of it. I don't know how.'

Every instinct told me to try to persuade Eliza that she didn't really want to get rid of it. That she couldn't. But I fought with myself, knowing that Eliza didn't want my opinion she just wanted my help.

I took another deep breath. 'I don't know how either.' Another sigh. 'But I can help you look at your options? If you want me to?'

She nodded.

'But you do need to tell Jerome.'

'No.'

'At least think about it?'

She shrugged.

And I went to get my laptop.

I could hear Ada humming to herself from her bedroom while I sat in a patch of watery sunshine that came through the window of her spare room. No one had used the room for perhaps forty years or more, and up until recently Ada had kept it dusted and clean. It was like a museum. In the walnut wardrobe there were dresses that must have belonged to her mother and suits and a dress shirt that had been her father's or her husband's. Putting those old clothes, from another era in a bag for charity was almost harder than getting rid of Ezra's things.

It made sense to add the things Ada would no longer need to the items I was giving to charity. In fact, once she'd realised what I'd been doing she was all for throwing out everything she had. I didn't mind helping, however I was a little uncomfortable going through her belongings. I felt as though I was rifling through her entire life and family history. Yet it didn't seem to bother Ada. With the move to Riverview imminent she was eager to make progress.

Ada had told me she didn't want to keep anything in the spare room but when I discovered a thick bundle of letters tied with blue satin ribbon in the bottom of the dressing table I hesitated. They were postmarked from France. I lifted the bundle out to take a closer look. As I did so, a black and white photograph slipped out and floated to the floor.

My heart almost stopped when I saw the image – it looked just like Torin. I picked it up and stared hard at the picture trying to get my head around what I was seeing. The man had the darkest eyes, solid black like a sharks but not cold, instead full of hidden amusement. His mouth was nearly covered by a thick moustache but I could still see the hint of a familiar smirk. I turned the photograph over and read;

Samuel Redferne, Redferne House, June 1953

I smiled. Of course, Ada's lover had been a Redferne and I was pretty sure Ezra's grandfather had been called Samuel.

Tucking the photo back into the bundle of letters I went to find Ada in her bedroom. She looked up from the blouse she was folding on the bed. She was quite adept at using her both hands now, despite still having the cast on.

'I found these letters,' I said.

It seemed to take her a moment but then recognition washed over her face.

'They're from Samuel?' I asked.

'Yes.'

From the half smile and subtle blink of her eyes I caught a glimpse of the young woman in love she'd been.

'Do you want to keep them?'

'Oh yes, well, maybe I should.' Ada paused. 'You can keep them safe for me for now Grace.'

I hesitated as I'd expected to hand them to her. I'd thought she would want to squirrel them away to reread in a private moment.

'Sure,' I said. 'Just let me know when you want them?'

'Yes dear,' Ada said, already looking down at the blouse once more.

I took the letters back into the spare room and placed them inside a shoebox, stashing it well away from everything else so I could take it to the safety of my house later.

We'd cleared all the rooms upstairs by lunch time. My slight thrill at finding out that Ada had been in a tangle with the Redferne's had already gone and I felt a little glum.

Ada was still bubbly and bright and asked me to come outside into the lane to get some fresh air. Perhaps she'd timed it as such or maybe it was coincidence but Jerome was just coming under the bridge, his breath clouding in the air despite the sunshine. I wondered if Eliza had told him she was pregnant. But something in his demeanour suggested she hadn't.

'Tell her your idea,' Ada called to him.

I saw Jerome smile. Then he looked at me.

'Me and Ada was thinking you should have her bike,' Jerome said.

'What would I do with a bike?' I asked.

'Ride it?' Jerome said.

'I'm not really a bike person.'

'But Ada wants you to have it.'

'You could use it to do your shopping,' Ada chipped in.

I could see Jerome grinning.

'I don't know.'

Jerome's smile fell. 'Is it because of what happen to your husband?'

'No,' I said.

'Then have Ada's bike? Please? We could like go for a bike ride together or something?' Jerome said, knowing he'd played his hand well.

'Okay,' I said to Jerome. I turned to Ada, 'Thank you.'

'My pleasure.' She was grinning in a similar way to Jerome.

'Come on then,' Jerome said and pulled the tarp off Ada's bike. He wheeled it onto the lane and looked at me with grin.

'Now?' I asked.

'Now.' He nodded.

I took the handles from Jerome and lifted my leg over the cross bar. I'd not thought of Ada and me as being the same height but the seat was perfectly positioned.

'Cycle all the way up to Eliza's and back,' Jerome instructed.

So I did.

And it was good.

So good that when I got back to Ada's I told Jerome to get his bike and come with me, as I was going again; we raced up and down Redferne Lane until my legs ached in the best possible way. Ada stood in front of her house watching us come and go with a look of pride on her face like a mother watching her children master a new skill.

Eventually we took ourselves back inside Ada's house. Jerome got the fire going and the three of us set about sorting downstairs. Jerome went home after an hour or two after Ada reminded him he must not neglect his studies on her behalf. Ada and I continued to pack more and more of her belongings into boxes.

When you realise you're no longer going to be cooking for yourself and almost all of your needs will be catered for, it appears there's not so much stuff you require anymore.

Or so it seemed for Ada. She was content to consign the contents of her kitchen to charity, and the effects of her living room too, including the large china Shire Horses on the mantel piece.

I was scared she was giving up, letting go too quickly until she reminded me I was doing something very similar myself. And the release of things physical did not necessarily mean letting go of the emotional ties.

Well into the evening we finally seemed to have finished. We sat sipping sherry and smoking and Ada made me another gift. I'd been explaining that I was going to give away much of my furniture and start again. She understood why I needed to do this. I'd thought the conversation was over as Ada sat silent, smoking her cigarette with her usual regal poise. Then she suggested I have some of her furniture, whatever of it I wanted. As she talked explaining that all the furniture from the spare room had come from Redferne House before she was born, a myriad of thoughts tumbled through my head. My first reaction was to dismiss her offer; I was starting again not going around in circles. But when I understood that the spare room had been her parents' room, and the furniture had been their wedding gift from the Redferne's, I felt the tide turn in my reaction.

'Of course,' Ada continued in her nasal tones, 'I will not feel slighted if you want to buy yourself something new. But it's yours, any of this,' she said waving her arms about, 'if you want it.' She inhaled like smoking was still sexy then said, 'And I have a few items I want to give Jerome. He's such a good boy.'

I smiled, restraining the scoff that lurked in my throat. Of course, she was right though, essentially he was a good soul.

'It's going to be quiet without you here Ada,' I said. 'Whatever am I going to do with myself?'

'Well, for a start you can walk ten minutes down the road and come to see me,' she said, and flashed her eyes at me. 'I shall want proper company in that place. I'll not be content to socialise with all those decrepit folk. I'm sure they all have dementia and won't remember a thing I say.'

Hearing both the humour and the anxiety in what she said I felt my eyes prickle at her bravery to face her old age with honesty and courage.

'I'll be there Ada,' I said, although I knew I didn't need to. She knew I'd be there.

Ada gave me a smile. We took each other's hands; cool fingers entwined.

'Will you take me to the chip shop? I should like to treat you to a fish supper,' she said. 'I haven't been in such a while, and I should like to exercise my freedom while it's still mine.'

'I'll get our coats,' I said, and went out into the hallway, grateful for a moment to quell the tears and take a few deep breaths.

'And wine,' Ada said, when I came back into her living room with drier eyes. 'We should have a bottle of wine.'

April 2004

'Welcome to Redferne House,' Noah said and kissed my cheek. 'And Happy Birthday.'

'Thank you.' I smiled at Ezra's brother, trying to hide my surprise at how much older than Ezra he seemed. And so different; in manner, looks and tone.

'It's my pleasure, I'm so delighted to meet you at last. We've heard an awful lot about you.' He gave Ezra a playful slap on the back at this last comment.

Noah ushered Ezra and me through the front door, into the cool hallway. The light dropped as Noah closed the door on the bright spring day. It smelt of beeswax and old wood, almost musty. I'd known from what Ezra had told me that Redferne House was a grand old place but I was taken aback by its size and majesty. The hallway alone was bigger than my parents' sitting room.

It was my first visit to Redferne House; the first time I was meeting Ezra's brothers. I'd wanted to spend my birthday somewhere with just Ezra but he so wanted me to meet his brothers that I did not mind so much.

We went through to the kitchen and my heart stopped. Torin was leaning against a large dresser, smiling at me, his head tilted to one side.

'I've heard so much about you Grace, it's great to finally meet you,' Torin said, as though we'd never met. He came forward to kiss my cheek.

I tried to step away so he couldn't put his lips on my skin. But I failed and, with his hands holding the top of my shoulders, I felt the scratch of his beard on my cheek. He smelt exactly as I remembered and memories flooded my body.

'You're even prettier than he let on,' Torin said, stepping back, holding me at arm's length. He still wore my bracelet.

I couldn't meet his eyes. My heart raced. I felt sick. My mouth was dry.

'Put her down Torin,' Ezra said, with a laugh. 'You're embarrassing her.'

Torin released me. 'Drink, you'll want a drink, right? Vodka and tonic? You like that right?'

'Yes.' I mumbled. I remembered the day we'd drunk vodka one sunny afternoon overlooking Bristol docks. I remembered going back to his hotel room too.

'Have a seat,' Torin said, indicating the long wooden table in the centre of the room. I couldn't speak but sat down relieved that Ezra and Noah's conversation filled the air. I watched Torin making drinks. He'd cut his hair, gone was the long ponytail. But everything else about him was the same.

Torin placed the drinks on the table and as the three brothers talked I took a long steadying sip, trying to compose myself. I took another sip and found I'd finished my drink in minutes. I was unable to fathom how I had not worked out that Ezra's brother was same the Torin I had met a year before.

'Ezra, you must come and see some plans I've been drawing up for a new client,' Noah said, already getting up from the table.

Ezra looked at me, 'I won't be long.' He turned to Torin, 'Look after her for me?'

'Of course,' Torin said.

After Ezra and Noah's voices had receded the only sound in the room was the electrical hum of the fridge and the hammering of my heart.

'You look like you need another drink Gracie?' Torin said.

Before, I'd liked the way he said my name but now it felt too familiar, too intimate.

I looked at him properly as if I might realise it was not him after all. But there was no mistaking those dark eyes and those tattoos that spanned his arms and chest.

'It's alright,' he mouthed looking down at me.

I shook my head and looked away. It was not alright.

I had finally let myself fall in love with Ezra and now it was ruined.

Torin sat down next to me with fresh drinks for both of us.

'So I sense you weren't expecting to see me here?' he said.

I turned to him. 'Why would I expect you to be here?'

'I thought you might have worked it out.' He pushed his hair from his face. My bracelet moved an inch down his arm. I wanted to rip it off of him.

'Why would I have worked it out? You don't even sound the same.'

'True, but we look quite alike don't we?'

I hadn't noticed until he said, but it was true, they did look alike.

'We take after our mother,' Torin informed me. 'And our fathers are why we sound different. He grew up here. I grew up in Scotland.'

I wasn't in the mood for family history.

'You don't seem surprised to see me?' I said.

'He showed me a picture of you. You're the only thing he's talked about for months.' He sounded so indifferent.

'Does Ezra know?'

'I haven't said anything.' Torin said. 'I haven't told him.'

'And that's meant to make me feel better?' The situation felt so cruel. I had done nothing wrong and yet guilt flooded my veins.

'Well, yeah, I mean, it's no problem right? We met, we had a lovely time together, and that was that. He doesn't need to know. It would only break his heart.'

I shook my head.

'You can't tell him,' Torin said.

I squeezed my eyes shut.

'Gracie?' Torin said, and he touched my hand.

I stood up so fast I knocked the table and somehow manged to knock our glasses over. I watched as they hit the flagstones with a sickening smash. The tonic bubbled as it spread, darkening the stone.

'You alright?' Ezra said, coming into the room, concern on his face.

'Just being clumsy again,' I said and bent down to pick up the pieces. I cut my finger on a shard of glass.

'Oh Grace, what am going to do with you?' Ezra said, helping me to my feet. He held my finger, squeezing it to stop the flow of blood.

'I'll clear up,' Torin said, bending down too. 'It's my fault, anyway. You take her upstairs to get that sorted.'

I perched on the edge of a roll-top bath in the old-fashioned bathroom. The room was shabby and dusty, unused. While Ezra was searching for plasters I knew this was the moment I should tell him. But I couldn't.

Torin was a huge part of Ezra's life. If I told him I wouldn't only be risking what I had with Ezra, but I knew I might ruin Ezra's relationship with Torin. And for what? As Torin had said himself, we'd had a lovely time, and that was that. There were no complications and no residual feelings, at least not anymore. I could be any one of the masses of women I didn't doubt Torin had met over the years. And I didn't want to ruin things with Ezra. He was so perfect and when I was with him I felt a little of that perfection rubbed off on me, making me a better version of myself.

'Here,' Ezra said, holding a box of plasters, 'finally.'

I smiled at Ezra. Whatever had happened with Torin would be of no consequence. It was in the past.

'Are you alright now?' Ezra said, after he'd wrapped up my damaged finger. He was a good nurse, tender and caring.

'Yes,' I said. 'Thank you.'

'My pleasure.'

He'd knelt before me, to tend to my wound and now it was taken care of, he nestled forward between my knees. I rested my head against his chest, as he stroked my hair down my back. Ezra placed a kiss on my neck. A thin breeze slipped in the window and I shivered.

'You want to come and see my room?' Ezra asked.

He took me down a long landing to the door at the end. His bedroom was enormous and unlike any other bedroom I'd been in. He actually had a four poster bed, with heavy blue curtains tied at each post.

'This is your room?' I asked, smiling with delight.

He grinned. 'Uh, huh. Kind of over the top isn't it?'

I took in the three windows that looked out over the gardens at the front, the thick carpet and imposing ornate furniture. He sat on the edge of the bed and patted the space next to him. I took my place beside him enjoying the desire in his eyes. He leant over and kissed me, cupping my neck with his hand. His other hand rested on my thigh, his forefinger ran back and forth.

After a minute I pulled back not able to let this run to its conclusion as Torin leapt unbidden into my thoughts.

'You alright?' Ezra asked, his voice full of concern.

I nodded, 'I can't.'

'Why not?'

'Your brothers will hear.'

He smiled. 'You have seen how big this house is, haven't you? They won't hear a thing.'

'It just feels ... funny.'

'Okay,' he said, ever understanding and accommodating to my wishes and desires. 'Then let me show you around the rest of the house.'

In the following few hours I visited every inch of Redferne House and Ezra was right, they wouldn't have heard us making love. After I'd seen the house we drank vodka with Noah in the conservatory. I began to relax as Noah and Ezra made me laugh with their banter. Torin was nowhere to be seen, neither Noah nor Ezra seemed to know where he was and I did not see him again until dinner.

I hadn't known there were other guests coming; they were colleagues of Noah's and their wives. I felt underdressed in my plain grey dress compared to the others. The men wore shirts and ties, the women pretty slinky dresses and expensive looking jewellery. Noah appeared in a tweed jacket. I was irked that Ezra had not forewarned me we were expected to dress for a dinner party.

Ezra smiled and pulled out a seat for me at the table, 'Why don't you sit next to Torin?'

I glanced at Torin who winked and smiled back at me. I wanted to sit next to Ezra, in fact, I'd have been happier if it was just me and Ezra.

'Oh aye Gracie, come sit beside me. This lot are going to be talking buildings all night. We can talk about something far more interesting,' Torin said, and patted the chair next to him.

'Behave yourself,' Ezra said to Torin.

'When don't I?' Torin said.

'Well, the list is extensive brother dear,' Ezra said, before he turned to kiss my forehead. Then he moved to the other end of the table to sit beside a woman with slick black bobbed hair, large gold earrings and a pinched mouth like a full stop.

I glanced around the table. Everyone else was seated. There was nothing else I could do but sit next to Torin.

'Has he kissed it all better for you?' Torin asked with a slight leer and he touched my plaster bound finger with his fingertip.

I moved my hand from the table and put it in my lap. 'Please don't touch me.'

Torin sighed. 'Aye, alright.' He paused. 'I'm sorry.' He sighed again. 'Maybe you'd like a drink?'

'Thank you.'

Torin picked up the bottle of white wine from the middle of the table and filled my glass.

'Maybe I wanted red,' I said.

'You don't like red wine,' he said.

I flushed wishing I had said nothing.

Ezra helped Noah serve soup to all the guests. Torin and I ate in silence but I was so aware of his every move and the heat emanating from him, I found each spoonful a struggle. I gave up and left my spoon swimming in the green soup.

'Not hungry?' Torin asked.

I shook my head.

'Gracie?'

I raised my eyes to his.

'Please don't fret so,' he said, so no one else would hear.

'But don't you think this is just a little bit weird? A little awkward?' I whispered back.

He shrugged, 'Aye, maybe a little, but it doesn't need to be.'

Noah cleared the soup bowls, and I stood to help. When I returned to my seat I turned to the man on my other side and asked him whether he was planning a holiday this year. By the time the main course finished I knew the finer details of the man's holiday to Thailand he was taking the following month.

As Thailand Man turned to talk to the guest on his other side Torin gave me a soft smile and a small flash of his white teeth. I tried to see Torin as Ezra's brother and nothing other. But as we looked at each other for a long minute, I struggled to forget what Torin had meant to me.

'You know that's a terrible dress you're wearing right?' Torin said, in a tone that suggested he was complimenting me.

I sat up straight. 'I like this dress.'

'Aye I suppose you do,' he paused, narrowing his eyes at me, 'but does Ezra?'

I stuttered something unintelligible.

'I mean it's not exactly a turn on is it?'

'What?'

'A word of advice Gracie, a woman needs to make an effort to keep a man's attention.' He gestured down from shoulder to knee. 'That dress doesn't make a man think you're all that bothered.'

'But…'

'You know what Gracie?' he interrupted and then didn't wait for me to answer. 'You may have him eating out of the palm of your hand right now, but when he finally works out that you don't want him as much as he wants you he'll stray into the open legs of another woman.'

'You're drunk,' I said.

'Aye. But I'm right. And you know it.' Torin said, staring right at me.

I was about to unload a deluge of obscenity at Torin when Ezra leant over and placed a large cake with countless candles on to the table in front of me.

The room burst into birthday song, still Torin looked at me and I felt my cheeks flare with embarrassment and my heart raced with guilt.

'Make a wish,' Ezra said, against my ear once the song was over.

I took a deep breath and blew out the candles on the cake wishing that something vile would happen to Torin, something unpleasant and violent. Then I wished that everything with Ezra and me would be okay.

Thailand Man moved allowing Ezra to take his place.

'Happy Birthday,' Ezra said, and gave me a small blue velvet jewellery box.

A wave of panic flooded me. I was not ready for this. It was too soon. I felt all eyes in the room watching me as I opened the box. But it was not a ring, and I smiled looking at the pretty silver pendant with a blue stone. Relief flooded me.

'Thank you,' I said, looking at Ezra. A lock of hair had fallen over his forehead. He looked so happy, his eyes shining with delight.

Ezra leant forward to whisper in my ear, 'I love you.' He kissed my cheek.

'I love you too,' I said. It was the first time I'd told him and I looked at his face wanting to see his reaction.

The emotion in his face was all the gift I needed. I threw myself against him, wrapping my arms around his neck and I felt him hold me. There was a collective 'ah' and then clapping. I closed my eyes. I heard the chair behind me being pushed back and Torin's footsteps walking away.

DECEMBER 2014

Eliza was calm but quiet as we sat in the waiting room that was awash with a strange grey light from the opaque window. There was no one else there save the receptionist; a well-tended woman of advanced years that held a kindness in her knowing eyes. Not once had Eliza waivered in her decisions and after an initial examination and consultation last week we'd come yesterday for the first pills and then I'd accompanied Eliza here again today for the final medication.

After Eliza told me, we'd searched online and found a local private clinic. From then on Eliza made all the arrangements herself, sending me texts to let me know when she required me to escort her. Periodically I'd asked if she was okay and every time she'd replied she was fine as though I was a fool for asking.

I didn't want her to go through with it but only because if I'd been in her shoes I'd have wanted to keep the baby. Since Eliza's revelation, I'd spent a fair few hours wondering what it must feel like to have a new life growing inside of you. I could at once see how wonderful or terrible it might seem. For Eliza, it probably was the right choice and yet I felt such a heavy sadness at her decision.

Eliza still refused to tell anyone. There had been a few times when I'd been near telling Jerome myself. He said

Eliza avoided him at school. He told me that since they'd broken up, they had not spoken. When he talked of her now it was tainted with disdain, he hinted that she'd be a mistake and yet I knew he cared for her still. Josie said Eliza had become more and more aloof, absent unless Noah insisted upon her presence. I was concerned for her. I knew how isolation and desperation felt, so I tried not show my sadness at her choice and I'd stopped trying to convince Eliza that she should tell Jerome and Noah because, for whatever reason, she had at least chosen to confide in me.

The receptionist called Eliza's name, and we both stood. But Eliza shook her head at me and asked me to wait. After the door closed swallowing up Eliza, the receptionist offered me a cup of coffee and I accepted, grateful for something to distract me from my whirling thoughts.

I'd written twenty-six job applications and so far had been invited for only one interview. The position was for a mentor at Eliza and Jerome's school. I'd applied at a point of mild desperation, when I'd exhausted all other possibilities, not for a moment thinking I would hear anything of the application. I wasn't even sure what the job might entail, but I was excited at the idea of doing something different. And if it didn't work out, I could try something else.

Tomorrow, in preparation for the interview, I would get my hair cut; it had grown out to just below my ears and I hoped a clever stylist could turn it from shaggy chaos to something more presentable. I also told myself I would buy some new clothes, having gotten rid of half of my own clothes as well as Ezra's.

There was so much change in my life that if I thought about it for more than a second I felt my chest constrict. I was determined to continue without my little white pills and despite the flutters of anxiety I still experienced, all these changes I was making helped to ease the knot of worry. I'd relinquished more than sixty percent of my furniture. I'd cleaned and decorated most of my house, mine and Ezra's bedroom was now empty and I'd moved into the back room. Accepting the offer of the bedroom furniture from Ada plus the addition of a new mattress I had a room that was mine and I'd been enjoying waking up and looking out over the meadow, with only my few clothes hung in the wardrobe. And for the living room I'd purchased a daybed upholstered in teal corduroy fabric I suspected Ezra would have hated, but it rather delighted me.

I glanced at the clock on the wall of the clinic and wondered if I had time to go outside for a cigarette but the door opened and Eliza came out. Pale and drawn.

She didn't talk in the taxi all the way back to Redferne Lane. We'd already agreed that she would come back to my house, so after I paid the driver we stepped under the bridge onto Redferne Lane. I glanced at Ada's house and noted the 'For Sale' sign that had appeared in the front garden. I'd known it was imminent, but I hadn't expected it so soon. It was only yesterday that Ada had spent her first night at Riverview. She hadn't let me take her, she'd wanted to do it alone. After my hair appointment tomorrow, I would visit.

Eliza sat in my living room on the only chair I'd kept, because it had once belonged to my Grandmother. I made tea and put the TV on. Eliza sat starring at the screen, cradling the steaming mug between her hands. But she didn't take a sip and an hour later I eased the cold mug from her fingers but I left the TV on even though I was sure she wasn't watching it.

'I need to talk to Jerome,' Eliza said.

My heart thudded.

'I really need to do it now.'

I checked the time on my phone, 'I expect he'll be home from school any minute.'

I waited by the window watching for Jerome and as soon as I saw him coming up the lane I stepped out of the door.

'Jerome, Eliza is inside,' I said. 'She'd like to talk to you.'

'What's going on?' He said, with a frown.

'Just come and talk to her, yeah?'

I left Eliza and Jerome in my sparse living room and loitered on the front wall, smoking a cigarette. Within a minute I heard raised voices.

The front door opened.

Jerome came out, pale with rage. He let out a shout. Then kicked the wall.

Eliza stood in the doorway and said his name.

'Fuck off,' he shouted at her.

'Jerome,' I began.

'Get her away from me. I can't even fucking look at her,' he said, with a strangled voice.

'Maybe you should go back inside,' I said to Eliza. I turned back to Jerome; he was holding his head with both hands, pulling his hair.

'I can't believe she didn't tell me,' he said looking up. 'And you. You should have told me.'

'I couldn't tell you. Eliza didn't want me to. I'm sorry.'

'Whatever.' He stepped back, grinding his bottom jaw against his top. He took another step back, glanced at my house and gritted his teeth. One more step back, he shook his head before he turned and started down Redferne Lane.

'Jerome?' I called.

He waved his hand as if to dismiss me, pulled his hood up and rounded his shoulders against the world. There was nothing I could do but let him go.

Back inside I found Eliza pulling her shoes on.

'I want to go home,' she mumbled through her tears.

As soon as we reached the house she went inside and upstairs. I could hear Josie was in the kitchen with the boys and went in with every intention of telling Josie what was going on. Yet as soon as I saw her rounded belly I knew I couldn't.

'Grace, what a lovely surprise, how are you?' Josie asked, coming over and placing a warm kiss on my cheek.

'I'm fine but I've just brought Eliza home, she doesn't seem very well. She went straight up to her room.' I said. My cheeks redden at concealing the truth from Josie.

'Oh dear, what's the matter?' she asked, only half her attention on the subject as she returned to slicing the rustic loaf on the breadboard.

'Women's troubles I think,' I mumbled, uncomfortable at not only the lie itself but the turn of phrase too. It was something my mother would say.

But Josie didn't seem to notice and made sounds of understanding.

Feeling as though I should have done more for Eliza I left knowing that at least she had Josie and Noah on hand if she really needed help.

As I neared the cottages at the bottom of Redferne Lane I was intensely relieved when I saw Jerome perched on the wall outside Ada's house. He was smoking and I could smell the skunk weed from more than twenty paces away.

'Alright?' I asked, when I reached him.

'Not really,' he said, as I took up the space beside him.

It was a clear cold evening, and the moon was a lazy crescent in the sky tipped up like an exaggerated smile.

'You want a drag?' Jerome asked, offering me his joint.

I thanked him and took it from his fingers. I inhaled a hot lungful and remembered why I'd stopped getting stoned years back. But I still took another drag before I gave it back to Jerome.

'Is she alright?' He asked after he'd inhaled the rest of the joint and dropped the end on the tarmac of Redferne Lane.

'She'll be okay.'

He nodded.

'I am sorry I didn't tell you Jerome. It just wasn't my place.' I tried to catch his eye as I spoke.

He looked away from me toward the bridge. 'It's alright, I don't blame you.'

'She was scared. I wanted to help her.'

'She should have told me. I'd have helped her.'

'I know.'

'Now I just hate her.'

As I watched him roll another joint I wished I knew of something I could say that would make him feel better, something that wasn't just some platitude. But there were no words. So we sat on Ada's wall in silent companionship and smoked while the moon traversed the sky. Then with a few words we bid each other goodnight and slipped inside our own front doors.

I walked towards Redferne Lane and despite the rain I still smiled from my visit with Ada. I'd been to her new house, as she liked me to call it, three times now and with each visit I was more and more sure she was okay. The first time I'd gone she'd seemed a little overwhelmed, disorientated even, and I'd kept my time there short, partly because I didn't think she seemed to be enjoying my company but also because I'd found the care home a challenging place to be. Unlike when we'd visited, the communal area was overrun with elderly folk barely holding on to their sanity or the contents of their bowels and it freaked me out.

When I'd returned to visit Ada for a second time the communal area was again quite full but this time Ada and I went out into the garden and I was pleased to see she wasn't using the wheelchair at all but shuffling along with just a stick. She'd begun daily physio with a charming young man (her words) that manipulated her hips. She'd giggled relaying that anecdote, and I was relieved to see the Ada I knew emerging once more.

I'd gone to see her again this afternoon straight after my job interview. I stayed for tea and played bingo with her and a table full of ladies most of whose names I'd forgotten the instant Ada introduced me. All of them seemed perky, jolly and of sound mind but Ada seemed to have a made a particular bond with a woman called Maudie. Maudie appeared an opposite to Ada in every way save her dirty sense of humour. Where Ada was petite Maudie was voluptuous, where Ada was diplomatic Maudie was blunt and at nearly six feet tall Maudie towered over Ada's five foot one and a bit. But those differences did not stop the two of them giggling like drunken teenagers. Maudie swore like a sailor and although I'd never heard Ada curse she seemed to find it utterly hilarious that Maudie was swearing every other word as she told us tales of her wild youth.

When I left Riverview, I picked up a bottle of wine, feeling like I might celebrate the day with a glass or two. Aside from my jolly visit with Ada, the interview had gone well. As well as I could have hoped. They would let me know on Monday. But I was quietly confident; a novel sensation. For a start there had been no other candidates, and I'd got on well with the Principle and the teaching staff I'd met.

I walked under the bridge onto Redferne Lane still grinning to myself, despite the fine drizzle dampening my face

My smile slipped when I saw Eliza running down the lane towards me, telling me to come quick. Josie was in labour. The baby wasn't due for another three weeks; he was supposed to be a Christmas baby.

I followed Eliza up Redferne Lane and she explained they couldn't get hold of Noah. Josie's parents were in York and Torin was on his way back to Redferne Lane but still more than an hour away.

We swept through the garden of Redferne House and the wet plants soaked my tights as I passed by and into the house. Josie was gripping the table in the hallway with both hands, groaning low in her chest and rocking her hips side to side. Her groan intensified, and she blew sharp breaths out of pursed lips.

I went to Josie and waited for the groaning to decrease before I spoke.

'Josie, what do you want me to do?' I would have liked to march in and take control of the situation but I had no idea what Josie needed or wanted.

'Oh Grace, I'm so glad you're here,' she said and reached her hand out to take mine. 'I can't find Noah. He's not at the office and he's not answering his phone. He should be home by now.'

I squeezed her hand. 'Don't worry.'

'I need to get to hospital,' she said and groaned again. Her grip on my hand intensified.

Eliza was still by the door, looking uneasy as she watched Josie.

'Where are the boys?' I asked her.

'Watching TV,' Eliza mumbled.

'Why don't you go and sit with them?'

She nodded and scooted past Josie and me.

The contraction appeared to subside and Josie began talking again. 'Can you call an ambulance? I need to get to the hospital.'

Noah burst in looking flustered. He took in the situation in an instant and was immediately beside Josie, rubbing her back. Josie started grilling him on his whereabouts until another contraction began and she swapped her words for low moaning.

Within minutes they had left the house, heading for the hospital, asking me to stay and look after the boys and Eliza.

A momentary flash of panic clutched my chest and for a moment I knew I needed a little white pill. Then I pulled a smile onto my face and reminded myself I wasn't doing that anymore. And I was only looking after two small boys and a teenager – no big deal.

The three of them were in the living room with the TV on. The boys were cuddled up together on the sofa watching Thomas the Tank Engine, and Eliza was as far away from them as possible on an uncomfortable looking upright chair gazing down at her phone.

'Auntie Grace, Auntie Grace,' Godfrey sang, when he saw me. He stood on the sofa and jumped up and down.

I went over to them and Barty took my hand and wordlessly pulled me to sit down. Godfrey climbed onto my lap. He smelt a little bit like a pet shop, sort of musty and hay like. It wasn't unpleasant but a little surprising. Barty fiddled with the seam of my dress, running his fingertips back and forth. It tickled a little, but I quite enjoyed the attention. As the little boys watched the TV, I looked over to Eliza wondering how I might connect with her.

I hadn't seen her since the abortion. I'd come to the house the day afterwards, to check she was okay, but she was in bed ill, according to Noah and I couldn't really insist on seeing her without raising suspicion. I'd texted her and received a reply informing me that she was fine.

Looking at her now she didn't look any different but I doubted she was unaffected by the experience. Yet I struggled to think of anything I could say, especially in front of the boys. After a time, she got up and started toward the door. I scooped Godfrey up and placed him on the sofa, telling the boys I'd be back in a moment.

'You alright?' I asked Eliza as she reached the door.

'Yeah.'

'You did really well, coming to get me,' I said.

'Josie told me to.' She shrugged.

I smiled. 'You'll have another little brother by tomorrow.' I realised straight away it was the wrong thing to say, and I felt stupid.

'Great,' she said, with distaste. She looked at me like the idiot I was.

I wanted to say something wise, but I doubted wisdom would ever be my forte.

'I'm glad I got rid of it,' Eliza said. 'I don't ever want to go through that.'

'I'm sure that when you're ready, the pain is worth it.'

Eliza shook her head. 'I'm never having kids.' She narrowed her eyes, daring me to contradict her, but I wasn't going to.

I let her leave the room without trying to stop her with anymore stupid words.

I snuggled back in between Godfrey and Barty. As the theme tune to Thomas the Tank Engine played, and the titles rolled I announced it was time for bed. I had a feeling it was well past their bedtime.

'You're going to have to tell me what to do as I've never put anyone to bed before,' I told them.

'We always have a story,' Barty told me.

'Well, I can read a story,' I said, giving him a smile.

'Piggy back!' Godfrey shouted, jumping off the sofa and running in circles on the rug.

I gave them both a piggyback upstairs and into the bathroom and they giggled all the way. We brushed teeth and washed faces and the giggling continued. Barty took himself to the toilet and Godfrey announced that he needed his bed pants. I had no idea what he was talking about until Barty explained that he wore nappy type pants at bedtime so he didn't wet the bed. After a little searching in the voluminous cupboard in the bathroom we located a packet of these pants and Godfrey pulled them on.

One whole wall in the boy's bedroom was decorated with an enormous picture of Thomas the Tank Engine. We sat on an oversized beanbag in the corner of their room and read a story about a train which both of the boys seemed to know by heart and joined in with all the sound effects. We read three more stories and then, it seemed I might expect the boys to get into bed. I turned on a moon nightlight that cast their bedroom in a soft golden glow and tucked each boy in under their little duvets decorated with trains.

'Night night, Auntie Grace,' Barty said.

'Night night,' I whispered.

'I love you,' Godfrey said.

I felt tears in my eyes and had to swallow them back before I could answer, 'I love you too.'

I stood at the end of their beds just looking for a while and wondering at the beauty of them.

Something made me look to the door, and I saw Torin leaning against the frame. He gave me a silent wave. I wanted to smile, but I wasn't sure if we were on smiling terms. Godfrey turned in his bed, making me look back toward the children but they both seemed settled. Holding my breath, I slipped out of their bedroom.

Torin and I faced each other for a moment on the shadowy landing. There were a million things we might have said to one another. But I just said, in a whisper, 'So now you're here, I'll get going.' And I didn't wait for him to reply before I walked down the landing to the stairs.

Torin followed me downstairs and to the hallway.

'Stay for a drink?' he said, as I pulled my damp shoes on.

I looked up. 'You think that's such a good idea?'

Torin shrugged, 'I don't know.' He gave a brief smile. 'But I would like it, if you'd stay for a bit.'

My heart leapt at the olive branch he was extending. I slipped my shoes back off and followed him into the kitchen.

We didn't talk as Torin opened a bottle of white wine. I watched his assured movements, letting myself drink in every inch of him, from his sock covered feet to the fall of an unruly curl on his forehead, from the thick silver ring he wore on his left thumb to the tail of his belt that had escaped the loop of his trousers.

He handed me a glass, catching my eye and giving me a wary smile.

'Shall we?' he said, indicating that we might go through to the living room.

The yellow sofa cushions still held the impression of Godfrey, Barty and me until Torin and I sat down. After a moments silence we began talking about Josie and the imminent arrival. Torin said he'd had a text from Noah half an hour earlier saying all was well, but labour had slowed a little. Torin told me he'd just returned from a couple of days back at his house in Scotland. There'd been snow on the hills. I hadn't even known he'd gone home, and I resented the fact. I didn't care to know about the snow.

'Would you like another?' Torin asked, looking at my empty glass.

'I should go.'

'Really? Can't you stay for another?'

I could feel a rising frustration. 'Why? Why would I stay?'

'So I can see you?'

I shook my head and stood up. I may even have done a little eye rolling. 'Oh, so you want to see me now?'

Torin stood up too. 'Gracie, I'm sorry. Of course I want to see you.'

'You haven't spoken to me for weeks.'

He tried to take my hand, but I pulled it away. 'I'm really sorry. It was all just doing my head in.'

'You've been doing my head in since I met you.' I folded my arms across my chest.

He huffed out a smile. I couldn't help but return a small smile. I'd never been able to stay angry with Torin for long.

'You're looking well Gracie,' he said.

'Thank you.' I felt self-conscious and tucked my newly styled hair behind my ear as though I could somehow hide behind the gesture.

Torin poured more wine in my glass, picked it up and held it toward me.

I hesitated before I took the glass. We perched on the edge of the sofa as though ready to get back on our feet at any moment, should the need arise.

'I really am sorry, you know,' Torin said, still staring ahead.

'Me too,' I admitted. 'I was being an idiot.'

'You were a little out of control,' Torin said, casting a sideways glance at me. 'I don't like seeing you like that.'

I rolled my eyes, giving him a faint smile. 'I didn't realise the state I was in until you came back. But I'm sorting myself out. I'm not taking those pills anymore.'

'Good.' Torin rubbed his hands back and forth over his hair. 'If it makes you feel any better that whole first year after Ezra died I was pretty messy. I mostly lived off a diet of cocaine and whiskey.' He shook his head. 'If I'm honest I was already well on the road to being a fuck up long before Ezra died. It's taken me all this time to get myself together.' He swallowed. 'This thing Gracie, you and me, it's been really hard over the years,' Torin said, with a heavy sigh. 'And I knew I couldn't see you when I was such a mess. But when I finally felt like I was together enough to see you I found you were a state and I hate it, I hate seeing you so messed up.' He looked at me. 'I'm tired Gracie, I'm so tired of this thing between us tearing me apart. I don't want to get hurt anymore.'

Watching the anguish on his face, I took a few steadying breaths and swallowed the lump in my throat. 'I don't mean to hurt you Torin.'

'But you do.' I felt stung by the undertone of venom in his voice.

I frowned. 'You hurt me too.'

'I know. I meant to.' Torin said, then he shrugged. 'You chose Ezra. Every time.'

'That's not fair Torin, you never gave me a choice. You made me choose him.'

'I did not. I never wanted you to be his,' Torin said, looking away toward the fireplace again.

'But you never wanted me to be yours either,' I whispered. 'You still don't.'

Torin turned back. 'I always wanted you to be mine.'

'But you left. You always leave. When Ezra had only just died you left.'

'I couldn't stay. I felt so guilty. So many times I'd wished he'd just leave you and then he died and it was like, it was my fault. I know it wasn't but I just couldn't stop thinking about all the times I'd wished he was gone so you could be mine,' his voice quivered.

'You never said…'

'How could I?'

'But even before I met Ezra, you left. Without even saying goodbye. Have you any idea what that was like?'

'Ah Gracie, I'm sorry. I really am sorry. I've regretted it ever since. But what was I meant to do? You were so young.' He reached his hand toward mine.

'I wasn't that young.' I kept my hands to myself.

'Come on, you were only nineteen. I was past thirty. I felt like a dirty old man. And I wasn't even going to be in the country. I thought you'd go and shag some college boys and forget about me.'

'But I loved you and I thought you loved me,' the words were out of my mouth before I could stop them.

He gave me a half smile. 'I did. I do. I always have.' His eyes shone with restrained emotion.

'I didn't want anyone else.' I said softly, 'I didn't even want Ezra to begin with. I wanted you. I've always wanted you.'

'Then why the fuck did you marry him?'

'Because you told me too.'

He blinked really, really slowly. 'You didn't have to say yes.' He said, so quietly I almost didn't hear.

'You broke my heart Torin. Ezra mended it.' I was angry that what I felt for Torin had always, always, been in conflict with what I felt for Ezra. And Torin never acknowledged that. 'He made my life mean something. He was so easy to be with. He took control of everything and I liked that. He made me feel loved. He made me feel safe. He made me feel like the most important person in the world. And I loved him.'

'Aye, I fucking know,' Torin said, as though I was forcing him to look at something unsightly.

Torin made to say something more but his phone pinged and then a second later, my phone vibrated.

Anthony Ezra Redferne, born at 9.43pm. Mother and son are both doing well. Noah x

We looked at each other and grinned, the tension from our conversation suddenly gone.

'Another little Redferne.'

'Aye, another little Redferne,' Torin said, raising his glass.

We drank a toast to our new nephew.

Eliza appeared at the doorway.

'What's going on?' she asked.

'Your brother was born an hour ago,' Torin announced with a smile in his voice.

'Whoopy-fucking-do,' she drawled.

'Eliza,' Torin admonished.

'What?'

'A new life is a miraculous thing.'

'No, it's just another burden on our already over populated planet,' she said, then turned with a flick of her hair.

Torin gave me a wide eyed look as we heard her walk back up the stairs.

'She gets worse by the day,' Torin said.

'Don't be too hard on her,' I said.

'Ah come on, that was well out of order, imagine if she says something like that to Noah or Josie?'

'Torin, I think there's something you should know,' I said, then I told him about the abortion.

We talked about Eliza for a while and then I put my empty glass on the table and stood up to leave.

'You're going?' Torin asked, and it sounded like disappointment in his voice.

'Yes,' I said. 'It's been a long day.'

I was pleased that Torin and I were talking again and glad we'd spoken some truths but I didn't know where that left us. I wasn't sure what I wanted from Torin.

I could feel Torin's eyes on me as I pulled on my shoes and coat, both still damp from earlier. At the door we faced each other. Then Torin suddenly pulled me into a hug, his arms wrapping around me, holding me tight against him.

The feel of him, the way he smelt and security of his embrace was almost overwhelming.

'It's so good to see you Gracie,' he said, into my hair. 'I've missed you.'

'I've missed you too,' I said. But then I pulled myself out of his arms and opened the door to leave.

The morning broke damp and windy, quite different from two years previously. It was not white and cold, no heavy silence of hoarfrost covered the lands. Winter was not pretty today. It had stopped raining but the icy temperature remained and the wind grabbed at me with violent hands.

I cycled down the lane and under the bridge. My hands were cold on the handle bars despite my gloves, but the wind against my face made me feel alive. I went through the town and out the other side to the cemetery, buffeted by side swipes from the wind that made the bike wobble.

I hadn't been for well over year and before that not since the funeral. Despite my absence I knew exactly where he was. I turned into the cemetery, got off Ada's bike and leant it against the notice board at the entrance. A pathway of greying tarmac lay in between rows and rows of headstones, manicured grass between each plot. The air was thick with fresh grief. The inscriptions on the headstones highly legible and bold in gold lettering. I couldn't help but look at them; scan the names and dates.

There were fresh flowers laid on the grave of a man twenty years dead. Would I still mourn Ezra twenty years from now? I could not imagine ever forgetting him but I had realised I did want to live. I wanted to move on.

I could not avoid the children's graves; Ezra was not far from those small plots. The air tinkled with the wind chimes hung from the willow tree that shaded those tiny resting places. Rainbow windmills spun too fast in the wind and cellophane wrapped teddy bears rested against the headstones. I was grateful that one of those graves was not my destination.

I walked around a bed of barren rose bushes, naked but for their thorns and there was Ezra's grave. There had been no headstone when I came last, just a thick wooden cross bearing a brass plate with a name and dates. Now the cross had been replaced with a pale grey slab with burgundy script:

Ezra Samuel Redferne
6th October 1983
6th December 2013
Resting Where No Shadows Fall

I hadn't chosen his headstone. I hadn't played any part in the funeral arrangements. If Mum had not physically put me into a black dress, and Dad had not pushed me into the back of their car, I doubt I'd have been at the funeral at all.

I'd watched as his banana leaf coffin was lowered into the frozen ground, knowing that Ezra, the man I'd thought I would spend the rest of my life with was inside.

Noah and Josie hosted the gathering at Redferne House afterwards. I had not eaten for days then drank a vast amount of whisky in a very short space of time. I vomited the whiskey back up over the cream rug in the living room. Mum and Dad took me back to my house. Mum put me to bed like I was a sick child.

Later that evening Torin came to the house. He sat on the edge of my bed and stroked my long hair like I was a kitten. I knew as he kissed my forehead he was leaving. I asked him not to go. Not yet. Not so soon. But it made no difference. I threw the glass jug, from beside the bed, at the door after he'd left and screamed obscenities after him. Then I just screamed. Even after Mum came up and held me like she hadn't since I was a little girl, I screamed. I only stopped when Dad came up and put a shot of something into my arm. Then he wrote out the first prescription for my little white pills.

I knelt on the damp grass in front of the headstone and traced Ezra's name with my fingertip. From my pocket I pulled out his wedding ring. Pushing my finger into the grass I forced a hole in the soil beneath. I kissed the ring and dropped it into the hole. Then I wriggled the wedding ring from my left hand and slipped that into the hole too. And finally I eased my engagement ring off. I rubbed the stone with my thumb and then placed it with the other rings. I squashed the mud filling the hole and brushed the grass with my hand. I could hardly see where I'd disturbed the earth.

Climbing back on Ada's old bike I left the cemetery with mud beneath my fingernail and a sense of relief. I cycled back through town, stopping at the toy shop and the florist before I rode all the way up Redferne Lane to meet the newest member of my family.

Eliza opened the door to Redferne House. Barty and Godfrey were rolling around wrestling in the hallway behind her.

'Alright?' I asked.

She shrugged and told me everyone was in the living room, all the while inching past me. She was wearing a tight top, skinny jeans and heavy eyeliner.

'Going somewhere nice?' I asked as she pulled on her coat.

'Anywhere but here,' she said, with a near snarl.

She went off down the garden path, her pretty fair hair flowing behind her, leaving me to shut the front door. I wished I knew some words I could say to her that didn't just piss her off. But I was well aware that I was witness to something she'd rather forget.

I took out the two new wooden engines I'd purchased from the toy shop, to go with the wooden train track the boys played with all the time. The boys stopped wrestling and squeaked with pleasure as I knelt down on the Persian rug in the hallway and helped them extract their new engines from the wrapping. Godfrey kissed my cheek then pulled Barty to the stairs so they could try out the trains on the track upstairs.

In the living room, Josie was laid on the sofa with Noah perched near her feet. She looked tired but happy and welcomed me with a broad smile and cooed at the flowers I gave her. I kissed her cheek and congratulated her, and Noah too. Then I looked around for the new arrival and saw Torin ensconced in a brocade armchair, holding the baby.

'Gracie,' he said and made my name sound beautiful with his rich warm voice. He stood and came towards me.

'This is Anthony,' he said. 'Anthony, this is Auntie Grace.'

I sat down on the primrose yellow chaise behind me before Torin put the baby into my arms. Torin's fingers brushed against my arm and I felt a tingle dance up my spine.

I looked down at baby Anthony. He wore a little white bonnet and was swaddled in a fine white crochet blanket. His face was red and puffy, his eyes closed and tiny white spots littered the bridge of his nose. He looked just as Godfrey had when I'd held him in the first days of his life. Soon this boy would be out there with his brothers wrestling and playing trains. I was struck by how much Godfrey had changed since he was born and since Ezra had gone; so much had changed in two years and yet also so little.

When I glanced up from the child again I found Josie, Noah and Torin watching me. And I knew they were thinking of Ezra too. I have missed Ezra so many times since he died and in that moment I felt his loss too. But it felt different because for the first time I was feeling how much Torin and Noah and maybe even Josie missed Ezra. There was a huge Ezra shaped whole in the room. How he would have loved to see his nephew. He'd loved babies. Somehow knowing how much everyone in that room missed Ezra, made it easier for me to miss him a little less.

'He's beautiful,' I said, to Josie and Noah.

'Thank you,' Josie said, glowing with joy. 'You know, while he's comfy in your arms, I think I'll just pop to see how the boys are getting on upstairs. I don't want them to feel left out.'

She shuffled slowly from the room, giving me a smile as she exited.

The phone rang and Noah stepped out to answer it.

As soon as the door was closed the baby started to grizzle. I stood and bounced gently in the hope that the baby wouldn't cry. Torin got up and walked across the room.

We held each other's gaze for a moment. A few fireworks went off in my chest. I think I saw some going off right beside Torin's heart too.

The baby made a noise and wriggled in my arms. Both Torin and I looked down at him.

'You look just right holding the wee boy,' Torin said.

Torin moved behind me, his body almost touching mine. He reached his arm around me and held it over the baby's head; his palm covered Anthony's scalp, his fingers overlapped on to my arm.

'So tiny, isn't he?' I could feel Torin's breath on my neck as he spoke in soft tones, his ring finger caressed my arm, rubbing back and forth.

'Yes. And perfect.'

'Aye, perfect.'

We watched the baby screw up his face; a precursor to a loud wail.

I rocked the baby in my arms and he seemed to swallow his cry. Torin stroked the baby's head. He stepped a little closer so his body was flush with mine; his front to my back. I longed to fall against him, to rest my head against his shoulder, to let his hands roam over me.

Noah and Josie came back into the room at the same time. Torin quickly moved away from me and I felt myself blushing as though I'd been caught misbehaving. When Anthony began to grizzle again, I handed him back to Josie on the sofa. She unbuttoned her top and eased her swollen breast free with her hand. I watched as the baby latched on to Josie's nipple and I couldn't help but wonder if I would ever experience that for myself.

'There's a little toy giraffe in the hall for him,' I said. 'Although I'm sure you don't need any more toys cluttering the house.'

Josie looked up. 'Thank you Grace. And for looking after the boys last night. They've talked of little else since I got home.'

I smiled, pleased with Josie's comment. 'There's a little something for Eliza too, when she gets back.'

'She's gone out?' Noah said.

'She left as I came in.'

'For God's sake,' Noah muttered.

'Well I'll leave you to it,' I said, more to Josie than Noah.

'Come again soon Grace?' she said. 'I'd love to see you.'

I nodded, knowing I would come back soon; I did not want to miss out on seeing Anthony grow.

Torin followed me out into hallway. He asked me to wait, said he had something for me and disappeared for a moment while I put my shoes on. He returned and offered an envelope towards me.

Inside was a card with a picture of a buff, half naked man holding a lily, standing in front of a rainbow. His jeans were undone and in his other hand he was proudly holding his erect penis. I glanced up at Torin. He was smirking at me.

I opened the card and read the messy looped scrawl,

Dearest Gracie,

Maybe this will give you something else to think about today?

Love always,
Torin x

I looked back at the picture on the front and smiled. It was the best sympathy card I'd ever received.

'Thank you,' I said. 'I think.'

He laughed. It was a sound I hadn't realised I'd missed hearing. 'Aye it's a good one right?'

'Well, it's certainly different.'

He chuckled again then sighed into seriousness. 'I wanted to get you a card, you know?' He paused. 'To let you know I care. To let you know I miss him too. All those sympathy cards are proper shite with the flowers and whatever and I just wanted to make you smile. You have such a lovely smile Gracie.'

I didn't want to look at Torin right then because I knew those fireworks would start going off in my chest again, so I spoke to the floor. 'Actually, I have something for you too.' I reached my hand into my pocket and retrieved the leather bracelet with tiny silver beads that I'd tied to the front door key Torin had returned.

'I'd like you to have these back,' I said, and placed them in his hand. 'You are always welcome at my house.'

I watched him finger the bracelet and then the door key. He seemed lost for words.

I leant forward, placed a kiss on his cheek and whispered goodbye.

I heard Torin clear his throat before he put the key in the lock and came into my house. He looked freshly laundered and I could see a few damp curls still clinging to his neck as though he hadn't had time to dry off properly. He hesitated before he came into the living room his eyes flicking around the room, noting the changes.

'You've been busy,' he said, still looking around at the new decor of the room.

'It was time for some changes.'

'It looks nice Gracie. I had no idea you could do tidy.'

I smiled. 'Neither did I.'

'I hope you don't mind me coming by?' Torin said.

'Of course not,' I said, moving the sketch book off of the daybed beside me so Torin could sit down.

'I heard you got the job. I wanted to give you these,' Torin said and produced a petite bunch of white freesias wrapped in brown paper, from behind his back. He put the flowers into my hand. 'Congratulations.'

'They're so pretty Torin, thank you,' I said and lowered my face to the flowers. I closed my eyes and inhaled the delightful scent.

Then I put the flowers on the windowsill.

'They like being in water,' Torin remarked.

I hesitated before I said, 'I don't have any vases.'

He gave a small laugh, 'Of course you don't Gracie.'

I shrugged, 'One thing at a time right?'

'Of course. So tell me about this job?' he said, and sat beside me.

I explained that I'd be working at Jerome and Eliza's school, with kids their age; young people that needed a bit of support. Senior management at the school were starting a new initiative. They were going to send me on some training in the New Year. I was looking forward to doing something new. Something that felt worthy.

As I talked Torin listened with a smile, his head inclined as though everything I said was fascinating.

'Sounds good Gracie,' he said. He reached out to rub my arm and I noticed the bracelet with the little silver beads around his wrist. 'I'm really pleased for you. And I'm proud of you too.'

I grinned at my new shoes, not quite able to look at Torin and receive his praise at the same time.

'I like this,' he said, tugging the sleeve of my new dress. 'And this,' he said, and tucked a strand of my newly coifed hair behind my ear. 'And these,' he said and tapped the toe of my shoes with the toe of his trainer.

Words got lost on their way from my brain to my mouth and all I managed was to look at Torin. A little bit rabbit and headlights.

He took hold of my fingers and ran his thumb over my knuckles. He discovered the bare skin where my rings had been for three and a half years.

'You've taken them off?' he said, lifting my left hand.

'It was time.'

Torin nodded as he threaded his fingers through mine. He squeezed my hand. I squeezed back. I was sure he sensed my heart pick up pace, heard the desire in the small gasp of my breath and saw the flush in my cheeks.

He gave me a gentle smile.

We hesitated.

A soft touch of his lips against mine.

I reached my free hand up to his neck, my fingers toyed with his hair. With a happy moan in the back of his throat he slipped his arm around my waist as we kissed. Torin ran his hands down my back, then skimmed the length of me, from the hem of my dress, up to my shoulders and neck. Torin gently pressed me to lie down on the daybed. He snuck his leg between my knees and I pressed against his thigh. His hand wandered beneath the hem of my dress. I couldn't stop the little groan of pleasure I made.

Torin paused and raised himself on his elbows. 'Is this really what you want?'

'Yes.'

'But you know I'm leaving after Christmas?'

I nodded.

'What happens then Gracie?'

'I don't know,' I said, pulling him down to kiss me again.

December 2003

My feet ached from working all day in the cafe. I wanted to get home, eat junk food and zone out in front of some trashy TV. After saying goodbye to my boss, I stepped into the dark evening, zipping up my coat against the ferocious wind. A movement across the street caught my eye. Ezra, my next-door neighbour walked towards me, smiling and waving. He talked while we were still yards from each other. The wind stole his words and threw them far from my ears.

Face-to-face Ezra placed a quick kiss on my cheek. He stepped back and looked down at me, a half smile on his face.

I should have said something, but I was surprised to see him and even more surprised by the kiss on the cheek.

'So?' he asked, his face looking a touch anxious.

'I'm sorry, I didn't hear what you said.' I shivered as the wind whipped around us and seemed to find its way under my coat. 'Tell me again?'

He sighed. 'It was a whole speech. I've been practising it in my head for hours.'

'Have another go?' I suggested, pulling up my hood against the rain. A gust of wind made me take a step to the side.

'I'm not sure if I can.'

'Go on.'

He hesitated. 'Do you want to go for a drink?' he said, in a rush so the words blended.

'Oh, uh, I'm kind of tired from work,' I said.

He looked so dejected.

'But, yes, that would be great,' I conceded, not wishing to upset Ezra.

He laughed. 'Great, come on then.' And he took hold of my hand.

In the three the months I'd known Ezra he had never once kissed my cheek or held my hand. In fact, apart from the moment we met and shook hands he had never touched me. He'd never met me from work either.

Ezra didn't let go of my hand as he pulled me along the pavement at quite a pace, the wind blowing rain into our faces making conversation impossible. He glanced back at me and squeezed my hand with his warm fingers. Again I was surprised, this time by the light and fluffy feeling in my chest.

'In here,' Ezra said and pulled me into the doorway of a pub.

We paused in the porch glad of the respite from the weather. I looked up at Ezra. He lifted his hand and wiped raindrops from my cheeks with his fingertips. He let his fingers linger on my cheek as he gazed down at me, his eyes hazy with something that might have been desire.

'Are you alright?' I smiled and frowned at this version of Ezra I hadn't come across before.

'Fine,' he said, unable to contain his grin. 'Although I might be a little drunk.'

He pushed open the door to the pub, and we were greeted with warm air; rich with damp people, stale alcohol and cigarette smoke. Pints of cider in hand, we found a small settle near the back of the pub that faced a window overlooking the carpark. Popular Christmas songs played, and the nicotine stained ceilings were hung with thick tinsel.

After a few swigs of my pint I made a cigarette and enjoyed sitting down. As I listened to Ezra talk about some building he'd been to see with his brother I slipped off my damp shoes, flexing my cold toes.

Ezra was always talkative but today he barely took a breath and there was something twitchy about him. He was a fraction dishevelled too; the top two buttons of his shirt were done up wrong and his hair was all over the place.

'What's going on with you today Ezra?' I asked, as I neared the bottom of my pint.

We sat bathed in the twinkling of fairy lights and it gave Ezra a warm glow. 'I've been with my brother,' he began as though this made everything clear.

'Right.'

'And he gave me some advice.' Ezra turned his body toward me and his leg rested against mine.

I smiled, intrigued by the notion that Ezra was flirting with me. 'I hope it was good advice.'

'So do I,' Ezra said.

We looked at each other. As though someone had shown me the answer to a tricky algebra equation I understood that Ezra was not just my slightly posh and geeky next-door neighbour. There was more to him than that, only I hadn't been able to see it before.

'You're all wonky,' I said. I reached over and touched the buttons on his shirt, so I could see how he'd react.

'What?' he said, flustered, trying to look down.

'Here, let me.' I took the buttons between my fingers. I let my knuckles graze his chin, darkened by day old stubble, as I pushed the button out of the wrong hole and slipped it into the right one. 'All done.' I touched my fingertips to Ezra's chest for a moment before I let them come back to rest on the table.

'Thanks,' Ezra said.

I couldn't help but note the slight flush that had crept up his neck. He swallowed and looked away.

'So, what was this advice?' I asked.

Ezra looked back at me and I noticed that his eyes were the shade of a newly hatched conker.

'He said I should stop talking to you.'

'Why?' I asked, taken aback. Ezra and I talked a lot, but I liked that, he was good to talk to and I liked the sound of his voice.

Ezra gave a slow blink, girding himself. 'He said I should stop talking to you and just take you to bed.'

'Oh.' My heart beat a little faster.

'He said I should stop playing at being your friend and seduce you.'

I smiled. 'So are you going to follow his advice?'

'I'd like to but to be honest I'm kind of terrified,' he said and gave a nervous laugh.

I felt as though I had his heart in the palm of my hand. Although I hadn't thought of Ezra in that way before, he was handsome and I rather liked that he was baring his soul. I leant forward, putting my hand to his face, and kissed him.

When I sat back, I watched him open his eyes as though he couldn't quite believe what had happened.

He smiled with delight and perhaps a little relief too. He took a shaky breath, then moved toward me, tilting his head.

First it was just the touch of our lips. He slid his arm around my waist and pulled me tight against him. Our kiss unfolded and I was lost in the taste of this man.

'I've wanted to do that since I first met you,' Ezra said, still cupping my face. He looked like he'd won first prize.

'Have you?' I asked.

'Yes.'

'I didn't realise ...'

'I didn't want to be all in your face after you told me about that wanker that broke your heart.'

At the beginning of my second year at university, not long after I'd met Ezra, I'd bumped into him at our local pub. Obscenely drunk I'd spent the entire night talking to him about a man I'd met in the summer. Ezra told me his brother's name was Torin too, and we'd laughed at the coincidence. When they'd called last orders Ezra had walked me home, and I'd puked all over the pavement in front of our houses. We'd been friends since.

'I could see you weren't interested in anyone, so I figured I'd wait,' Ezra continued. 'But I've been driving my brother nuts talking about you and today he said I should go for it.' Ezra caressed my fingers with his, looking at me through his foppish fringe. Then he was kissing me again as though it was written in the script.

I woke up with a dry mouth and sense I'd made a terrible mistake. Ezra's warm exhale brushed my naked shoulder. I felt the heat of his body along the length of mine as we lay in his single bed, his hand resting upon my hip.

Recollections of the mediocre sex we'd had blazed through my thoughts. I had wanted Ezra, but the experience had been a rushed fumble in the sheets.

I eased my legs out, placed my feet on the floor, letting Ezra's hand slide off my hip, and slipped out of his bed. A floorboard creaked, and I froze hoping I hadn't woken him. I listened; his breath was still gentle and regular. I scanned the room but my clothes and his were indistinguishable dark shadows on the floor.

I managed to locate my top but looking through the other clothing I struggled to find my jeans and the more I moved the more the floorboards groaned.

'Grace?' Ezra said, from the bed, his voice thick from sleep.

'Hi,' I said, my heart hammering in my chest at having been caught trying to leave.

Ezra sat up and I could make out his outline in the dawning light outside the window. 'You alright?'

'Yeah.' I swallowed, knowing my voice had given me away.

I didn't know what to do. I didn't want to hurt Ezra, but I didn't know how to leave without doing that.

'Are you coming back to bed?' he asked.

I didn't answer and stood frozen to the spot in nothing but my top.

'Don't go yet.'

'I…' I stopped, unable to articulate what was going through my mind.

'Come here,' Ezra said.

I obeyed, going to perch on the edge of the bed.

'What's the matter?' he asked.

I hesitated before I said, 'I'm not sure how this will work.'

'Nothing has to change if you don't want it to.'

'We can't pretend last night didn't happen.'

'Do you wish it hadn't?' I could hear the anxiety in his voice.

'It's not that, it's just… I like being friends.'

'Can't we still be friends?' Ezra slid behind me, his knees either side of my hips. He gathered my hair and brushed it all over one shoulder. Ezra placed a row of kisses down my neck and put a hand on my hip. It felt good, and I didn't know why I was resisting this.

'You're so beautiful Grace,' he murmured. His hand slipped beneath my top and his fingertips traced tiny circles on my stomach.

'Friends don't usually do this,' I said, as his hand moved to my thigh.

'Maybe not, but it's nice isn't it?'

'Yes.' There was desire in my breath.

'So stay?' he said, kissing my neck again, as his hand slid between my legs.

Desire robbed my thoughts, I could only respond to Ezra's fingers caressing me.

We fitted together just right. No awkward positioning and nothing uncomfortable. He felt so familiar. And I was all caught up in him, my doubts discarded, like this was supposed to happened.

December 2014

'Can I show you something?' I asked Torin, as we lay facing each other, sharing my pillow.

'Have you not shown me enough of yourself already?' Torin said, running his hand over my naked hip.

I smiled. 'Funny. But what I want to show you isn't about me.'

'Now I'm intrigued.'

Rolling over, I leant out of bed and picked up the shoe box that held Ada's bundle of letters. I pulled the photo free and handed it to Torin.

First he frowned, then he glanced up at me, before he looked back down at the photo. He flipped it over and read the name.

'Why are you showing a picture of my grandfather?' he asked.

'I wasn't totally sure he was your grandfather,' I began. 'I found the photo at Ada's.'

'Tell me more?' Torin said.

I pulled the duvet up to cover my nakedness as a few more drops of rain hit my bedroom window and told Torin that Ada had had an affair with his grandfather.

'Christ, there's no hope for my family, we're a bunch of reprobates unable to keep our hands to ourselves,' he said, with amusement as he gave me back the photo.

I tucked the photograph of Samuel back into Ada's bundle of letters, then stowed the bundle back in the shoebox. I laid my head against Torin's shoulder, placing my fingers on his bare chest so I might trace his tattoos with my fingertip. He snaked his arms around me and talked about his grandfather. He hadn't known Samuel, having grown up in Scotland away from Redferne Lane; he remembered only meeting him a handful of times. Torin explained that Samuel was his mother's father. She'd been his only child, inheriting everything. At Samuel's instruction she'd kept her surname on marrying and passed it on to her children, defying tradition. I sensed in Torin, a deep respect for his grandfather.

'I'm sure his ring is languishing in a drawer somewhere. If we find it, we could give it to Ada,' Torin said.

'Really?' I said.

'Yes, she'd like that right?' Torin asked. 'We could return her letters and give her the ring?'

'Okay,' I said.

Torin climbed out of my bed. 'Come up to the house with me?' Torin said, doing his trousers up.

'I don't know,' I said, reluctant to share Torin with anyone.

'Please?' he said, lifting my chin. 'This is the first whole day I've been able to spend with you and I don't want to leave your side.'

I smiled and agreed to go with him. I didn't want to be apart from him either. Every morning this week he'd had to leave my bed to finish a job, and I'd hated his departures. And now the job was complete I relished the thought of all the hours we might have together.

It was past midday before we left my bed and walked up Redferne Lane hand in hand in the intermittent rain.

Unusually, there was no one home, and the house seemed odd without the bustle of family. Torin lead me first to the library, a room rarely used, but filled with a plethora of old books and a dusty smell. I tried to dislodge a memory of coming in here to steal kisses with Ezra once upon a time. Torin rummaged through drawers but couldn't find the ring. I was grateful to leave the library and go into the living room where Torin continued to search, first in a solid bureau and then finally in the drawers of an art deco sideboard.

'Here it is,' Torin said, holding a small gold signet ring between his finger and thumb. 'This was my grandfather's.'

I took the ring and rolled it between my fingers. It was solid but almost feminine in design.

'Do you think Ada will want it?'

'I don't know,' I said, thinking of Ezra's rings I'd buried. 'But it's a lovely gesture, so we can give it to her anyway. Like you said, it's just sitting here, untouched otherwise.'

'Alright then,' Torin said, holding out the velvet box so I could slip the ring back inside before he put the box in his pocket. 'Here, look at these.'

Torin handed me a battered old photograph album. I recognised Samuel in the first images, first as a young man in rolled shirt sleeves and in the latter photographs a distinguished gentleman in tweed. In many photographs Elizabeth, Torin's grandmother, was beside Samuel. She was a beautiful, elegant woman dripping with cultured breeding. Perhaps it was indicative of the period but in the photographs her mouth was rarely smiling. I could see the likeness in both Noah and Eliza whereas Torin and Ezra had seemed to favour their grandfather's genes.

'And this is my favourite picture of my mother,' Torin said, and handed me a photograph in a silver frame. Of course I'd seen a photograph of her before but I'd never looked at one and seen her as Torin's mother, only as a connection to Ezra. 'My father took this.'

She had a happy glint in her eye as she looked at the camera as though she was flirting with the man behind the lens. I could almost feel her deep affection for Torin's father from that look alone. I realised it was akin to a look Torin gave me at times and a bubble of excitement and trepidation rose in my chest.

'She's very beautiful,' I said, handing the photo back.

'Aye. And trouble.' He placed the photo back on the sideboard. 'Like someone else I know,' he said, with a grin.

As I looked at Torin I was surprised by the desire I felt, it was as fresh and new as though we'd never kissed.

He slipped his arm around my waist and pulled me close. He kissed me and I moaned, ready to let his kiss evolve. I felt him smile against my mouth and his hands wander my body freely.

Clothes were untucked, unzipped and pulled aside as Torin pressed me against the sideboard.

We heard the front door and sprang apart. Giggling as we adjusted our clothing, so we were decent once more. We were still chuckling as Eliza walked in. She stopped in the doorway.

'Hi,' she said, slowly, giving us an assessing look. 'Something funny?'

'We were just looking at some old photos,' Torin told her, smoothly.

She looked between us. Back and forth.

'Good day at school?' Torin asked, breaking the silence.

'Yeah, like totally amazing,' she said, rolled her eyes, and left the doorway.

Torin and I looked at each other, smiling, as we heard her walk up the stairs, then both winced as she slammed her bedroom door.

'Maybe we should go and visit Ada?' I said.

Torin took my hand. 'Aye, let's do that.'

Ada was dozing in an armchair beside a window overlooking the garden. We sat sipping tea with her until she had woken up fully.

'You've had the cast taken off?' I said.

'Yes, they took it off yesterday.'

'And how is your arm now?'

'A little weak but I'll be arm wrestling again soon.' She gave a cackle at her joke.

'Good,' I paused. 'We brought you something.'

Torin placed the shoebox on the table before Ada.

'Now you're all settled, I thought you might want these?' I said, indicating the letters from Samuel inside the shoebox.

She looked at me, her eyes watery with emotion. 'How thoughtful of you.' She picked up the bundles of letters and ran her fingers over the paper.

'I haven't read them,' I said.

She gave a small laugh. 'I wouldn't have minded if you had. There's nothing racy in these letters.'

Perhaps they weren't explicit, but I expected they held love and affection, something private between Samuel and Ada.

Ada took the photo from the box and I felt a pang of guilt at bringing the letters as I saw a wave of sadness wash over her normally cheery face.

'I'm sorry,' I said. 'I shouldn't have brought them.'

'No,' Ada said, looking up at me. Her pale blue eyes were watery from unshed tears. 'It's so lovely to see him again. It's a long time since I read these letters.' She ran her fingers over the ribbon holding the letters together. 'It will be nice to read them again.'

'I thought you might like this,' Torin said, and passed Ada the small jewellery box.

Ada opened it to look at the gold signet ring inside.

'His ring,' she said, more to herself than anyone else. 'He always wore it on his little finger.'

Ada sat gazing at the ring as though looking upon her lover himself for long silent minutes.

Ada looked up at Torin. 'You look so like him.'

'Aye, that I do. Loveable old rogue wasn't he?' Torin said, with a gentle smile.

Ada gave one of her naughty cackles, 'A rogue, yes. That's exactly what he was.'

Torin and I exchanged a look and a smile.

Ada put the ring, the letters and the photo back in the shoebox and placed the lid on top. Then she indicated the Christmas tree that had been put up and started a jolly conversation about a Christmas crafts workshop they were having next week.

When Ada gave a yawn I suggested it was time Torin and I should go.

Ada gave a sighing smile. 'You two take care of each other now.' And she winked at me as though she knew exactly what Torin and I had been up to all week.

After we'd had dinner Torin and I lounged on the daybed; I lay between his legs with my head on his chest. We were watching a film but I could almost hear the whir of Torin's thoughts.

'What's the matter?' I asked, raising my head to look at him.

He looked sad. 'I was just thinking about Noah. I mean Ada seemed to know what was going on between us and

Eliza too, maybe. It's only a matter of time before Noah finds out.'

'So why don't you just tell him?'

'He'll think it's weird.'

'Do you think it's weird?' I asked, sitting up.

Torin sat up too. We were no longer touching. 'No.' He paused. 'Well, maybe a little but I think that's more about history than it is about now.'

I didn't like his words. 'History?'

'There have been times in the past when I've struggled with the fact that I fancy my brother's wife,' Torin said, in a tone that implied I was a little stupid.

'You don't have to say it like that.'

'Sorry.' He reached over, tucked my hair behind my ear and ran his thumb along my jaw. 'It's just been complicated over the years. You know that as well as I do.'

I gave a faint smile and tried to suppress the spark of lust that rippled through me as Torin ran his fingertips along my collarbone.

'It doesn't have to be complicated anymore,' I said, unable to stop the slight sigh in my voice as Torin continued to caress my skin.

'Maybe, maybe not.'

'What do you mean?' I placed my hand on his thigh and traced invisible patterns with my fingertip.

'I'm wondering what happens next? What happens when I leave again?'

I shrugged. 'Where are going when you leave Redferne Lane?'

'Home first, for a week or so. Then Toronto,' Torin said. 'For a couple of months probably, maybe more. Then we have a whole string of festivals all over the country which will take up May to September.'

'Woah,' I said. 'That's almost your whole year mapped out.'

He gave me an apologetic smile. 'It's kind of how my life is Gracie. It's been this way for years now.' He scoffed. 'Pretty much since I first met you, actually.'

'It's given you a good excuse to keep on leaving.'

'Aye and yet I keep coming back too.'

'Don't you want to stop moving around so much? Don't you miss being home?' I asked.

'Sometimes it's been hard. And yet other times I have been so grateful to be able to be far away.'

I knew he meant that he'd been glad to be away from me and I hated that I'd hurt him, that he'd felt like he couldn't be near me. But I noticed that he hadn't answered my question. He hadn't said that he wanted to change his lifestyle. He hadn't said that he might want to stop leaving.

'You could come with me? When I leave?' Torin said.

'You know I hate flying,' I said, before I could even think.

'Aye, I do.'

'And I've just got a new job.'

'Fine, so you don't want to come with me,' he said, turning his body away from me.

'I don't mean it like that,' I said reaching over to him, disliking his closed posture.

'It's exactly what you meant.'

'Well it's not like you're going to stay, is it?'

Torin turned his head to look at me. He reached over and brushed the back of his fingers down my cheek.

'Let's not talk about this now,' I said, and moved to kiss him.

Torin let me kiss him and took my tongue into his mouth. He eased me to lie down beneath him on the day-bed, nestling between my legs. After a moment he raised his head and looked down at me.

'We will talk about all of this Gracie, sooner rather than later,' he said, before he kissed me again and slid his hand down to the hem of my skirt.

Torin placed his hand on my thigh and traced an arc back and forth with his finger. I loved him touching me but sat with the rest of the Redferne clan I wished he'd stop. I was sure they would notice the catch in my breath and flush of desire in my cheeks.

'Pass the salad poppet,' Noah said to Eliza.

She silently gave the bowl to her father not raising her eyes from her plate.

'When I said no phones at the table, it was so you'd be sociable. Stop sulking child and say something,' Noah said, as he heaped green leaves on to his plate.

'What do you want me to say?' Eliza asked.

'Well, I don't know, you're supposed to think of something,' he gave a gruff sigh and raised his palms as if in despair.

Torin continued to caress my thigh, and I had to shift in my seat in an attempt to quash the ache between my legs. I slipped my hand beneath the table and placed my hand on top of Torin's, to still his actions. But he slipped his hand on top of mine and moved both of our hands up my thigh.

I glanced at Torin. He smiled at me, pressing our hands between my legs.

We'd had no intention of joining the family for lunch but when we'd come up to the house so Torin could get some clean clothes and his phone charger before we went out for lunch together, we were ambushed by nephews. And

Josie had set places for us both at the table before we'd realised what was going on.

Godfrey, on Torin's other side, knocked his plate onto the floor. Torin leapt up to retrieve the plate and food from the floor. Noah muttered words of annoyance while Josie got to her knees to help Torin. Godfrey looked like he might start crying so I offered him a piece of bread from my plate. He took it with a wobbly smile.

'At least thank your aunt if she's going to reward your silly behaviour,' Noah said to Godfrey.

Godfrey gave his father a wounded look; clearly didn't understand what Noah had said.

'Say thank you,' Noah snapped.

'Thank you Auntie Grace,' Godfrey said.

I grinned at the boy. 'Do you want another piece?' I handed him the rest of my bread and caught Noah rolling his eyes.

Torin put Godfrey's plate back in front of the child and returned to his seat beside me.

Josie sat down and a second later we heard Anthony crying through the baby monitor. Josie stood up again to get the baby from his cot.

'For God's sake, can't we sit still for a meal anymore?' Noah said and poured himself some more wine.

Barty began telling Noah about an episode of Thomas the Tank Engine. Noah did little to hide his boredom. I felt the press of Torin's leg against mine and wondered how long it would be before we could leave the chaos of lunch at Redferne House.

Josie returned to the table with Anthony grizzling in her arms. She unbuttoned her lime green blouse, unhooked the cup of her bra and exposed her breast. With a faint smile on her face, she latched the baby on to her nipple. She watched him feed for a moment, giving his cheek a stroke with her finger. She picked up the bread from her plate and took a bite before looking back down at Anthony.

'Oh my God, do you have to do that at the table?' Eliza said, her words dripping with distaste.

Josie looked up from the baby in surprise but it was Noah that spoke.

'I beg your pardon?' he said.

'Does she have to get her tits out while we're eating?' Eliza said.

'How dare you?' Noah said, loud and abrasive.

Eliza stood up, shoved back her chair and threw her cutlery down on the table. The fork bounced and hit the jug of water with a loud clang.

'Sit down,' Noah bellowed.

Baby Anthony startled at the loud noises and lost the nipple. He started a frantic cry and then Barty started to sob too.

'Noah, it's fine, I'll go in the other room,' Josie said, while she struggled to latch the baby back on to her breast at the same time as standing up.

'You'll stay right there,' Noah said.

'She goes or I do,' Eliza said, with defiance.

'You'll both bloody stay,' Noah said.

Eliza suddenly burst into tears. She sank down on her chair and screwed up her face as though it might stop her from crying. But her shoulders shook, and another sob escaped her lips.

'Eliza,' Torin began but Noah talked over him.

'What's the matter with you?' Noah said, in exasperation.

'Nothing,' Eliza said, as more tears streamed down her face.

'Then stop crying?' Noah continued in a belligerent tone. 'You're always crying.'

'Noah, stop,' Torin said. 'She's reason enough to cry. Leave her alone.'

Both Eliza and Noah looked at Torin in surprise.

'Maybe it would help if you just told them,' Torin said softly to Eliza.

'You told him?' Eliza snarled at me.

'I was worried about you,' I said.

'Would one of you like to tell me what is going on?' Noah asked.

No one said anything and all I could hear was the little snuffling sounds of the baby feeding.

'Well?' Noah asked.

Torin glanced at me, then at Eliza. 'She had an abortion.'

Noah took a sharp inhale.

Eliza stood up. 'You promised you wouldn't tell anyone,' she said to me through gritted teeth.

'Eliza, I'm sorry,' I said, knowing my words were woefully inadequate.

'In the long run it's better not to have secrets,' Torin said.

'Secrets?' she said and gave a hollow laugh. 'This family is full of secrets.' She turned to Noah. 'You know all about secrets don't you Dad?'

'Eliza,' Torin said, in a warning tone.

She spun to look at Torin

'And what about your secret Uncle Torin?' She looked at me. 'What about you and Auntie Grace?' Eliza turned back to Noah. 'You do know they're fucking each other right?' She paused, watching the confusion on her father's face. 'Thought not.'

Noah looked at Torin, and I could see by the frown on his face he wished it wasn't true.

Through another heavy silence Torin rubbed his face with his hand. Half of me wanted to throttle Eliza, the other half just wished I was somewhere else.

'Well, I think it's lovely that Torin and Grace make each other happy,' Josie said in a jovial tone.

I gave her a grateful smile but as I did Noah slammed his wine glass down on the table, breaking the stem from the cup, spilling the contents. A dark red stain spread across the tablecloth.

'I cannot believe you actually went there,' Noah said to Torin, his voice dripping with distaste.

Eliza said, 'You're a fine one to talk Dad.'

'Eliza, seriously, don't,' Torin said, shaking his head.

'What? Don't tell everyone he's been shagging the cleaner?' she said. 'Haven't you Dad?'

We all looked at Noah and he didn't deny the accusation.

Josie made a funny sort of squeak.

'There was really no need for that,' Torin said to Eliza.

She shrugged. 'In the long run, it's better not to have secrets, right?' Then she walked from the kitchen and a moment later we heard the front door bang closed.

Josie stood, clutching Anthony to her breast, 'I'm going to just finish feeding him upstairs…' she mumbled and fled the kitchen too.

I made to go after her but Torin grabbed my wrist, stopping me. 'Noah?' Torin prompted.

'I'm going, alright?' Noah said, getting up from the table and following his wife, leaving Torin and I in the kitchen with Barty and Godfrey.

'You knew about Noah and Sam?' I asked in a whisper, surveying the debris of lunch on the table, before I looked up at Torin.

'I had my suspicions,' he said, releasing his grip on my wrist and sliding his fingers between mine.

Torin squeezed my hand as we shared a look that communicated a myriad of feelings we couldn't discuss in front of the children.

'Have some jelly?' Godfrey asked, with a bright smile.

I looked down at his blonde curls and smooth cheeks. 'Of course, let's all have jelly.'

July 2003

Torin stood half naked in the middle of my bedroom. His T-shirt was crumpled from its night spent on my bedroom floor. The tendon in his neck pulled taut under his skin as he turned to adjust the sleeve. He straightened, and I noticed that the hem didn't reach beyond the thick weave of pubic hair. His cock hung between his legs not quite limp. I admired the tone in his thighs and the soft arc of his calves. He picked up his jeans then continued to look around the floor.

The sight of him took my breath away. I would never grow tired of looking at Torin.

'Morning,' I said, sitting up.

'I didn't mean to wake you, Gracie,' Torin said, coming to sit on the edge of the bed.

'I don't mind.' I made to reach for him, wanting to initiate intimacy but he took both of my hands in his.

He smiled, but it didn't quite reach his eyes. 'I have to go in a bit,' he said looking at me with a small frown.

'So soon?'

He touched my face with his hand, leant forward and kissed my forehead.

I sighed.

Torin stood up and looked about the floor of my room. 'Don't suppose you've seen my pants?'

I shook my head.

'Never mind,' he said and pulled his jeans on without underwear.

He tucked his cock down the left side of his jeans. Before he'd done up the buttons, he stopped and said, 'Have you seen my wallet?'

I shook my head again. He lifted items of my clothing from the floor in the search for his wallet and located it under one of my tops. While he moved about my room I saw the dark curled hairs in the V of his open jeans.

'What time is your dad coming?' Torin asked, still searching the room.

I glanced at my phone beside the bed and sighed. 'He'll be here in about half an hour.' Half an hour until I had to go back to my parents for the summer. Half an hour until I had to say goodbye to Torin.

Torin moved a little quicker. He finished doing up his jeans before picking up his hoody and slipping his arm into one sleeve, the bracelet of mine that he wore disappearing beneath the fabric. His delicate bicep formed a smooth curve as he moved to pull the hoody across his back. The veins on the inside of his wrist were visible. The silver ring on his thumb caught the light.

Again he searched my floor and found one dark grey sock almost at once. He stood on one leg and slipped the sock over his long toes; over the low instep, round the curve of his heel and over the thin bulge of his ankle. The hem of his jeans stayed a little raised on his calve exposing an inch of pale skin covered with dark hairs.

I could smell Torin in my room; in the air, on my sheets, on my skin. The taste of him was on my lips and every place his fingers had touched glowed with heat. I didn't want these weeks to be over. Sunny days during which we'd laughed and talked, sharing intimate details of our lives. I hadn't known I could feel this way about another person, about Torin. It was bordering on the ridiculous the number of things I adored about him. And now he was leaving. He had never concealed his imminent departure to Australia since we'd met but somehow I had never quite felt it would happen. But it was happening now.

Torin cursed again unable to find the other sock. He ran his hands over his hair and adjusted the bands holding the ponytail in place. I watched him for another minute as he found his other sock and pulled on his trainers. He located his keys on my desk and slid them into the pocket of his jeans. Torin paused in the middle of my room but he was ready to leave.

'Torin?'

He looked over and his eyes dropped to where I'd let the duvet fall to expose my naked breasts. 'Yes?' he said and lifted his eyes to my face.

'I'm so glad I met you.' They were not the words I wanted to say, but I couldn't tell him those three words after just a month. Even though I was sure I'd heard him whisper those words last night as he moved inside me.

Torin sucked in a breath as though I'd just punched him. He rubbed his face with both hands and came back to the bed. He pulled me against him, his hand in my hair. We stayed in that secure embrace for long minutes, breathing each other in as though to stock up upon one another until we would see each other again. He kissed my head and held me a moment longer.

'You take care now Gracie,' he said, and placed his palm on the cast covering my wrist. 'No more accidents.'

I nodded.

He kissed my lips, then stood up.

'Call me when you've landed?' I said.

The slightest of frowns ran across his forehead. 'Aye.'

He came back for one last kiss then left my room, closing the door behind him.

I took a few deep breaths and decided I wouldn't cry. I would speak to Torin tomorrow and I would see him soon. He'd already said he'd be back in the country in a month or so.

Dad arrived as I finished pulling my clothes on. He rolled his eyes at the mess in my room and tutted that I hadn't finished packing my belongings. He opened the window and silently folded my clothes and put them in the suitcase he'd brought from home. Within an hour Dad had packed the car with my things and we were driving out of Bristol. As we went up the M32, passing from inner city to green space in minutes I gazed out of the window and thought of Torin. I'd only known him for a month and yet I loved him. They had been the best and funniest weeks of my life. I hadn't known that someone could make me smile and laugh like Torin did. And Torin had shown me there was a difference between sex and making love.

I pulled my phone out of my pocket meaning to text Torin. Instantly I knew something wasn't right. All the texts I'd had from Torin during the last month were gone. Not one remained. In the call history there was no evidence we had spoken at all and yet we'd spoken every day. When he'd been at work he'd phoned me at least once, often twice or three times, as though he couldn't last from leaving my bed in the morning and seeing me again in the early evening. But there was no trace of this. And in my contacts list there was nothing; his name was not there. I scrolled through my phone over and over again but there was nothing of him.

I couldn't work out what was going on with my phone. Of all the times for it to malfunction. The tears I'd decided I did not need to cry silently slipped down my cheeks and I failed to stop them. I turned my face away so Dad would not see. I told myself I would just have to wait for Torin to call me.

December 2014

The clouds drifted apart, and the primary coloured rubber matting was slowly washed in pale sunlight. First the toes of our boots, then our knees, then the whole of Torin and I gained a grain of warmth as the sun came out. We'd already spent an hour at the swings and climbing frames with Barty and Godfrey before we'd taken them to the cafe for fairy cakes and milk and now we were back in the park. The boys were content to let Torin and I observe from a bench while they played side by side in the damp sandpit.

'Eliza phoned last night,' Torin said. 'She's coming back from her mother's the day before Christmas Eve.'

'How is she?'

'A bit of a mess. But she had a long talk with Josie and they decided that she should come home. Both Josie and Eliza are happy enough with that. Noah was worried she'd want to stay with her mother, but she wants to come home,' Torin said.

'It's probably done her good to go away for a bit.'

'Aye, I think it has. And I think Noah and Josie needed her out of the way for a bit too.'

'Josie seemed a little happier today,' I said.

'Aye,' Torin agreed. 'I think now Josie knows Sam is going to move she feels like her and Noah can sort their marriage out.'

'It seems harsh on Sam and Jerome,' I said.

'Aye maybe, but you can't blame Josie for wanting Sam gone.'

'No, of course not.'

We sat quiet for a time. I watched Godfrey and Barty playing together, glad they had no idea of the turmoil their parents were in. I hoped in time Noah and Josie could be happy together again.

Torin had his hands clasped loosely, resting between his knees as he looked into the distance and by the frown on his brow I could tell he was thinking at a million miles an hour. I reached over and with a gentle tug separated his hands so I could lattice our fingers together. I shifted closer to Torin, relishing his warmth and his scent. Torin looked at me with a quizzical smile.

'What are you thinking about?' I asked.

He gave me a wonky smile. 'You.'

'You don't need to think about me, I'm right here.'

'Aye,' he said, 'but soon I'll be gone.'

'And then you'll come back.'

He sighed. 'Is that what you want? You want me to come back to you?'

'Yes.'

'You don't want to see if there's anyone else out there for you?'

'Why are you asking that?' I said.

'I'm tired Gracie, I'm tired of moving around all the time but I need a reason to stay still,' he paused. 'You could be that reason?'

'Could I?'

'Aye.'

'You'd stop leaving?' I asked with a smile.

'Aye, maybe.' He returned a wary smile. 'I was thinking I might sell my place in Scotland.'

'Really?'

'Aye.'

'And where would you live?'

'Maybe with you?'

I blinked a few times and didn't say anything and instantly wished I'd spoken because Torin looked wounded and turned away.

'Torin ...'

There was a sudden cry from the sand pit and I looked to see Godfrey in tears. We both ran over. Barty talked at speed explaining that his little brother had sand in his eye but he was certain it wasn't his fault. Torin cuddled Godfrey and after a moment or two Godfrey calmed down and then told us that Barty had thrown sand at him.

'It was an accident,' Barty said, looking as though he might cry too.

'Say sorry,' Torin commanded.

Barty mumbled an apology to his brother. Godfrey suddenly smiled, wriggled free of Torin's arms and went back to digging in the sand.

'You're good with them,' I said, as we stood watching them play.

He shrugged. 'So are you.'

I said his name but he cut me off, saying we should take the boys home before there were any more tears or fights.

Godfrey sat in the pushchair and Barty stood on the buggy board while Torin pushed the two of them. The sun was peeking out from behind a cloud once more as we came under the bridge onto Redferne Lane. The boys were quiet, tired from playing in the park and Torin and I were quiet too. For my part I was thinking about what would happen when Torin left. But more about when he came back. It was so difficult to know how we might map a path together but I knew I didn't want to be spend my life without him. A few months absence I could contend with but after that I wanted us to be together.

I stopped and Torin stopped too looking at me with a question in his face.

'Move in with me?' I said.

He frowned, as though he didn't trust my words.

'I love you,' I said.

He laughed and gave a small shake of his head. 'I love you too Gracie,' he said, and pulled me into a hug.

'I don't want be without you anymore Torin,' I said. 'I don't know how it'll all work but I want to be with you.'

He pulled me harder against him. 'I don't want to be without you either,' he said, softly with his cheek pressed against my head.

We stayed in each other's arms until Barty spoke.

'Uncle Torin? What's wrong with him?' he said, his voice uncertain.

We both looked up to where Barty was pointing across the meadow to the large oak tree where a figured huddled at the roots, his head bent, his body shuddering as though he was either cold or crying.

My heart juddered as I realised it was Jerome.

'What is he doing?' Torin asked.

'I'll go and see,' I said, already taking a step into the damp grass of the meadow.

'Wait Gracie, I'll come with you,' Torin said, concern on his face.

'You should take the boys home,' I said, and gave his hand a quick squeeze.

'Take care,' Torin said.

The grass soaked my shoes in an instant. I could hear the train going over the bridge; the familiar grate of metal on metal and the clickety-rumble of the trucks. Jerome sat on his haunches, his whole body shook with sobs. His hands were bloodied and swollen; he rested his wrists on his knees. I slowed to a stop a few paces from Jerome; close enough for him to hear me say his name.

Jerome looked up, and I saw his face was a tear stained mess. His fringe was matted into a clump that hung to the side of his face and his T-shirt was dark with sweat and smears of blood and it stuck to his chest.

I took the last few steps towards him. 'What's happened?'

'This day is so fucked up,' he said, with shuddering breaths as I knelt down next to him. 'I hate that family. I hate them all.'

I could only assume he was talking about the Redferne's – my family.

'What's happened Jerome?'

'My Mum's been shagging Eliza's Dad.' Jerome stuttered out. 'How fucked up is that?' Jerome shook his head. 'He came to the house and started telling Mum about me and Eliza and the abortion. He told her they couldn't see each anymore but he didn't know I was there and then I could hear Mum crying and then he said we had to leave the house and he said he never wanted to see either of us again. And I ran out of the house because I had to get out because I just wanted to hurt him so bad and the next thing I know I was punching the tree and wishing it was him.' He looked at his hands, bloody and swollen.

'I'm so sorry Jerome.'

He crumpled putting his face in his stiff bloodied hands as sobs over took him again. I hesitated then put my arms around him.

We stayed that way for a long time, long after Jerome had stopped crying and his breathing calmed. My hands grew numb from the frosty weather and the blood on Jerome's T-shirt began to stiffen in the cold. The light of day was fading and I could feel involuntary shivers from us both.

'Shall I take you home?' I asked.

'I'm never going back there,' he said, lifting his face up. 'It ain't my home no more.'

I paused before I said, 'Would you like to come to my house?'

He stood slowly, stiff, as though every inch of him hurt and we walked to my cottage. In the kitchen I bathed his hands in warm water but he didn't want bandages and the only thing he asked of me was a cigarette. But as well as giving him a cigarette, I made him a cup of sweet tea and draped a hoody of Torin's around his shoulders.

I suggested to Jerome that Sam might be worried about him, that maybe we should go and see her but he refused. Again he told me he wasn't ever going back.

I heard Torin unlocking the front door. Leaving Jerome in the kitchen I met Torin in the hallway.

'Is he here?' Torin asked.

I nodded. 'He's pretty upset. He won't go home.'

I felt tears threaten and Torin pulled me against him, stroking my hair as my head lay against his chest. 'Hey don't cry.'

'But it's so unfair. Jerome hasn't done anything wrong.'

'I know.'

'What's he supposed to do?'

'I don't know Gracie. I suppose he'll have to go and live wherever Sam finds a new place.'

'He could stay here?' I said, before I'd really considered it.

Torin sighed and kissed my head. 'Gracie, please think about it before you offer.'

But it was too late because Jerome was stood in the doorway, watching Torin and I. And I could see the look of hope on his face.

June 2003

'Have you got a light?' a man with a soft Scottish accent asked, leaning over from the table next to mine with a cigarette between his fingers.

'Sure,' I said, handing over my purple lighter.

I watched him light his cigarette and inhale. Tattoos decorated his fine shaped arm from wrist to up beyond the sleeve of his T-shirt. The flex of his tendons made the inked skin ripple.

'Do you know what the time is?' I asked.

'A little after seven.'

'Thanks.'

'Is your boyfriend late?' he asked, with a smirk as he handed my lighter back.

'I don't have a boyfriend. I'm just waiting for my housemates.'

'Going out on the town?' He rubbed his thick gingery beard with his thumb and forefinger and it made a static crackle. He smiled showing white even teeth.

'Yes. We've all finished our first year. It seemed like a good idea to mark the occasion.'

'Student are you?' As he spoke he looked at me with dark, near black eyes. I'd never seen eyes like his and his gaze set my heart running a little faster than normal.

'Yes.'

'What are you studying? No wait, let me guess.' He looked down the length of me, taking in my plait, my white shirt, black skirt, tights and black ballet pumps; my work uniform. He licked his lips and looked back to my face. His scrutiny made me blush.

'English?'

I shook my head.

'History?'

I shook my head again, smiling, amused that he could think I had the faintest idea about the significance of the past.

'Maybe you're an architect? My brothers are architects.'

'No.'

He sighed with smile. 'Alright then, tell me.'

'Fine art,' I said.

'What's your preferred medium?' I liked his voice, not only the accent but the soft melodic weave of his words.

'Pencil and charcoal.'

'People or things?'

'People.'

He nodded and blinked as though this was enlightening news, then continued to look at me as he asked if I'd like company while I waited for my friends. Holding out his hand, he told me his name. My cool fingers touched his warm leathery palm as I gave him my name. He had hard working hands, a callous on his finger rubbed against the back of my hand as he repeated my name, rolling the 'R' as though committing it to memory. He picked up his pint and moved from his table and joined me at mine. I shuffled over a fraction to make room for him.

'So what do you do Torin?' I asked, enjoying the feel of his name in my mouth.

He'd recently started a stage construction company that built temporary platforms for all kinds of events from gigs to fashion shows to business conferences. The business was small but doing well. He fished in the pocket of his black jeans, looking for a business card to give me but he'd left them in the hotel where he was staying. Torin stayed in a lot of hotels, B&B's and hostels, all over the world he told me; he travelled a lot. He was off to Australia soon.

'I've only been to Nice,' I said. 'I'm not good with flying.'

When I was seven, my parents and I went to Nice for a week, it was my first and last holiday abroad. I spent the entire flight throwing up and freaking out – I've never been so terrified. I was still being sick twenty-four hours after we'd landed. Even when I kept some food down I still felt so dizzy I had to lie in the hotel room with the blinds closed against the dazzling sunshine. The day before we were due to go home my parents dragged me around the Russian Cathedral but I was so gripped with fear, knowing we had to fly home again that I don't remember much of the experience. I was sick three times in the airport and retched repeatedly as we took off. When we returned home I was suffering from dehydration and had to spend the night in hospital on a drip. Dad said he would never take me on an aeroplane again.

Torin laughed at my tale and said, 'It's a right shame you don't fly. I love flying. It's that feeling when you're taking off and your stomach is still on the ground but the rest of you is in the air; it blows my mind every time.'

I felt woozy at the thought of it. 'That's the bit I don't like. That and knowing you're in the air and there's nothing sensible keeping you there.'

'Aside from an aeroplane.'

'Exactly, nothing sensible. I can't get my head around how a big tin can stay in the air.'

He laughed again, a great warm sound that tickled me inside my chest. His phone rang and vibrated on the table.

Torin spoke with warmth to the person calling him. Turning away, he looked out of the window overlooking Bristol Docks. The top section of his hair was long and tied with a series of hair bands at intervals down the length of it; the rest of his scalp closely shaved. He was not broad shouldered but had a strong physique. He made me think of a Viking lord. I could imagine him painted in woad and charging into battle ready to meet Odin in Valhalla.

Torin turned back and looked straight at me, catching me staring. He grinned and ran his tongue along his teeth, he gazed right back at me while still listening to whoever was on the phone.

'I gotta go,' he said into the phone, then hung up.

'Was that your girlfriend?' I asked.

'There is no girlfriend. That was my brother,' he told me, putting his phone back down on the table. 'He's just about to go traveling in Thailand for a couple of months.'

'Sounds nice,' I said, twirling the end of my plait around my finger. 'If you like flying.'

Torin laughed again. 'Aye, I'm sure he'll have a good time.' He paused and looked at me with his head on one side. 'Can I buy you drink? While you wait for your friends?'

I rarely accepted a drink from a man as it was often code for granting access to my knickers but I smiled at Torin and let him buy me a drink.

The pub was filling up as Friday night got started, but there was no sign of my housemates, I suspected they weren't coming. It was a student pub and was already quite rowdy. Torin had shifted his seat close to mine so we could hear each other. I could feel his leg ever so slightly pressing against mine and he looked right at me throughout our conversation as though I was the most interesting thing in the whole place. We chatted as though we'd known each other for years. He was so easy to be with, to talk to and laugh with. He was funny without being crass.

'So you reckon they've stood you up?' Torin asked.

I looked down at the dregs of my drink. The last few bubbles rose to the top of the amber liquid and popped when they reached the surface. 'Probably. It wouldn't be the first time.'

I wasn't part of the gang. I didn't dress right, I didn't like the right music, and they thought I was posh because I said castle and bath with an 'ar' sound.

'Ah, that's mean,' Torin said.

I shrugged.

'You think they'll turn up here later?'

'Maybe.'

'Why don't you call one of them?'

'I left my phone at home.'

'Want to use mine?'

'Thanks, but I don't know any of their numbers.'

He smiled. 'Will you wait?'

I shook my head. 'I think I'll just go home.'

'Aye, me too. It's been a long week.'

We left the pub together. Torin shook my hand again and told me what a pleasure it had been to meet me. I felt a sudden sense of loss knowing I would probably never meet him again. I'd never met anyone I'd been able to talk to so easily. Nor anyone as handsome. He crossed the road, but we both walked in the same direction. Once then twice, then three times we glanced at each other smiling. Then my clumsiness took charge.

I tripped over nothing and crumpled like a wet paper bag. Landing hard on my knees, I fell sideways onto my forearm and felt the bone snap as I hit the curb. I needed get up out of the road but all the air had gone out of me.

'Come on Grace,' Torin said. I felt his arms go around me and lift me onto the pavement.

'I think I've broken my arm,' I mumbled. My knees screamed hot pain and the dull ache in my arm was increasing. I'd laddered my tights, exposing bloody knees encrusted with grit.

'Let me have a look,' Torin said. He held my wrist and elbow gently in his hands. 'Aye, I think you're right.'

I looked at my arm and wished I hadn't when I saw an odd lump in my forearm. I wave of nausea swept over me. The back of my neck felt hot and my mouth felt funny.

'Breathe in Grace,' Torin said, 'and out. Now in again.'

The nausea passed, only to be replaced by a shooting pain in my arm.

Torin conjured a taxi. He put his arm around me as we drove through the traffic to the hospital. Throughout the short journey he talked softly, telling me I was going to be fine. I believed him.

He sat in the waiting room with me and I found my voice again as the shock subsided. I told Torin about my numerous visits to A&E departments over the years. My first visit I don't remember as I was only one and a half. I'd broken my leg after falling down the stairs at home. But I remember all the other accidents. The worst was when I was thirteen and I broke my collarbone and three ribs after falling out of a tree. I'd been with Jamie, my first boyfriend and I said he could kiss me if he could beat me to the top of the tree. I let him win. When I got to the top branch I closed my eyes and Jamie put his free hand on my waist. I put both of my hands on his chest and felt his heart beating wildly beneath my palm. It was a sweet kiss. When I opened my eyes again somehow my balance was all wrong, and I fell. I remember lying on the ground and looking up through the branches, still able to see Jamie at the top of the tree.

'How's it feeling?' Torin asked after we'd been waiting for an hour.

'A bit odd.'

He gave me a gentle smile.

'You don't have to wait with me, you know,' I told Torin.

'I'd like to, if you don't mind?'

'Thank you.' I said and felt a surge of tears push behind my eyes.

'Hey, it's alright.' Torin put his arm around my shoulders. I leant my head against him, finding a perfect space in the crook of his neck. I took a deep breath, trying not to cry. Torin smelt earthy and natural and male and I couldn't help but inhale again, this time letting the scent of him fill me. He pulled me against him a fraction tighter and I felt his hand stroke my hair. I couldn't remember ever feeling so cared for.

'Shall I take this off for you?' Torin said, touching one of the silver beads on my leather bracelet. 'They'll probably cut it off otherwise.'

I watched his fingers undo the thin leather ties. He was so careful not to nudge my arm.

'I'll look after it for you,' Torin said, holding the bracelet in his fingers.

A nurse called my name and took me to a cubicle to assess the damage. She helped me out of my ruined tights and cleaned my grazed knees. They took X-rays of my arm and told me I'd snapped both the radius and ulna. Nice clean breaks.

When I emerged with my arm in plaster from wrist to elbow the waiting room was filling up with drunks, noisy and boisterous. Torin stepped forward and put a protective arm around my shoulders.

'Can I see you home?' he asked.

It seemed natural to ask him in after he'd cared to wait for me and bothered to see me home. My housemates were in the living room, loud and drunk so we went into the kitchen. The kitchen always smelt odd as though something had died in it and was rotting unseen. It was always dirty to the point of a health hazard. Torin found an unopened bottle of white wine in the fridge that must have belonged to one of my housemates. He held it aloft with a question in his face. I nodded, and he opened it, took a swig then held it toward me. I took a sip and then another. It was like drinking nectar.

Torin and I looked at each other and exchanged a smile at the sound of my drunken housemates in the living room.

'So, you want me to leave so you can join the fun?' Torin asked, at the same time as I asked him if he wanted to come up to my room.

My bedroom comprised a single unmade bed, a desk covered in sketches and pieces of broken charcoal and an enormous dark wooden wardrobe. But most of my clothes were strewn across the floor. It smelt of stale cigarette smoke and incense.

We sat side by side on my bed, leaning back against the woodchip papered wall, swigging from the bottle. The noise of my housemates' downstairs was still audible but now only a distance tinkle of giggles and talking.

Torin told me about his house in Scotland, someplace east of Perth, as we drank the wine as though it was water. I could feel Torin's arm just touching mine. My skirt was riding up my legs and the fabric of Torin's trousers brushed my naked thigh.

'Does it hurt?' Torin asked as he placed his finger on top of the cast, leaning over me a little.

I shook my head. 'They gave me some painkillers.' At that moment nothing hurt.

I touched my finger to my bracelet Torin was now wearing on his wrist. 'Looks better on you,' I told him. My fingers strayed onto the skin either side of the bracelet and I ran my fingertips over his wrist, then up his arm, following a line in one of his tattoos.

Looking up I saw Torin was watching my face. I leant forward and kissed him. It was like my first kiss, sweet and gentle and chaste.

Torin smirked at me.

'What?'

He let out a laugh. 'You needn't have broken your arm to get my attention, Gracie. You had my attention the moment you walked into the bar.'

Torin kissed me and this time there was nothing chaste about it.

December 2014

'Do you want a mince pie Mum?' Jerome said, holding the plate towards Sam.

'Thanks love,' she said, taking one, giving her son a bright smile. She held the foil dish between her fingers. Her nails were painted to look like Christmas puddings. She wore tinsel earrings too.

Jerome didn't return Sam's smile, instead, he bestowed a beaming grin on Ada, and sat down on the daybed next to her.

'I know you'll want one,' Jerome said to Ada, putting a mince pie in her hand.

'You know me well,' Ada said and gave Jerome an indulgent look.

I wondered if perhaps it hadn't been such a good idea to invite Ada at the same time as Sam. I'd hoped that having Ada present would diffuse the atmosphere between Jerome and Sam.

'So, how was your journey?' Torin asked Sam.

Seemingly grateful to have something to say Sam went into great detail about the drive from her sister's house in Weymouth, where she was now staying, to Redferne Lane. Torin was adept at keeping the conversation with her going. When they'd exhausted the topic Sam seemed to have relaxed a little.

'So I've got you all a little something,' Ada said, as I cleared up the leftover mince pies and coffee cups. She handed Jerome a bag and said, 'You give them out, they all have labels.'

'I've got some presents,' Sam said. 'You give mine out too,' she said to Jerome.

We watched Jerome hand out the gifts. Ada had indeed got all of us a present. She'd given Sam some pretty handkerchiefs and I could have kissed Ada for thinking of Sam, because I could see by the look on Sam's face as she opened the simple gift that it meant a lot to her.

For Torin, there was a bottle of whisky. For me a Delia Smith recipe book and a floral apron.

'Time I learnt to cook?' I asked Ada.

'Yes dear. Jerome is a growing lad, you need to feed him properly,' Ada said, in a serious tone.

'Lucky you Jerome, Grace can test out her cookery skills on you,' Torin said, with delight.

'She might have poisoned me by the time you get back,' Jerome said to Torin.

'Do you two mind?' I said, with a smile. 'My cooking is not that bad. I just don't do much of it.'

'Right,' Torin laughed.

'Open yours Jerome,' Ada said, tapping the box on Jerome's lap.

To Jerome, Ada had given a shiny red bike helmet and a sturdy looking bike lock. For a moment I thought Jerome was going to be disappointed by his gifts but his face lit up and he pulled the helmet from its packaging and stuck it on his head.

'Thanks Ada, it's perfect,' he said, kissing her on the cheek and knocking her with the helmet in the process.

'I shan't worry about you whizzing about on your bike so much if I know you're wearing that,' Ada said and knocked her knuckles against the shiny coating. 'And you make sure you use that lock too.'

'I will,' Jerome said, still wearing the helmet and grinning.

Sam had given Torin and me a large tub of Quality Street. Her present to Ada a bar of lavender soap. And her gift to Jerome was a neat pile of new clothes; jeans, hoody, T-shirt and a pair of trainers. By the labels and logos, I doubted the pile of new threads had been cheap. But I suspected the hug Jerome gave Sam was worth every penny.

Sam was subdued as she watched her son receiving his gift from Ada and I was glad that her own present to Jerome outshone mine (I'd given him a new sketch book and pencils earlier). Before Sam left to live with her sister she'd told me how she felt as though she was losing Jerome. I couldn't contradict her because even though he was now talking to her and even discussing a possible visit in the New Year, I knew he was still so angry with her for losing their home. I was glad to help the both of them navigate this but I sensed Sam found my involvement difficult to swallow. It had taken a fair bit of persuading for her to agree to let Jerome stay with me. She'd only really agreed when Jerome had made it clear he wasn't going to live with her in Weymouth or anywhere.

'So I'm going to get the keys for my flat in the first week of January,' Sam said, to Jerome.

'Right,' Jerome said, his smile gone, suddenly wary.

'It's only got one bedroom but I'm going to get one of them fold out beds, so you can come and stay whenever you like,' Sam said.

I watched as Jerome clenched his jaw before he spoke. 'What's it like, your flat?' he asked.

'It's nice,' Sam smiled. 'It's got a little garden, and it's done out really nice inside, with a new bathroom and carpets. And the landlord says I can do what I like with the garden.'

'It's lovely to have a garden I always think. A little piece of earth to call your own,' Ada said. 'You must plant some flowers dear, everyone should have a garden with flowers to look at.'

'Yeah, I will,' Sam said.

After another coffee Sam said she should get back because she didn't want her sister to be waiting to serve the turkey. I was pleased when, after Sam had said goodbye to Torin, Ada and me, Jerome went outside with his mum and walked her down to the bottom of Redferne lane to where she'd parked her sister's car.

Torin and I helped Ada get ready to go, packing the gifts she'd received into a bag. She gave me a hug and told me she'd see me in a few days for a game with Maudie and her. Jerome came back into the house. He smiled but I could see the moisture on his eyelashes.

'So, we'll see you later?' I said.

Jerome grinned and glanced at Torin. 'Actually, I'm going to stay at my mates tonight.'

I made to disagree but Torin squeezed my fingers. 'It's alright Gracie.'

Jerome gave a chuckle. 'Think of it as a gift yeah? A night without me in the house?'

It was true that since Jerome had come to stay Torin and I had been sneaking around, snatching private moments.

'Alright then but write down the address of this friend and give me his number,' I said.

Jerome rolled his eyes but did as he was asked.

With one last hug each, Jerome and Ada set off down Redferne Lane towards the bridge, passing the sold sign that had been put up outside Ada's house. The 'For Sale' sign would go up outside Jerome's old house in the New Year. Torin slipped his arm around my waist and we turned the other way and began the walk up the lane to Redferne House.

Noah was laying the table in the kitchen. The worn wood was covered with a thick white tablecloth and a wreath of holly sat around three wide candles in the middle. Each place was laid with the silver cutlery that had been in the Redferne family for generations. The air smelt of roasting food and the goose already sat on top of the Aga, resting before it was carved.

Torin and Noah embraced, and I was glad to see they were making the effort to be civil to one another. Noah greeted me with a restrained hug and kiss to the cheek.

'Let me get you a drink and then you must go through to see Josie and the boys,' Noah said.

Noah poured us each a glass of Champagne and ushered us through to the living room before he returned to the kitchen. He had a humbleness about him since the revelation of his relationship with Sam and I knew he was making every effort to make amends. For now, Josie had allowed him to stay but, she'd told me, the future depended upon whether Noah changed his ways.

Josie sat feeding the baby and Godfrey and Barty were on the rug with their grandparents, Josie's parents, playing a board game with brightly coloured plastic hippos. Eliza sat on the uncomfortable upright chair at the side of room, I'd seen her inhabit often before. After initial greetings and the exchange of pleasantries Torin and I gave Eliza and the boys their gifts. We sipped Champagne and enjoyed the squeals of delight that the boys emitted as they unwrapped their presents.

Noah announced that lunch was ready and as we all trooped through to the kitchen Eliza stopped me. She waited until we were alone in the living room before she spoke.

'Thanks for this,' she said, holding up the little jewellery box that contained a necklace.

'My pleasure,' I said, smiling. 'Ezra gave it to me.'

'Really?'

I nodded.

'Don't you want to keep it?'

I shook my head. 'I think he'd like you to have it.'

'Thank you,' she said again.

'Shall I help you put it on?'

Eliza handed me the delicate chain and turned around. She scooped up her mass of pale blond hair and held it aloft so I could fasten the clasp at the back of her neck. Releasing her hair, she turned and touched the pendant that sat against her skin.

'The stone matches your eyes. It looks lovely Eliza,' I said.

She gave a half smile, the first I'd seen on her face for a while.

'Are you alright?' I asked.

She nodded. 'Josie has talked to school and they're going to arrange some counselling for me.'

'I think that's a good idea.'

'Yeah.' She swallowed. 'Is Jerome coming for lunch?'

I shook my head. 'He's gone to have lunch with Ada.'

'I thought he might come, now he's living with you?'

'I don't think he feels very welcome here,' I said.

'No.' She looked at the floor. When she raised her eyes again she said, 'Do you think he'll ever forgive me?'

The word on my lips was no, but it was not my place to say whether Jerome had the capacity to forgive Eliza. I shrugged and said, 'It's hard for him Eliza. Not just because of you but Noah too.'

Eliza nodded.

I held out my arm. 'Come on, let's go and have lunch.'

She slipped her hand into the crook of my arm and we walked into the kitchen. I smiled to myself when Eliza took the chair in between Barty and Josie when I'm sure she'd have rather sat beside Torin. As I took my place beside Torin he slid his hand onto my knee and began a gentle caress with his thumb.

'Well, Happy Christmas one and all,' Noah said, holding his glass aloft. 'Here's to absent friends and of course my dear brother Ezra.'

Ezra had been at the back of my mind all day and it was nice to acknowledge him here at Redferne House. But as I took a sip of Champagne in his memory I realised that we'd never spent a Christmas at Redferne House with his brothers. Never had I spent a Christmas with Torin. I was glad to be making new memories and glad to be here with this family; my family.

CPSIA information can be obtained
at www.ICGtesting.com
Printed in the USA
LVHW01s1543100518
576716LV00004B/799/P